KNIFE'S EDGE

A KATE STARK THRILLER

M. L. BUCHMAN

PRAISE FOR M. L. BUCHMAN

Tom Clancy fans open to a strong female lead will clamor for more.

— *DRONE*, PUBLISHERS WEEKLY

Superb! Miranda is utterly compelling!

— *BOOKLIST*, STARRED REVIEW

Escape Rating: A. Five Stars! OMG just start with *Drone* and be prepared for a fantastic binge-read!

— READING REALITY, MIRANDA CHASE
SERIES

The best military thriller I've read in a very long time. Love the female characters.

— *DRONE*, SHELDON MCARTHUR, FOUNDER
OF THE MYSTERY BOOKSTORE, LA

Meticulously researched, hard-hitting, and suspenseful.

— *PURE HEAT*, PUBLISHERS WEEKLY,
STARRED REVIEW

A fabulous soaring thriller.

Buchman has catapulted his way to the top tier of my favorite authors.

Nonstop action that will keep readers on the edge of their seats.

M L. Buchman's ability to keep the reader right in the middle of the action is amazing.

The only thing you'll ask yourself is, "When does the next one come out?"

I knew the books would be good, but I didn't realize how good.

SIGN UP FOR M. L. BUCHMAN'S NEWSLETTER TODAY

and receive:
Release News
Free Short Stories
a Free Book

Get your free book today. Do it now.
free-book.mlbuchman.com

Other works by M. L. Buchman: (* - also in audio)

Action-Adventure Thrillers

Kate Stark
Final Taste
Ice Burn
Knife's Edge

Miranda Chase
Drone*
Thunderbolt*
Condor*
Ghostrider*
Raider*
Chinook*
Havoc*
White Top*
Start the Chase*
Lightning*
Skibird*
Nightwatch*
Osprey*
Gryphon*
Wedgetail*

Science Fiction / Fantasy

Deities Anonymous
Cookbook from Hell: Reheated
Saviors 101

Contemporary Romance

Eagle Cove
Return to Eagle Cove
Recipe for Eagle Cove
Longing for Eagle Cove
Keepsake for Eagle Cove

Love Abroad
Heart of the Cotswolds: England
Path of Love: Cinque Terre, Italy

Where Dreams
Where Dreams are Born
Where Dreams Reside
Where Dreams Are of Christmas*
Where Dreams Unfold
Where Dreams Are Written
Where Dreams Continue

Non-Fiction

Strategies for Success
Managing Your Inner Artist/Writer
Estate Planning for Authors*
Character Voice
Narrate and Record Your Own Audiobook*
Beyond Prince Charming: One Guy's Guide to Writing Men in Romance

Short Story Series by M. L. Buchman:

Action-Adventure Thrillers

Kate Stark
Miranda Chase Stories

Romantic Suspense

Antarctic Ice Fliers
US Coast Guard

Contemporary Romance

Eagle Cove

Other

Deities Anonymous (fantasy)
Single Titles

The Emily Beale Universe
(military romantic suspense)

ABOUT THIS BOOK

A brewery explosion wipes out Kate Stark's newest television team. An exploding wedding cake on a cruise ship exploring the Icelandic coast almost kills Kate herself.

Former Secret Service agent and now owner of Cooks Network, she despises this feeling—when labeled as Hunted. Her small team is like family: a geek, a US Marine, and her conman twin brother.

But does she dare trust even them? Are they headed toward being collateral damage, or are they the targets and she's the one caught in the chaos?

Kate must walk the knife's edge for a chance to survive.

———

A list of characters and locations may be found at:
https://mlbuchman.com/people-places-planes#KS
And return afterward for a free bonus story
and a recipe from the book.

PROLOGUE

HE STEPPED INTO HEAVEN. OR AS CLOSE AS HE'D EVER IMAGINED while still walking upon this mortal Earth.

Bad boys don't go to Heaven, Raymond Chandler! He could hear Mam's favorite saying. He'd prove her wrong yet.

This moment was all prearranged, of course, but he pulled into the reserved spot directly in front of the Twin Lights Pub as if he'd randomly pulled off the road in his Ford Ranger. Not a tough-guy, I-own-the-freaking-road black F-150 or Dodge Ram designed to terrorize normal drivers on New England's narrow, twisted streets. But neither was it some suburban sedan, and definitely not imported.

Hitting the right tone was key in creating television shows. *Don't stiffen up, be yourself.* His producer Shari had beat those words into his head until they'd become his own mantra.

For the television videographer pre-positioned for his arrival, he'd look like just an average Joe. Driving into the seaside town of Gloucester, Massachusetts in a three-year-old deep-red pickup to park in front of a pub on a sunny June afternoon. He resisted grinning over at Shari as she hovered close behind the camera position.

She'd picked the truck's color because it popped on video when parked near the inevitable forest green and dark wood that defined so many pub exteriors—especially the Irish ones he intended to highlight as much as the television network would let him.

Shari and the camerawoman slipped in behind him.

The first thing was the smell: they'd nailed it. Not stale beer, of course. But the air in most American-built pubs tasted sterile. No character. No life. The Twin Lights smelled of the hops that hung from the old wood beams, of generous plates of steaming food. Of home. A good pub was Ray's favorite place in the world.

The owner had decorated in classic Irish style, right down to the painted board of a flagon of beer glowing between two shining lighthouses, which dangled above the entry door. Inside it sported comfortable booths, plenty of tables for groups both big and small, and a corner stage for three-nights-a-week bands. Twinkle lights added to the homey touch.

About twenty patrons were seated at the bar and three tables clustered together in the otherwise empty pub. They were enough for the place to look packed from the right angles and add to the general burbles of conversation that marked a friendly pub, without creating any problems for the filming. Being *friends-of,* they would also be his casual interview subjects.

"Mr. O'Connor?" He greeted the portly gentleman wiping down the bar—for probably the fiftieth time in anticipation of their scheduled arrival. "I'm Ray Chandler. I heard that you have the best Irish pub 'round these parts."

"Best north"—pronounced *nawth*—"of Boston 'til you cross the wide Atlantic. Welcome to Gloucester," pronounced *Glosta.* "And call me Mike." They clasped hands over the bar as Ray slid onto a stool.

The place was perfect. Gloucester was America's first

seaport and dated back over four hundred years. Still small enough to feel friendly. How to make it relatable? Twice the size of MIT's student body? *No, too elitest, Ray. Those folks aren't your target audience if you want broad appeal.* "So, Mike, what made you open a pub in a town that's a chunk smaller than the student body of BU?" Boston University had been his own alma mater, but Mam never let him forget his sister getting into MIT where both of their first-gen-immigrant parents were professors. He'd always been the black sheep.

They chatted over the attractions of small towns for a bit.

"That's quite a collection, Mike." Ray pointed at the wall Shari had already briefed him on from a prior scouting mission. It was covered with hundreds of beer coasters, perhaps thousands—without a single repeat that he could spot. There were plenty in Gaelic, but Shari's research said the collection came from over ninety countries and covered sixty-five languages.

"Every one of them are Irish pubs, Ray," his lifelong Gloucesterman accent shifted from North (Nawth) Shore, Mass., to Irish with pride. And the man relaxed as he started talking about something so familiar. "If we're missing one from Ireland herself, it's not for lack of trying."

Ray stayed attentive as Mike pointed out a few favorites that patrons had collected and brought back from various travels.

"The Irish Pub in Nepal, that's the most remote one there is by most reckoning, along the trekking route to Everest. The Dublin is a common last stop before leaving Tierra del Fuego for the Antarctic ice. There's Uganda, Cambodia, and Dessie O'Dowds is up to the top of Western Australia. Not much else there except crocodiles and red sand. Fetched that one myself."

Mike tossed Ray one from the bar. "Here's ours for your own collection."

"Now that's a beauty." He held it up for the camera to get a good look, not speaking for long enough that they could cut the zoom in and zoom out without any sound problems. Yellow lettering on a kelly-green background. Around the rim, it read, *The best beer is the one you drink with friends. Twin Lights Pub, Glosta, Mass.* The central graphic showed the towering twin lighthouses of Thacher Island. On the back, a simple bit of history: *The Twin Lights. Built in 1771, rebuilt in 1861. They mark the end of an Atlantic crossing for ship captains. When you reach the twin lights, turn due south for Boston. When you reach the Twin Lights pub, turn in at the door and you're home.*

Ray thumped a fist against the center of his chest. "You got me right in the heart, Mike. Right in the heart." He made a show of tucking it carefully in his shirt pocket. Off the rack, light blue, one button open.

Ray added that dream of his own Irish pub collection. Not in mere coasters but rather growing into such a media sensation that he'd be paid to travel to the world's most remote pubs. He filed that idea away to discuss with Shari as he prompted Mike for more of the pub's background and origins. Most of it wouldn't make it into the show, but that wasn't the point. He let his own Irish gift o' the gab prepare the opening of other doors.

Ignoring the camera and the woman behind it, yet leaving the best angles open for it, had been drilled into him by Shari during unending practice until it became second nature. His producer was tough. Shari stayed in the background, but she was the one who had found him. He'd been hustling as a sous chef at The Dubliner, the best Irish pub in Boston. She'd convinced him there was a whole vast world beyond Boston that he'd never really considered, then trained him until he could pass the toughest test in the industry.

At Shari's insistence, they'd started at the top and pitched to the largest food television network of them all. The actual owner of Cooks Network, Kate Stark, vetted every show personally. Five-ten, black Irish—fair-skin, jet black hair, and the bluest eyes he'd ever seen—she ruled as the uncontested queen of the media-driven side of the food world. And somehow, without crapping his pants, they'd pitched the show to her.

Ms. Stark ran the craziest interview process.

He and Shari never even had a chance to sit down in her office. *I watched your audition tape and read your prospectus and pitch,* Kate had said as she rose and shook their hands. *Nice enough. Let's go. This is Rikka, ignore her if you can. Something I've never managed.* She'd waved a negligent hand at a tiny slip of a Japanese woman holding a camera far too big for her and an even bigger smile that could only be read as evil.

Without any other explanation, Ms. Stark had led them from her skyscraper office in Rockefeller Plaza in the heart of Manhattan, out onto the New York streets and a block south to the Pig 'N' Whistle. *It's a casual place. I didn't give them any warning.* Her idea of casual needed a serious downgrade. Even his former job at The Dubliner in the core of Boston's financial district looked closer to a dive bar than this upscale watering hole of the city's broadcast elite.

They'd called out Kate's name in greeting as she stepped in. *Hey, Clive. I haven't had lunch; would love a bowl of your stew. And would you mind showing Ray here what you do?* Kate Stark sat at the bar, ordered a pint, and spoke directly to him for the last time. *One tip: it's not about you. Make them look good. You have until I finish lunch to capture enough film for a solid fifteen-minute spot.*

He and Shari hadn't traded a panicked look, no matter how much they'd felt it; there just wasn't time. He'd plunged in. Shari orchestrated everything, including getting interview releases from some patrons also dining at the bar by the time he'd left the kitchen. Through some form of voodoo magic, the little camerawoman had always been precisely where he needed her.

Back at the studio, Cooks' head of production might have been cliché flamboyant, but Mac Olson knew his shit. He'd taken the footage Ray and Shari had shot and polished off all the rough spots that neither of them had even imagined. This first shoot of *A Brew and a Bite* was transformed into television art, and Ms. Stark's nod confirmed it worthy with only one note: *The history. These pubs often have deep history; add that element going forward.*

Shari had said that was part of the plan, but this was only a fifteen-minute segment. It actually hadn't been, but it would be now. *Flexibility!* He and Shari were willing to flex however necessary to rocket into the network's firmament. At the moment, that was a pilot with an option on ten episodes in the full-hour format, way more than they'd ever dreamt of. Well, maybe Shari had when she fished him out of The Dubliner. No...by the awe on her face, it blew her away too. Ms. Stark had laughed at them both, but it had been a good-natured one that was easy to join.

After the pressure of that shoot, today's felt easy; anything would, out from under Ms. Stark's watchful eye. She'd scheduled the Twin Lights shoot for her return from a two-week trip overseas. He and Shari wanted to have the first three episodes in the can to present upon her return. They'd jiggered the schedule, found a videographer, and launched up the highway to Gloucester. And it was working!

At the Twin Lights' taps, he poured and pulled a Black and Tan, his favorite beer. He'd thankfully long since learned the tricks to that. Mike nodded his approval at the clean line he'd achieved between the heavier Harp lager filling the bottom half of the pint and the dark Guinness he'd floated on the top by using patience and dribbling the latter over the back of a soup spoon to make it land easier in the glass.

Shari gave him a smile, then shifted out of his peripheral vision. She'd be ten steps ahead of him, making sure the kitchen was prepped, the owner's favorite patrons were ready, and anything else he'd never think of. Damn but that woman twisted him around. Six months ago, she'd taken a single lunch hour to fill his heart with the dream of cracking into network television. Every day since she'd remade him in *his* own image. His own best self. Polishing off his rough edges just as Mac Olson had done with that audition video—Ray Chandler knew he'd never shone through like this in his life.

Highlighting Irish pubs was only the start. After Kate Stark approved the show and took them back to the Pig 'N' Whistle for a celebratory dinner, he and Shari had sat there straight through to closing. They'd scribbled down structures for three other shows on the bar napkins. Then, in their hotel room, had fleshed them out into full detailed proposals. They hadn't even stopped for sex until they had it down. They were that perfect together.

Shari wanted nothing to do with being on camera, though she certainly had the looks. Her African-American heritage and coloring—except for the bleached blonde hair that looked so good on the tall, slender woman—would play great. And she positively vibrated with her high energy and inner vision, but she'd insisted on being the background. And maybe she was right. The way Shari made the shoot flow around him as she did now at the Twin Lights was almost as good as she felt in their bed at night.

Mike O'Connor wasn't only the pub's founder, it fast became clear that he was much more the back-room man. The camerawoman, Dana something, filmed him and Mike making a Full Irish together—bacon, sausages, eggs, beans, black-and-white pudding, home fries, toast, and roasted tomato slices. Then they whipped up Mike's secret recipe for a curry chicken over jasmine rice.

"Ireland isn't about boiled potatoes anymore. Embracing everything good is in our nature, Ray, isn't it?"

He couldn't agree more. That was how Shari hooked him, uncovering his love of *just sitting* in an Irish pub. A single beer could see him through a whole night; it was being there that felt best—especially when Mam was on a tear at home.

Mike was so perfect that he wanted to ask if Kate Stark had prepped him earlier, but he knew she hadn't. It was true Irish hospitality, with a heavy slice of Shari's scouting work.

"Now, tell me about that." Ray pointed to the glass wall that backed the kitchen. "That is one serious setup. How did that happen?"

In a narrow room seen through the glass ranged the shining steel tanks, intricate weavings of connecting pipes, and all the other paraphernalia for small batch beer brewing. He knew the gear already from Shari's notes. It was built for a hundred and fifty-gallon batches, about ten kegs. But at Kate's reminder that it was about *them* not *him,* he let Mike tell his story.

Ray had already noted that six of the bar's taps were for Irish beers but that six more had strictly local names—Mike's own brews. Fisherman's Fancy was an IPA. Old Pear was an Irish red, but an homage to the oldest cultivated fruit tree in the United States. The Endicott Pear Tree stood not twenty miles away—Shari had known and they'd visited it for a photo on the way here. Rockport Bitter might point to an old rivalry from the township breaking away in 1840, but the bite was good and the malt sweet had been balanced well against the hop bitter. There was even a Ledge Hard cider; ledge was what they called the granite bedrock quarried here that made the area world-famous in the 1800s.

"It took a big grant from IPI. That's Irish Pubs, Inc."

Ray knew about them. They rescued ailing pubs and helped launch new ones. He'd have to ask Shari where they got their money—Mike had said *grant* not *loan.*

The camerawoman suggested that she'd go into the

brewery alone to find the best angles. She also wanted to film the whole line without any people in the way.

While she did that, he, Shari, and Mike had simply sat together over the good food they'd made while she did her job. Dana wasn't as exceptional as that Rikka woman had been, but Cooks' people were definitely top grade. He wished for a second camera, but there hadn't been one available, so they often repeated one step or another to be shot from different angles.

Dana signaled she was ready for them just as they started discussing finances and history. But he could see how eager Mike was to show off his pride and joy, so Ray tabled those questions for now.

"Must have taken a bit to learn the brewing trade," Ray teased Mike as they faced all the gleaming equipment efficiently packed into the small space. There was barely room to maneuver between the various tanks and piping.

"That it did, laddie. But time and patience can bring a snail to County Cork. Come let me show you." Mike sighed happily as he led them along the brewery line. His descriptions of each stage blew past Ray's studied knowledge. Where Mike had been awkward at the front of the house, he turned erudite in here. Ray knew they could make a special episode, *Brewing Basics,* from this tour without any additional shooting costs, just editing and his own studio voiceover.

With that in mind, he focused on asking leading questions.

The questions.

Like the special one he wanted to ask Shari about the ring burning a hole in his pocket right now.

"That's fascinating, Mike." How would she answer? Shari had been many things, but predictable wasn't one of them. But he knew it was right; he'd never been in such sync with a woman in his life. The sex rated spectacular, but the wonder of the woman made that fade into being a mere bonus. Nobody had ever believed in him so hard.

Last into the brewery, Shari squinted at him.

Something going wrong? But it felt so smooth.

Then he spotted the direction of her gaze. Not the camera or their host. No, she stared at his right front thigh, where he hadn't thought to hide the lump of the ring box deep in his pocket.

Her eyes opened wide and her gaze shot up to his.

One heartbeat.

Two.

Three...

And her smile blasted brighter than radiant.

Yes! Ray wanted to dance a hornpipe, sing a sea shanty, do—

"That's odd," Mike was tapping a dial.

It didn't change.

He thumped it harder.

Still no change.

"What is this tank?" The stainless-steel vessel stood seven feet high and as big as a shower stall that would fit two if they wanted to be as close as he and Shari usually were when washing each other down.

"It's the Brite tank, the finisher." When Mike tapped the dial again, the needle moved up, not down. "We use a method here called Forced CO_2. Rather than adding more yeast to create the carbonation, I can do a multi-week process in hours with far more control by forcing the carbon dioxide into the finished beer under pressure."

Ray focused on the dial. "Is it supposed to be that high?" It was graded: white, green, yellow, and red. Even as he watched, the needle shifted into the red, heading for the pin stop at the end.

Mike shook his head as he squinted at the top of the tank. "Pressure relief should have popped by now."

Shari edged closer.

All three of them looked up at the valve but none of them saw the broken-off shaft of a #2 pencil pinning the valve closed.

Stepping to the control panel, Mike pressed the Close Valve control.

The wire to transmit the electrical impulse to the valve that would stop the CO_2 had been cut. He tapped the Open Valve; the needle began moving faster. He pounded on the Close Valve multiple times, but no signal was sent. The tall supply bottles could provide one thousand and seventy-one pounds per square inch of pressure. The tank was designed to operate at fifteen psi and be safe to thirty.

It held to sixty-seven—

Then it detonated.

The first seam to fail was to the tank's side, sending a storm of stainless-steel shrapnel right through where Shari had been watching from before moving closer. The sideways blast of beer didn't touch any of them. But, with no human flesh to slow it down, the shrapnel slashed into the rack of five-foot-tall CO_2 cylinders, snapping off one of the regulator valves. This turned the tank from a resource into an eighteen-inch-wide high-pressure rocket. The chains designed to keep the tanks from falling over weren't up to the task of stopping the unstoppable force of a full tank with a missing valve.

Mike was the first victim as the CO_2 cylinder ricocheted off the back wall, shot beneath the Brite Tank still spewing a hundred and forty-six gallons of Shoebert the Seal Porter, and the cylinder's butt end took him out below the knees. He landed face down in the dark brew that had been named for a grey seal. Shoebert had become a favorite of the neighboring town of Beverly when he spent a few weeks trapped in a freshwater pond, then crawled to the police station's back door for help in returning to the sea. Knocked out cold, Mike lay awash in his own beer.

With the safety chain broken, the four other CO_2 cylinders toppled to the floor. Another valve broke after it clipped a pipe. This tank skipped twice before going airborne and punching into the side of the Brewing tank. A hundred and fifty-three gallons of boiling wort poured onto the floor as well. Forensics would never be able to determine if Mike fully drowned before he was cooked to death.

The first cylinder, still ricocheting about the floor, severed the propane gas line to the wort boiler ahead of the step-down pressure regulator. The bolt of flame killed Shari instantly, not by burning her, but by the pressure wave that slammed her against the five-hundred-liter beer Serving Tank, freshly filled with the very popular Swordfish Stout. It was Mike's bestseller and had earned him his first contact by a national brewer wanting to license the recipe for a decently obscene amount of money. Ten percent would go to Irish Pubs, Inc, but that was the deal he'd cut on all his income when they'd helped him initially.

Unaware of Shari's demise, Ray Chandler stood in the sea of unfinished brew, so far spared by the perfect storm of sloshing liquid, flying objects, and fire as the disaster wrecked the small Gloucester brewery. The CO_2 gas cylinders ran empty and came to rest, the beer flood retreated from apocalyptic to ankle deep, and he stood well clear of the continuing flare from the broken propane pipe.

"Ha!" Ray pumped a fist in the air. The combination of three separate weather systems colliding to form *The Perfect Storm* had killed the Glosta swordfish boat *Andrea Gail.* They'd gone down—and become famous because of the George Clooney movie. Well, he'd survived his own three-disaster storm, maybe that would make him famous too.

But Ray didn't realize that a fourth element had joined this particular storm. The two cylinders had released two thousand cubic feet of pure CO_2 into the compact brewery's limited air supply. That caused an initial overpressure, which had blown much of the normal air mix out of swinging doors and ventilation shafts. The fire erupting at the snapped propane line continued consuming the marginal amounts of remaining oxygen in the room at a prodigious rate.

Ray's balance wavered. He reached out a hand to regain his balance, barely noticing as his palm was sliced open by the torn steel of the tank that had initially detonated.

Instead, he stood there, weaving like a leaf in the wind. No longer able to find the oxygen to breathe, he suffocated standing up.

His knees folded first.

As he flopped onto the hard concrete, the last pain he felt was the ring box tucked safely in his pocket being driven into his thigh. His last thought was one of Mam's favorite admonitions: *Bad boys don't go to Heaven.*

No one would be adding to the pub's collection of coasters anytime soon.

The camera operator was nowhere to be seen.

1

THREE DAYS LATER

OFF REYKJAVIK, ICELAND

So First-Class! Exactly how she wanted everything to run all the way through.

Bret's hand rested over hers as Savannah laid the big knife on the icing of their wedding cake's lowest tier.

All hundred passengers and several of the smaller, expedition-class cruise ship's crew crowded together on the after deck. The sunlit sea the perfect backdrop in every direction. She'd arranged to have the captain turn the ship for the cake cutting so that the low sun of the Icelandic summer evening caught her best profile. The scents of sea and sugar wafted over those assembled, reminding them of happy times or their own weddings.

The only awkward aspect about the whole setup was that Bret was lefthanded and she was righthanded. But because of the camera's angle, he had to stand to her left, forcing them both to use their off hands. Bret didn't seem to mind, but she always felt awkward and clumsy using her left land. She was sure it would show in the film. However, she took a deep breath to fortify herself as there was no choice. Kate Stark, the owner of Cooks Network, had decided to film the wedding, and the camera had to be positioned to her right—it was only proper that the bride be front and center.

Because she and Bret were both using their off hands on the knife, neither one felt the additional resistance as the long blade snagged the thin wire hidden beneath the icing.

The knife tip connected to the metal base plate of the tier.

The circuit was closed: wire, knife, base plate.

A small battery buried in the cake's bottom layer sent a pulse of electricity through the circuit.

Neither Savannah nor Bret felt anything. They were insulated by the handle carved per tradition from the wood of a hinoki tree.

That's when things started to go very, *very* wrong.

2

FIVE HOURS EARLIER

THE CUSTOMER IS NEVER WRONG.

Executive Chef Marnie Girard of the Oceansaway ship *Ice Adventure* reminded herself of that. Again. But it lay so far from the truth that she often considered writing a book entitled *The Cruiser's Guide to Never Being Right*. Perhaps that was inaccurate. They were never wrong, being the ones with the money. Maybe, *The Ultimate Cruiser's Guide to Terminal Stupidity!* With the exclamation point and a heavy dash of powdered habanero pepper in their breakfast cereal for revenge upon them. They'd probably talk about the piquant finish selected by the chef like it was a fine wine—while it scorched a hole straight through their tiny little brain pans.

Her current least favorite guests had been the very first aboard ship this afternoon, Savannah Sachs and Bret Calder. Savannah had earned it personally; Bret merely guilty by association of being her fiancé.

Dial up the meet-cute story: celebrating their shared birthdate with friends at neighboring tables in The Bedford. Where better for your happy-ever-after story to begin than in Martha Stewart's Las Vegas eatery where the Fettuccine Alfredo ran sixty dollars—and (breathless surprise) *Only a hundred-and-seventy-dollars for the caviar add-on. Oh, just so luscious! You simply must try it next time you're there.*

True love found in an overpriced casino restaurant? Gamble much?

Oh, and don't you just love how our names fit together? Bret and Savannah, Savannah and Bret. Why anyone named their kid after a hot, sweaty city deep in the American south, Marnie couldn't even guess. She shouldn't let them get to her, but she was a French chef on a British ship; when she felt emotions, they blasted to the surface.

She had half-seriously considered taking a chef's knife to one or both of them for the betterment of the species' gene pool. She'd thought her own Millennial generation owned the biggest market share of annoying. They'd proven her wrong. The Zoomers had them beat hands down—rich ones times a thousand.

Savannah had clearly entered some altered mental state requiring absolute perfection. And she was smart and driven enough that Marnie could almost believe she'd pull it off. She was also polite and terminally pleasant about having a rod of titanium up her butt. The woman had elevated micromanagement into an art form of frenetic need driven who cared what.

And where better to have an annoying yet poshly perfect wedding? On a cruise ship, of course. Nothing ostentatious; they weren't dropping a thousand guests on a massive Disney ship or even five hundred on a luxurious Crystal ship.

No, they'd decided to have their *lovely little do* on *her* cruise ship. Just fifty of their nearest and dearest to join them on Marnie's expedition-class ship at thirteen thousand pounds sterling a head—more for the upper deck suites with balconies, of course. The ship carried a hundred guests and sixty crew, a quarter of which were Marnie's own culinary staff, with another eight as servers.

She'd had to meet the couple for multiple online consultations. Damn those stupid satellite constellations; even being out at sea hadn't let her escape Savannah's thousands of questions, pointers, tips, suggestions, and other noise. Then they'd flown out to *Inspect the Venue* (more effusive bubbling) when the ship reached port—twice!

After all the video calls—with zero awareness of time zone differences as her ship moved about the world's oceans— there'd been the first personal site visit in Punta Arenas six months ago when the ship had been sailing out of Chile and down to the Antarctic Peninsula. Not the couple; Savannah had visited with her venue scout in tow.

During that first visit, Bret had appeared as an afterthought in the form of an engagement photo.

Savannah had dragged him along for the second visit in Stockholm a month ago to review the final details. Yet he'd somehow sat placidly through it all with a vague smile on his lips. He showed less dynamic range than British members of the ship's crew.

During that hellish twelve-hour layover, Marnie had seen to neither the provisioning, which she always managed personally, nor Vicente. His ship had been in port the same day, a rare overlap, during which they typically took full and primarily horizontal advantage. As a French chef, she had very discerning taste in both food and lovers. Vincente might be a decade older, but neither that nor his sailing on a big ship for Carnival proved to be a sufficiently notable shortcoming after they got naked together with a suitable supply of condiments. Some things definitely went down better coated in a warmed dark chocolate-Courvoisier ganache. There was also the joy of a swirl of mint-infused honey drizzled on and tongue-laved away to pine after.

Still, she kept her complaints to herself—the premium that Savannah paid for a wedding aboard ship nudged the meter from the *lovely* category straight into *startling*. It also wasn't often as a ship's chef that her commission included an extravagant wedding cake, which she'd rather enjoyed. Marnie had started her career as a pastry chef before ships floated into the picture and set her culinary path upon a new course.

The stupidest part, in her unsolicited opinion—of what might actually be a lovely wedding—was their choice of wedding date. Yes, the couple shared a birthday, even if they were both sad enough to celebrate it in Vegas. And yes, getting married on the one year anniversary of their meeting offered a nicely full circle feel to everything.

But years of observing too many shipboard honeymoon and anniversary cruises made Marnie a fair judge of marital longevity. Savannah and Bret had three years painted all over them—maximum.

Year One, keeping up the face of the marriage to convince themselves. Year Two, keeping up face to convince each other. Year Three, pure hell. And then the *stupid* bit: a lifetime of hating the date of your own birthday because it was also the date of trading vows and wasting your best years on that bitch / bastard. Take your pick and both would be right by the end of it. Maybe she was wrong...she hoped so for their sakes.

But she just couldn't picture them like the gray-hair cruiser couples who habitually walked hand-in-hand. And did it twenty, thirty, forty years on when she asked. Marnie hadn't found anything inside her that thought settling down made more sense than American cheese as a food product—at least not yet.

That Savannah and Bret chose *stupid* wasn't her problem. They were merely an annoyance that paid far better than average. All part of the smaller, expedition-class cruising ship experience. Unlike Vincente, Marnie wasn't the Food Manager on a big ship with a staff of hundreds to serve a cast of thousands of human cattle on seven-day jaunts. She was an executive chef with a staff of thirteen serving two to three-week cruises to a hundred guests.

No, her *real* problem was Kate Stark. She was the grand dame of food television. Her shows were fun, entertaining, and educational. Marnie had never heard of her breaking careers, but she had certainly made them with a stroke of her magic TV wand. Ever since this filming had been arranged, Marnie had been forced to confront her life choices. She'd been drifting along on ships, with nothing but utter contentment for her lot, for over a decade.

But having snagged the notice of Cooks Network and Kate Stark herself, she became far too aware of all the choices that had landed her here. She didn't like being forced to think about what else she might ever want. And yet, now she was—with no clear answer popping aboard either. She'd been unmoored from one shore, yet had no idea what other shore she could possibly want to land upon.

She could feel Kate's arrival on the ship like a split cream sauce frothing out of the pot to scorch on the burner—a frisson of blind panic overlaid by nausea worthy of bad oysters and the sweet scent of burnt dairy. It was ridiculous, as Marnie's galley lair lay a deck below the entry level on the opposite side of the hundred-meter-long, twenty-meter-wide ship.

But still...she felt Kate Stark's arrival.

3

KATE STEPPED OFF THE RATTLING METAL GANGPLANK ONTO THE
Ice Adventure.

The ship felt comfortingly solid. She wasn't sure what she'd
expected, but that wasn't it.

"You've never been on a cruise?" Rikka asked from close
behind, of course not missing Kate's tentative first step aboard.

"I haven't been to Iceland before either." She also couldn't
recall the last time she'd been away from Cooks Network for
two full weeks—twelve days aboard, one in transit at either
end. Certainly not since her parents had died and left it to her
and her twin brother. Probably not since she'd quit her six
years in the US Secret Service.

Looking out from the deck, Reykjavik's harbor spread wide
about them. The angular glass facade of the Harpa Concert
Hall rose beside the ship, dominating the harbor's skyline.
During the pre-trip briefing that her people put together, they
said sixty percent of the country's population had seen a show
there. She'd intended to go last night but, once again, her twin
brother had taken the family jet off somewhere—after she'd

been clear that she needed it. She should have learned by now that telling Paul was never sufficient. Mental note, again: *Talk to their pilot in the future.* Paul wasn't nasty, simply oblivious to anything that wasn't about him.

Thankfully, her assistant scrounged a pair of red-eye seats out of New York for Rikka and herself despite it being the height of the season.

She hated flying red-eye. Kate had never figured out if Rikka thrived on such things, or simply never slept—ever. They'd talked the whole way across and then set off at sunrise to tour the city until it was time for the midafternoon boarding call. Rikka looked ready to roll; Kate felt ready to collapse.

Reminding herself to be present, Kate leaned on the railing and took a slow, deep breath. The late afternoon light washed over the city. Though it was only four o'clock and the local sunset wouldn't happen until almost midnight, she couldn't think of the time any other way. For the first half of this trip, it would never be darker than twilight during the three hours that the sun ducked below the northern horizon. She was actually hoping to see that...after she caught up with her sleep.

The city itself rose on a low hill past the harbor. What little she'd seen of the country coming in from the airport was a strange mix of rolling flatland with an occasional blunt peak of a volcano punching upward. Even now in mid-July, some of the lower ones still boasted snowy caps. Reykjavik was the farthest north national capital in the world, so maybe she shouldn't be surprised.

The thick blanket of purple lupines was set off brilliantly by the green grass and the blue tones of sky and ocean. Those were the only vibrant colors. The houses, which she'd expected to be brightly painted to offset the long winter grays, were uniformly white with red or gray roofs. More surprising for their *lack* of variation than anything else. Though the city was over a thousand years old, it had been little more than a village of a few thousand before the twentieth century. Now home to over a third of Iceland's four hundred thousand residents, the city revealed no hint of its age.

A lone church steeple, in gray concrete making it a distinct color, towered above a skyline boasting few buildings over five stories. Yet Reykjavik locals claimed a vibrant food culture that had been featured on her network but she'd never experienced. She'd intended to visit her team's top three spots by arriving early in the city.

"I bet your brother's been on dozens of cruises." Rikka never missed a chance to scoff at Paul—it was a full-time sport between them. His career was primarily focused on bedding lovely women. Her development of her half-share of Cooks Network had made him richer than even most heiresses. For Paul, that appeared to be a moot point; he was wholly impartial about his companion-of-the-moment's wealth. He was absolutely in love with each one, until he wasn't. Yet, by some magic formula she'd never understood, he remained friends with each one afterward.

Her recipe for remaining friends with ex-lovers was mostly about keeping her emotional distance throughout and the affairs too brief to become acrimonious. Neither was intentional, but she hadn't found the missing ingredient to fix that either.

How she and Paul had been born of the same mother remained a deep mystery. That they were twins simply ranked as annoying.

"Welcome aboard, Ms. Stark. Ms. Albert. I'm Mister Charles, the ship's Cruise Director. You might like these." He used a pair of tongs to hand them each a rolled-up white washcloth, freshly dampened with hot water. It was lovely to wipe it over her face and hands—not as refreshing as the eight hours' sleep she'd missed last night, but it instilled some energy back into her system.

A glance around revealed no readout used to garner their names from their dockside check-in. Perhaps it wasn't hard to figure out how he knew her. She might own Cooks Network, Number One in the North American market and Top Three in both Europe and Asia, but her passion was the cooking. She spent as much time as she could in the studio with her guest chefs. Which meant she was more prominently on the air than even her mother had been.

This trip would only add to her unsought fame. The first episode of *Wedding Chefs Far Afield* would start with the wedding but mostly feature Executive Chef Marnie Girard as the chef catered a society wedding aboard ship.

Kate knew she herself was also a draw—the marketing department made sure she was aware of that—but that's not why she always did the first episode of any new series. She wanted to set more than the theme and tone for each Cooks Network show. Far more importantly, she wanted to set a standard for how the guest chefs were treated and highlighted. This wasn't about her, but rather the true masters of their craft.

"Chef Girard," Mr. Charles continued as he held out a wicker basket for their used towels, then handed each of them a flute of champagne, "is presently busy in the galley, but looks forward to meeting with you later."

"Meaning you've scared her to death, Kate, and she's hiding."

The merest flicker of concern in Mr. Charles' eyes confirmed Rikka's assessment. One of the many reasons she didn't wish to be *The Kate Stark*. So often they had to throw out the first half hour or so of footage before the chef finally relaxed around her. Some never did. Ray and Shari had leaned right in, their passion overriding any fear. It would be fun to reconnect with them once she returned.

She and Rikka moved to the side to sip their champagne as more people came in behind them. It had a nice lemony note and a smoothness behind the fizz rippling over her tongue that spoke of above mid-shelf. Very pleasant.

Kate finally spotted the smartwatch facing inward on the cruise director's wrist as he greeted the next couple by name. Yet he hadn't checked his wrist upon her own arrival. The man probably studied the guest list for prominent people before the boarding began. She vacillated in the borderland between charmed that he'd taken the trouble and creeped-out that she had somehow become a *prominent* person worthy of special attention.

"So, do we turn this into an episode of *Kate's Kitchen Raids?*" Rikka hefted the camera case that she hadn't handed over with their other luggage at the base of the gangway.

Staging a camera-in-the-lead raid on the chef's kitchen was a thought, but Kate wanted Marnie Girard cooperative, not panicked. "You know as well as I do, that series isn't about ambushing chefs." It was about getting behind the scenes in kitchens at major events, like the Superbowl or the G-7. Though that conclave of world leaders had turned rather more challenging than intended.

"Spoilsport!" Rikka's view of the world. She hugged her camera case close as if seeking another target.

At the base of the loading gangway, a team had been waiting to take their luggage, but Rikka had refused to let anyone else touch her camera case. The team was led by a grizzled old salt and included four slight men dressed in ninja black—black deck shoes, black jeans, black turtlenecks, and matching worker-guy gloves. They even wore those sports cowls—black, of course—up past their noses, probably to avoid catching every passenger-borne cold. Black woolen caps against the cool afternoon (Iceland's only other kind were cold) and dark sunglasses completed their outfits. Based on her briefing for the cruise, they were probably Filippino—not that there'd been much to see of them. Most were closer to Rikka's five-foot-zero (she always specified the zero) than Kate's five-ten, but they manhandled heavy luggage aboard as if were oversized pillows.

They didn't mar a single one, but Rikka was as protective of that camera as she was of her sushi knives.

More and more people were gathering in the lounge area, armed with champagne glasses and overly bright smiles. Some obviously trying to hide jet lag, like herself. Others, young enough to not care, and therefore intensely annoying.

The half of those aboard that were wealthy Gen Z guests for the wedding set about mingling and pretending that they knew each other. The elder half were on the trip for their own reasons and clustered in small groups. Most of the latter would be here for the exceptional birding that existed around Iceland in the summer months.

A cluster of eleven ladies-of-an-age were also here on a knitting-group expedition. Several of them had already taken over a corner of the lounge and pulled out their projects while sipping their champagne. Kate wasn't a knitter, but she made a mental note to spend some time hanging out with them—they certainly looked to be enjoying themselves.

Everyone had received wedding invitations as part of their on-boarding package—including Kate and Rikka. Fifty unknown guests at your wedding apparently earned some kind of Gen Z points that she didn't understand, even after Rikka had tried to explain it. As a cusp-year Millennial, she at least had a chance. Being eight years older clearly placed Kate in the middle-late, out-of-touch category of their shared generation.

There was an additional danger beyond polite cruise directors—several women from both the older and the younger crowd had recognized her. By their glances at her and away, and a growing buzz among themselves, Kate knew she had seconds before she'd be surrounded by fawning supplicants who'd simply *love* to share grandma's county-fair-prize-winning recipe—*live* on one of Kate's shows, of course.

Several men were eyeing them as well, but that was probably Rikka's doing. It was the lure of a stunningly cute Japanese-Eurasian with straight hair long down her trim frame and mystical green eyes. She wore her usual form-fitting black turtleneck, black jeans, and black sneakers. She'd fit right in with the crew ninjas except her sneaker laces were bright purple today, which—if Kate called them purple—Rikka would come up with some completely bizarre color name that had nothing to do with purple, *Oh no, it's ultra-mauve* or *the color of the Boy Scouts of America's flag* or something far more obscure than she could guess. Kate had quickly learned to never comment on their ever-changing variety beyond saying, *Nice.*

"Let's settle in our room first, then we'll find our chef." That should give the chef a few minutes to get over at least the first wave of panic at her arrival. Kate had long since learned that chefs tended to freak out when meeting the owner of the top cooking network. Their reactions varied, but she'd seen what Rikka called *The KS Effect*—which she'd insisted was short for Kick Ass rather than for Kate Stark, when Kate had been foolish enough to ask. It transformed even the most arrogant of the chef breed into bumbling fools for a time. Them she rather enjoyed scaring the shit out of; innocent cruise ship chefs not so much.

Rikka smiled, "Right. First, we establish our base of operations. Then we go on the hunt."

"You've been spending too much time with Sam. He's rubbing off on you." The hulking Marine Force Recon (retired) made Kate look as small as she did Rikka. A decidedly odd couple, but it seemed to work for them. Rock steady and dead silent versus Rikka's live-wire energy who always had the fascinating or the funny to impart—thankfully without tipping over into annoying chatter.

"I'm rubbing against him every chance I get." Rikka's grin was wicked and reminded Kate of how long it had been since she'd found someone she wanted to rub against. Wouldn't be happening on this trip as she and Rikka were sharing a suite.

"We're up two decks," Rikka opted for the stairs over the small elevator. Probably a good idea with how generous she'd heard shipboard meal portions were.

Kate stopped to glance at the ship's deck-layout diagram posted by the stairs. It showed five decks, with rooms forward on the first three levels and only in the middle on the top two. To the ship's rear, from lowest to highest were: dining room and galley (where Chef Marnie would be hiding), lounge (where the champagne welcome service continued), a library and a secondary lounge that included a bar and was labeled as The Captain's Club, then an outdoor dining area tagged as the Quarterdeck. The Bridge lay at the very forward end on that fourth deck. The topmost deck was smallest and had a beauty salon to the rear, the best rooms middle, and a viewing platform forward. Machine spaces and the crew's deck below didn't appear on the diagram, though the ex-Secret Service agent in her would certainly be watching for the access points.

As she viewed the deck names, Kate puzzled at their implications. This cruise line specialized in the far north and far south cruises, right to the edge of the ice pack in either direction. She knew that they owned a sister ship to the *Ice Adventure* that had each deck named for one of the great polar explorers.: Amundsen, Byrd, Mawson, Scott, and Shackleton.

Rikka had actually slowed down enough to read the names as well and let out a happy sound.

"What?"

"It's not the explorers; these decks are all named for lost ships."

The sheer mass of esoteric knowledge that Rikka carried around shouldn't fit in a single individual's brain. But Kate knew just enough to see that her friend was right.

Rikka stabbed a finger at each one as she cataloged them from the lowest deck to highest.

"Shackleton's *Endurance,* crushed and sunk on the way to Antarctica, undiscovered for a century. They recently found it three thousand meters down, under the ice pack of the Weddell Sea."

She pointed at the deck they'd entered on and still hadn't escaped. Kate kept a weather eye on the lounge guests, but they looked uncertain if this was the opportune moment to reenact a streaming ice-floe-like charge of humanity to crush down upon her. For the moment, the passage of escape remained open. Though it might snap closed at any second and spell her doom to sinking beneath overeager cooks.

"I don't want to suffer the same fate as the *Endurance.*"

Oblivious to her dilemma, Rikka remained firmly blocking her direct line to the stairs and continued. "The *Jeanette* got all crushed up in 1881 after being trapped in the polar ice north of Russia for two years—thirteen of thirty-three survived."

"How do you know that one?" Kate didn't know why she ever asked. It was some kind of deep Pavlovian response that she couldn't help around Rikka.

"Great book about it by Captain Edward Ellsberg titled *Hell on Ice.* I can lend you a copy. Neat guy. Did you know that he—" Rikka could launch into a lengthy lecture at the least provocation.

Kate preempted this one by pointing at the next deck's name on the ship's diagram.

"Oh, the *Erebus* shouldn't have its own deck—abandoned in the ice, no survivors, rediscovered a hundred and seventy years later on the ocean floor. Her sister ship, the *Terror,* didn't get listed at all—the pansies."

Personally, Kate felt that was a wise choice. She wouldn't particularly like having a cabin on a deck named *Terror*.

"What's really weird is that after they abandoned both ships, the *Terror* did travel ninety kilometers south on her own from where she was abandoned. I bet she sailed right past Franklin and his gang, who had considered her lost before becoming lost themselves."

"Is this ancient Greece?" Deck Four was their deck, *Octavius*.

"That one is seriously cool. Back in the 1700s, a trader reached the orient and decided to sail back from China to the UK through the Bering Strait. He planned to traverse the uncharted Northwest Passage to Europe. They were found by a whaler thirteen years later. The ship had made it through—she floated off the coast of Greenland. The captain still sat in his chair, logbook open and pen in hand—frozen in that position for the whole span of years, based on his final log entry."

A shiver up her spine almost convinced Kate she'd have been happier on a deck named for the *Terror*.

Rikka didn't bother commenting on Deck Five's name, *The Flying Dutchman*. Instead, she began climbing the stairs and chanting the dark chorus from the finale of Wagner's opera *Der fliegende Holländer*, "Yohohoeh! Yohohohoeh! Scream, storm-wind, howl!" Her mezzo soprano voice did little to offset the spookiness of the basses and baritones Wagner had written for.

They'd seen it together over the winter at the Met and, typically, Rikka remembered the words as she did everything else. Kate and Paul had inherited the Met subscription when their parents died. Whenever he wasn't around—not much of an opera fan, he made a point of becoming scarce on opening nights—Rikka typically joined her.

The chorus of the cursed sailors wending their ship once more to sea, to spend another seven years in the shadowy realm of lost souls, led her up the short flight.

"You choose the most fun places to go, Kate," Rikka broke off the chant as they reached *Erebus* Deck, temporarily escaping all of the aspirants to TV stardom in the ship's lounge down on *Jeanette* Deck.

Maybe she could hire a passing ice floe as a bodyguard, ready to intervene on a moment's notice and freeze out anyone seeking to corner her during the voyage.

"Glad we aren't on the top deck. Damned by Satan to wander the high seas? Ick!" Rikka shuddered like a dog trying to shed a recent swim.

"But the Dutchman and his crew were redeemed in the end."

Rikka blew a raspberry. "Only by a perfectly ridiculous soprano casting herself into the sea and killing herself to prove that love carried beyond death. Not *my* idea of redemption. I mean, would you want to kill yourself to save those ladies eyeing you like a golden ticket without even offering you a lifetime supply of chocolate Wonka bars?" She waved her hand down toward the lounge, of course not missing a thing.

Rikka guided her off the stairs to tour the third deck. In addition to early photographs of the command crews, there were numerous, painfully vivid paintings. Both the *Erebus* and the *Terror* setting forth from England, becoming caught in the ice, and finally abandoned. Behind the bar in The Captain's Club, there was an encased model of the *Erebus* caught in the ice. It included the crew laboring to drag their small boats over the rough ice, seeking an escape they never found. The small library had several shelves of Arctic and Antarctic exploration disasters, outnumbered only by an amazing collection of birding books.

Octavius, their own deck, was even more macabre. The luxury of the dark wooden walls and thick carpeting were offset by the tastefully spotlit paintings screwed to the wall against movement in violent weather. That ship had been found with weather-tattered sails and rough icebergs all about, but it had long predated photography and only been seen that one time by rough whalers. From their meager description, the artists' imaginations took flight.

Close by their own cabin's door hung a pen-and-ink of the whaler's rescue crew fearful of the captain frozen to death in his chair. The near mythic nature of the finding inspired modern renderings to appear far more ghostly and misty because—unlike the *Erebus* and *Terror*—she had truly been a ghost ship, not merely lost to the ice.

Kate decided to skip touring the uppermost deck for now. She would need to feel far stronger to face the truly mythic emanations from the murky shadows of Richard Wagner's mind. There were some things better left to the imagination.

Rikka pointed at the small sign on the door across from theirs. It read, *Groom's Suite.* "Did you know that the bride and her immediate entourage claimed all six luxury cabins at the uppermost level? And as a bonus, the ship's beauty salon is up there too." Kate had left that chore of dealing with the bride to Rikka and intentionally not asked for any report. She didn't need to, Rikka heaped more than her usual share of disdain upon the woman's head *in absentia*.

That the groom didn't even rate a place on the bride's floor told Kate that Rikka's disdain might be well justified.

Their own cabin was pleasantly devoid of dead-ship reminders. No hint of foul seaweed, rotting timber, or whale oil lanterns. Twin beds, comfortable chairs for lounging, a private bath with a surprisingly reasonable shower, and a balcony big enough for two chairs and a small table.

Rikka wasn't admiring the view and had barely glanced at the room's fittings. Instead, she paced about as she inspected some app on her phone. She gave a loud, "Ah-ha!" when she returned to the head of the bed closer to the door. "This one's mine. The ship's Wi-Fi signal is seven percent stronger at the head of this bed than anywhere else in the room."

Kate dropped her light traveling pack on the bed nearer the window without complaint. Since the day she'd taken down one of the world's foremost hackers back in her days as a Secret Service agent, she'd come to rely on Rikka's skills with a computer. Several times. It had taken washing her through the Witness Protection Program twice, but Rikka's current identity as her right hand and chief camera operator whenever she went into the field seemed to be working.

In seconds, Rikka had unpacked the camera. The fifty-thousand-dollar Red V-Raptor XL was massive overkill for television, but it had made Rikka so happy that Kate hadn't argued for long. Rikka slid on a shorter zoom lens, suitable for close-up to general work. After dropping the macro and a longer zoom into the camera bag, she held it out without turning from her task.

Kate knew better than to argue and took it. More than once she'd appeared in whole segments with Rikka's bag slung forgotten over her shoulder. Rikka also held out a lapel mike. Kate clipped the battery pack to her belt and ran the wire up under her hair. She anchored it just below her temple and forward of her ear with skin-tone tape as Rikka had taught her —invisible with her hair down but affording exceptional voice pickup.

I could pick you up just fine with the camera mike, but this way I can EQ one line specifically to highlight the best tonal quality of your voice.

Kate had nodded in agreement, unsure of what adjustments Rikka would be making. She considered asking—for the length of three heartbeats. No, better not to know.

In the time it had taken her to prep the mike, Rikka had turned the nightstand between their beds and much of the lone desk into technology stations of chargers, adapters, and the pair of laptops she was rarely without. *One for editing and work, one for play while the other tries to keep up.*

"No hacking the ship." Kate was always careful to *not* ask whose secure database Rikka was *just fooling around with* as she called it.

"No promises." Rikka patted her laptop like a puppy dog but left it closed. "Let's go find that chef."

4

CHEF MARNIE GIRARD FELT THE AIR CHANGE IN THE GALLEY.

Wasn't one of her chefs. Her sous chef and the line cooks wouldn't be on for another hour. Only herself and the two prep chefs were in the galley at the moment. Percy's turn to select the music had her nodding along to the French rap that he favored. It also set a fine rhythm for working the fish she was prepping.

No need to turn—the air change told her plenty.

If they were servers, they'd have whooshed into her galley through the swinging doors from the dining room, which wouldn't open for dinner for another three hours. Mr. Charles, the tour manager, always entered with a swift brusqueness in sharp contrast to the elegant gentleman he presented to the passengers. The only other person to typically brave her galley, the expedition leader Alli Rydell, always arrived as swiftly as Mr. Charles but invariably called out a friendly greeting before asking after sixty box lunches or to report a compliment for the outdoor dinner service up on the Quarterdeck.

How the tall woman stayed so slender was a mystery, as she never failed to hit the cookie jar Marnie had learned to keep handy for her. Perhaps because she somehow managed to be everywhere at once: whether out and about on hikes with the guests, giving presentations in the lounge, or at meals split between the First Deck dining room and the Fourth Level Quarterdeck.

This time the door opened slowly, barely enough to disturb the air, as if someone were peeking in, unsure of whether or not they should be there. Any ship's guest would either gasp in surprise and depart, or call out a tentative *Hello?* if they were curious to look about.

Which only left…

She stopped slicing the tuna steak that she'd put on the first night's menu as the chef's special. Marnie closed her eyes for the length of two deep breaths before putting on a smile, which she hoped looked more genuine than terrified, and turning.

"Am I really that scary?" The taller of the two women asked. "I don't feel that scary. Honest."

Marnie inspected her, the first time she'd seen Ms. Stark on anything bigger than her laptop's screen. She didn't loom. Nor did she overfill the space around her. Shockingly human-sized, Marnie still didn't know what to say to her.

Cooks Network was the only one that she actually subscribed to so that she could watch any content that included this woman. Her hosting was pleasant and her judging a fine translation of taste into description for the small screen. Her words also revealed a world-class palate. But Marnie knew that her interview questions were incisive, slipping past a chef's guard more smoothly than—

"Is that a Shiratsuru *maguro?*" the camerawoman hadn't aimed the lens at her face, instead focusing on her hands. Actually, on the half-meter-long tuna knife—*maguro* named both the fish and the knife she still held, pointed at the new arrivals. She set it quickly on the cutting board behind her, then had no idea what to do with her hands.

"Uh, yes."

The woman had tracked her big camera onto the knife. "I use a Takayuki, the three-hundred-millimeter Genbu, for my sushi and sashimi. I always found the big tuna knives a bit intimidating."

The Genbu cost over seven hundred dollars. Half the cost of her own blade but...still. Either the woman was utterly spoiled or—

"Forgive her," Kate's spoke softly enough to invite Marnie to lean in without forcing her to. "Rikka is an *itamae*. She gets even stranger than I—a mere cook in her eyes—do about knives."

"Don't mind Kate." Rikka lowered her voice conspiratorially, "She uses German knives, Henckels. Stainless steel, not even carbon steel."

"I grew up using them. They were my mother's, so don't mess with that, Rikka."

The camerawoman's grin said that was exactly the reaction she'd been expecting. Marnie saw that Kate also caught on a beat too late that it was a tease and grimaced.

Marnie didn't know what to say to that. But now this Rikka might be the daunting one. Marnie could debone and portion tuna better than most she'd met—the reason she was portioning the lovely fish herself. But she was not a sushi *itamae*, one sufficiently trained to literally *stand in front of the cutting board*. Had she ever met one? "What is an *itamae* doing behind a camera?"

"I like the toys Kate lets me play with." She patted the side of the camera, which looked as complex as her own *maguro* looked simple, then she seemed to disappear behind it. That left Marnie face-to-face with Kate Stark.

"Uh, hi."

"Want me to try the entry again?"

It was a nice offer, but Marnie shook her head. "No, I wouldn't do any better than the first try."

"Sure you would. A couple deep breaths. And imagine that Rikka actually makes sense more than ten percent of the time."

Marnie couldn't stop the laugh at that.

Kate stepped up after the laugh finished but before the smile had faded, holding out her hand. "Hi, I'm Kate Stark."

"Marnie Girard, welcome to my kitchen."

"Thank you, Chef."

Marnie noted that the handshake was as friendly as the woman and wanted to laugh again. She let herself actually look at the woman as they both joked about the tiny expanse of a small-ship galley producing over four hundred meal services per day.

They were much alike in build, though Kate Stark's eyes were a startling, brilliant blue. Offset by her pale skin and midnight-black hair that formed happy waves down to her shoulders, it was easy to imagine her striding through the Garden of Eden and befuddling the crap out of a clueless Adam.

"So, tuna steaks on the menu tonight, what else?"

And just that smoothly she was leading Kate through the menu as they toured each of the kitchen stations that were in various stages of prep. "Clifford is developing the mushroom-and-wine reduction for the chicken breast. We also have a steak au poivre and a butternut squash-eggplant lasagna."

As she continued the tour of the galley, Kate asking deeper and deeper questions about how such a small kitchen served fine dining to such a large crowd, Rikka always managed to be in the right place at the right moment for filming. Was there a Japanese word for someone good enough to *stand behind the camera*—an *itamae* for television?

Finally circling back to her station, it seemed only natural to demonstrate advanced techniques for portioning tuna steak. Soon Kate was trying her hand. Marnie could do better...but not much better. Right, Kate had asked about the techniques for the camera's sake, not her own. When she glanced aside at Rikka—with the camera presently focused on Kate's latest cut —to offer her a chance, she received an infinitesimal headshake. The camera didn't waver when Rikka repeated her answer.

Kate didn't look up from her task. "It's okay, Rikka. You can down the camera. I can feel you judging my cuts on Chef Girard's tuna. I'll let you clean it up."

In seconds, the camera was tucked on a high shelf. The lens no longer aimed at the workstation, but rather at her and Kate. It seemed to be staring at her, but thank God it was off and she could relax—a little. Or did the red light indicate it was still recording? *Merde!*

Marnie didn't see a thing wrong with Kate's work. However, she had to struggle to hide her wince as Rikka took her precious knife and inspected the blade carefully.

"The cutting board is a goal, not a target, Kate. With a knife like this, you aren't chopping onions. You're feeling your way down the grain of the fish." She pulled out a sharpening steel before Marnie could stop her.

A single bad stroke could require hours of work to fix on the long blade and she had a lot more fish to cut.

Rikka took three quick swipes of the blade along the steel with a bright, *shick, shick, shick,* then inspected the blade again. Nodding to herself, she plucked an apple from the supply basket for the dessert crumble. With a flick of the wrist almost too fast to follow, she peeled half the apple. Then she inspected the inside of the skin closely. No discernable white left attached to the skin nor red skin to the apple. Taking a big bite out of the apple, she set it aside. Marnie realized that she'd done the peeling in a single long stroke that used every millimeter of the long blade; she would see any imperfections down its length in the apple's flesh. Marnie would have to practice that move—when no camera could see her.

After a long moment staring at the blocky tuna steak and the knife, Rikka leaned forward. She shaved the merest sliver of tuna and tossed it aside.

"Really, Kate. You're better than that." Then she began slicing in rapid clean strokes of the long blade. After the third cut, she began talking without any change in her cut. "Oh wait, I keep forgetting that you're left-handed and this is a right-handed blade. In that case, not too shabby at all."

"Thank you so very much for your sanction of acceptability, I feel deeply honored." Kate's glance at the blade said that she hadn't noticed the handedness—the left-side flat and the right-side beveled.

Marnie ignored the small bite of jealousy at Rikka's non-reaction to Kate's sarcasm. They possessed a deep enough friendship it merely constituted friendly banter. The kind of friendship that didn't happen when you shifted from ship-to-ship and staff-to-staff as schedules demanded.

"You're welcome. Single bevel knives aren't all that common outside of Japanese fish knives, anyway." Rikka said it matter-of-factly enough that it was giving Kate an out without making any big deal of it.

If Kate wasn't here, and that camera with the disconcerting red light wasn't staring at her, she'd have asked for a class. Marnie could see that there were techniques she didn't have, but she couldn't begin to replicate.

Rikka paused in her slicing. "Marnie? Do you ever use the last quarter of the blade? I can't tell if it's my adaptation to my shorter sashimi blade or not knowing the proper technique for a *maguro* that's stopping me."

"Uh, I only use the last of the blade for the larger pieces of fish. If I'm splitting the length of it—"

Rikka made a long, slash gesture perpendicular to the grain

but in the air above the fish, as if splitting a whole fish flank. "Oh, I get it." And she fell back into her fast rhythm. "How many pieces do you want?"

"I was planning on fifty-five. I've already cut—"

"Twenty-seven plus Kate's five and now mine. Okay," and she continued slicing portions that Marnie knew she couldn't match.

5

THESE WERE ALWAYS KATE'S FAVORITE MOMENTS. ACTUALLY, running Cooks Network afforded her a lot of favorite moments. The peaceful, if not quiet, sounds of a well-run kitchen doing what it was supposed to do. Discovering a new chef in one of her competition shows, getting to know one in the interview shows. She didn't mind when Rikka or someone else showed her up on technique, though she still didn't see what was wrong with the sliver that Rikka had shaved away.

She leaned in to take the slice.

Without breaking rhythm, Rikka swung the knife over close by her fingertips, cut the piece in half, and went back to her portioning. "Oh, I do like the length of this blade. I should get one for Sam next Christmas." Kate could feel Rikka's wicked smile even though her back was turned.

"So that you get to use it, of course." Kate picked up the two halves of the sliver and handed one to Marnie.

"Of course."

"Or you could drop a hint so that he gets it for you." The raw tuna tasted perfect: meaty yet dense, and finally so creamy that it melted away on her tongue. She was definitely ordering the Chef's Special at dinner.

Rikka paused, "See, that's why you're the boss. I always miss the people hacks. I get the computer ones, but the people... That's you all over, Kate."

"Thanks, I think." She traded a smile with Marnie. "So, what's your favorite dish to make today?"

"I'll show you."

A woman with an impossible bounty of gently curling deep-brown hair breezed into the kitchen.

"Or maybe not," Marnie whispered to her with a sigh.

6

"OH MY GAWD! LOOK AT THAT ADORABLE KNIFE."

That voice! It had invaded Rikka's nightmares over these last months of video, text, email, phone, and every other kind of consultation.

But she would do anything Kate asked of her—ever. And Kate had asked her to liaison with Savannah for the wedding, so she had for every single, agonizing moment. Each time Kate called her for a job or to join her at the opera, it still turned her into a jabbering idiot. At least on the insides. Kate was awesome. If Rikka could grow ten more inches and develop a real figure just to be more like her, she would. Of course, nothing Rikka did would measure up, but she'd known that for a fact since birth. Being dumped in an orphanage at the age of zero wasn't the first step in a self-esteem-building trajectory.

She cut the last piece of tuna with a waver worse than Kate's first cut—as if she needed a reminder of her failings. She really shouldn't have said anything about Kate's cut, especially as this one was so much worse. But there were certain topics she knew she lost her sense of humor about, and a well-cut piece of fish ranked near the top of that list. The master she'd apprenticed under had called it the *itamae* disease. *You will never be happy ordering fish in a restaurant again.* He'd been right.

Rikka turned slowly, still holding the *maguro*. She briefly considered how the blade might look plunged to the hilt in Savannah Sachs' chest. Even an image of her as a cartoon character pinned to the refrigerator behind her, looking down at the knife and commenting on its *adorable* metallurgy, didn't make Rikka smile. Her sense of the absurd had been stretched past its limits by this woman.

Over the last two months of preparations this filming aboard ship, which *just happened* to include Savannah's wedding, the bride-to-be had hounded Rikka about everything from camera angles to exposure settings—proving, without a doubt, that she knew nothing about filming, cameras, light angles, or self-control. To her credit, she'd learned fast. To her vast discredit—leaving her still far down a dank hole in Rikka's consideration—Savannah then tried to turn around and tell her how Cooks Network generally and Rikka specifically were going to film the event right down to the lens and f-stop.

But this was Chef Marnie's blade, so Rikka cleaned and dried it thoroughly, inspected that the edge remained unblemished, and sheathed it. As she did so, she swore that she'd never be a bride like that. A *bride?* Where on this little blue planet had *that* thought come from? Nope, nope, and more nope.

"Oh, I just have to use that for the First Cut," capital letters clear in her over-excited tone (the only tone she had as far as Rikka could tell). "It will look so First-Class on camera."

Rikka almost said it would look utterly ridiculous but, for once—as she considered the angles, the slender length of the bride's arms, and the ginormous scale of the specified cake— Savannah was (impossibly) right. It would make great theater. Especially if the cake really was as large as promoted in the press packet (and the four revised designs that had followed).

"Oh, Marnie, can't you just see it? And—" a gasp of shocked pleasure "—you must be Katie Stark."

"*Kate* Stark," her tone should have chilled anything short of an erupting Icelandic geyser. But Kate was always too gentle. Her tone didn't stand a chance against a bride in the erupting volcano category.

"Oh, I'm just so excited that you're showcasing my wedding. Yours is the only channel I really watch."

"I'm so pleased." How Kate managed to say that without any outward sarcasm counted not as magic but as the purest of mystical powers.

Rikka couldn't match that even if she had magical mystical powers of her own. No genie in a bottle could ever grant her that skill. No—

"We're actually here to highlight Chef—"

"Oh yes, her too. Now, Katie—"

"Kate," Rikka snarled at her since Kate never would.

"Right," Savannah rolled blithely on, further proving Rikka's failure at even defending her friend's name. "Do you think we should do the formal photographs of the wedding dress before or after the ceremony, Katie?"

"We aren't doing—"

"Oh, I know," Savannah fluttered a hand at Rikka's reaction. "Not part of your plan, but my sick bridesmaid was also my wedding photographer. And I absolutely *must* have some First-Class photos of me in the dress."

"After!" Rikka snapped it out.

Kate raised an eyebrow from out of Savannah's view. They both knew that the light would be better before. But Rikka didn't change her opinion. She was counting on Kate, or anyone else, please, to kill off the bride before then.

7

HE SAT ON THE PARK BENCH HIGH ATOP TABLET ROCK IN STAGE Fort Park. From his perch, he had a clear view across the harbor to the town of Gloucester. The Twin Lights Pub, closed until further notice, lay hidden behind the Beauport Hotel and the harborside fish-packing plants.

The evening light showed the small town at its best. Dusk also provided the worst visibility, making it unlikely anyone not looking for him would see him. The three main church steeples caught the last of the sunlight. The Unitarian Universalists, St. Ann's Catholic, and Our Lady of Good Voyage with the Madonna cradling a Gloucester schooner in her arms for its safety—little good that had done the ten thousand fishermen who'd left this harbor over the last four centuries on a one-way trip to the briny deep. Lobster boats coming into port and an old schooner heading out on a two-hour cruise for tourists left wakes on the harbor's smooth waters. An hour earlier, it had been returning from a sunset cruise. They knew their marketing.

He opened the *Boston Globe* app on his tablet. The story hadn't made the first page. He had to tap through Metro,

Around Mass, and North Shore to find it. Even then, it wasn't a lead story but two screens down in the scroll.

Not that having a headline had been likely. The famous target who would have taken it to Page One hadn't even been present to die in the disaster—nor the main target, her assistant. His hands clenched around the tablet until they ached. To make matters worse, he'd had good money invested there; sadly, a write-off now.

A woman stepped into the small headland area of the vast park where the old fort once stood. Now it was little more than a splendid view and four black-painted replica canons. She spotted him, then hurried up the steep slope and steps carved into the back of Tablet Rock's massive prominence. It rose six stories high and as long and wide as an NHL hockey rink. This side faced the town and the vast harbor that had made Gloucester America's very first major seaport.

At his nod, she sat on the bench. Dana Winston's main distinguishing feature was the padded camera backpack she'd slid off and rested carefully between her knees. Other than that, she was neither pretty nor overly plain. Average height and definitely on the light side, nothing about her would draw your attention in a crowd. Perhaps that's why she'd become a videographer.

Dana set a pair of memory cards in a small plastic case on the open bench between them.

"Is that the only copy?"

"As promised. I'd like my freedom now. Give me what *you* promised." They'd agreed to meet here after a three-day cooling-off period.

He didn't feel any cooler. The whole point of the goddamn—

Taking a deep breath helped no more now than it had over the intervening days.

"I did exactly as you asked. It was..." her skin blanched

white and she swallowed hard "...horrible. But I know how to keep a secret."

He could see that there was no way Dana would keep this a secret for long, with or without video evidence. Sadly for her, there were two details she knew nothing about.

First, she'd failed in her assignment without knowing it. He hadn't cared about the Twin Lights Pub, its owner, or the couple trying to launch their careers in cooking shows. Because they'd jumped the filming schedule, the target he'd cared about hadn't been in attendance. Kate Stark and her right-hand assistant had been departing New York for Iceland when the *accident* had happened here in Gloucester. There he'd lost all trace of them.

In hindsight, part of that was his fault. He knew that Kate Stark always attended the filming of every first episode produced by her network. When he'd coerced the assigned videographer's services, he hadn't anticipated *A Brew and a Bite's* team jumping the gun on the schedule. He hadn't asked the videographer about the reason they were shooting two weeks ahead of the original schedule. By the time he'd found out, it wouldn't have mattered. She would have already been filming by then, so she'd probably had her phone off anyway. No real consequence.

Second, Dana wasn't versed in her Benjamin Franklin quotes: *Three may keep a secret, if two of them are dead.* Unfortunately for her, videographer Dana Winston counted as one person too many.

He raised the hand he'd kept draped over the back of the bench and rested it on the woman's slender neck.

"Hey, back off, creep. I have Mace."

As she reached for a pocket on her camera pack, he brought his other hand across sharply. Keeping her slender neck immobile in one hand, he slammed his palm into the side of her head. He felt her neck bones shatter. Then she went limp in his hands, only her wide eyes searching about in frantic shock. She managed a vague croaking sound, the last sea air that would ever pass her vocal cords.

While she continued with dying, he lifted her camera pack onto the bench and opened it. Her camera was already assembled with a long lens attached. He wrapped an arm around her slender shoulders and, with little effort, lifted her passive body enough that her feet didn't drag for the ten steps to the front edge of Tablet Rock. Not much to her. On this side, the rock rose sheer above the hard-packed path below. A six-story fall should prove sufficient.

He slid her hand into the camera's strap, hit record, and panned across the view, remaining carefully outside the frame himself. At the end of the pan, he shifted her body one more step. She tumbled backward into space, landing with a very convincing crunch at the base of the rock.

He scanned the park from his elevated view. A few cars remained at the off-leash dog park across the wide meadow and the road. The earlier ball game had disbanded and no dog walkers were in view along the park's many paths. Perfect. The only witness was the bronze tablet embedded in the face of the rock. It described the founding of Gloucester in 1623 and claimed that Myles Standish achieved less assholedom here than at the founding of Plymouth.

Puritan bastards.

They hadn't come to America to escape repression, they'd come to found a new land where no government existed to stop them oppressing whoever they wanted to. He didn't want to oppress anyone. But the right to revenge? It was the land of the free, after all. And that right was one he'd always appreciated. Too bad for the woman that she'd gotten in the way.

Returning to the bench, he retrieved the memory cards and his own tablet computer, leaving Dana's camera case opened on the bench. He peeled off and pocketed the flesh-toned micropore gloves that had been invisible in the twilight. They were biodegradable, so he'd flush them when he stopped for dinner farther down the highway—he'd heard that the Anmol Indian Restaurant in Beverly was exceptional. He reminded himself to keep an eye on the Wikipedia page for selfie-related deaths to make sure that was the ruling in Dana's mishap.

He still must solve the real problem—permanently.

8

THANKS TO RIKKA'S MANEUVERING, THEY'D MANAGED TO SHARE A dinner table with a group of birding enthusiasts. After the initial round of introductions at the six-person table, they showed only marginal interest in discussing Kate's strange world of cooking shows and television—a First-Class relief. Gads! The woman was already rubbing off on her.

Kevin Bragason, a recently retired Icelandic ambassador to Uganda—"Farthest south embassy we have, you know," he informed them with a softly British accent. "Just a hop, skip, and thirty kilometers to the equator. Plenty of relations south of the line, but we're the *lowest* embassy." His friendly wink invited them to take that however they chose.

He also admitted to having perhaps overindulged his passion for the winged creatures of that region by "Just a tad bit. What with Lake Victoria outside the front door, the wildlife was truly exceptional. Must say, now that I've been bitten by the beak, so to speak, I can't wait to truly see the birds of my homeland. Such a treat you gave me, my dear." He squeezed his wife's hand before he happily launched into a discussion of his life list with the other birders.

At Kate's glance, Clara smiled. "I managed to arrange this trip at the last minute in celebration of his retirement. I knew it was perfect when I saw all the rare birding sites we'd be visiting." She leaned in with a conspiratorial whisper. "I think he has as much fun with the camera gear as he does with the birds."

Kate winked back.

It turned out that Clara was one of the Knitting Gang that, she assured Kate, just might have a little more in common with street gangs than seemed likely. She'd knit a 3D bird of each species her husband had cataloged.

"Quite the lovely flock," the ambassador interrupted his conversation long enough to kiss his wife on the temple as if it was the most natural thing to do despite decades together. A romantic part of Kate envied that; the realistic part sighed that it wasn't going to happen in her life anytime soon.

"I'm self-admittedly not a rabid birder," Clara explained after Kevin's attention had returned to the others. "I grew up in the Yorkshire Dales, up in England's north. Though I met Kevin at Oxford. The other knitters still allow me to be a remote member of the Yorkshire Yarnbombers all these years on. Though I visit as often as I can as I still miss the Dales country."

Kate dug for details. Clara said they would choose a target —a rock, an old statue, or one of those imposing British red phone boxes—and would create knit art for it. Sneaking out at night, they'd attach the knitting of a lush garden over an electrical supply box or a pack of Corgis with crowns to preside over the local celebration during the king's coronation. Then, they'd head off in triumph to celebrate their bad-ass ways over a pot of tea and sweet scones.

Kate wished she'd taken up knitting just so that she could join them. Perhaps she would learn, then she'd travel to Yorkshire and yarnbomb an unsuspecting sheep or Shetland pony. Though Rikka would probably tell Mac, Cooks Network's creative director, and between them they'd turn it into another Kate Stark Production. The last thing she needed.

She added shows far more rarely than most people thought because she wanted each one to be important and receive the attention it deserved. *A Brew and a Bite* had captured her attention despite herself. She gave them a hard test at the Pig 'N' Whistle. Her intent had been to offer them a lunchtime's worth of training and then wish them luck.

But Ray and Shari had operated with a smooth but friendly efficiency that shone as pure quality on screen. And they'd treated one of her favorite pubs as a shrine, not a job. *That* she hadn't expected but was always looking for. They still had a lot to learn. As soon as they returned from Iceland, she and Rikka would go out in the field with them for a couple of shows and see if they could learn the needed depth and polish. Her money was on Shari to make it happen.

The other couple at their table were pure birders—Kate couldn't tell if they even owned a television, never mind watched one. They were soon installing bird identification apps onto her phone and talking about lens focal lengths with Rikka. When she admitted having a twelve-hundred-millimeter behemoth in the cabin, Kate wondered if they'd die of ecstasy.

Kate, on the other hand, really wanted to talk to Chef Marnie and Clifford the saucier about what they'd used on the tuna. There was a subtlety to the marinade that emphasized rather than masked the gentle flavor of the lightly seared protein. The choice of spring asparagus, just coming into season in midsummer Iceland, and roasted new potatoes with an unexpected ginger drizzle had complemented it wonderfully. The aroma alone had filled her senses, except it was even richer on the palate.

For dessert, after the apple crumble, there would be wedding cake up on the Quarterdeck, the aft dining area up on their own *Octavius* level.

That's where Chef Marnie had guided them once they'd managed to shed the bride by reminding her of her salon appointment. Kate hadn't known if there was one, but she'd made a bet with herself. Sure enough, Savannah had rushed from the kitchen as if someone had announced they were about to toss her curling iron overboard.

The Quarterdeck had been closed off to set up for the wedding. Marnie recruited Kate and Rikka to help with the massive cake's final assembly—layer by layer, then tier by tier. Which they'd managed with only a few dozen interruptions—three of which had them retreating to the galley for a bit of consulting on sauces, an issue with a mis-stowed protein that took some hunting to find, and stepping into prep while a chef suffering from too much shore leave soaked his brain in hot black coffee and a freezing cold shower.

Once the cake had started taking shape, Kate asked carefully—not wishing to cause offense—*Isn't it a little...sizeable?*

The bride is convinced that everyone will want a large piece of each flavor. It could feed our entire crew and all the guests for a week.

The flavor choices did indeed sound good, but a single forkful of each one would be sufficient as the various tiers sounded incredibly rich. The lightest was a chiffon-honey cake base, but even it sported thick layers of ruby chocolate ganache and a whipped brandy cream frosting—dyed dark blue and formed into waves. Four layers tall and a yard square, it alone could feed the entire ship's complement twice over.

Elevated on six-inch-tall, overly fat Greek columns and only marginally smaller, the second tier was a rum carrot cake thick with dried apricots, currants, and more figs than any fruit cake ever boasted. All coated in night-sky-dark blueberry cream cheese.

Perched atop slenderer columns, the third was a Kirsch Black Forest gateau hidden under a dark chocolate ganache.

The top layer was a strawberry-cashew-peppermint-schnapps fudge with a blackened chocolate icing and silver paste stylized winter snowflakes.

They're stars, Marnie had explained (her cruiser's manners not quite masking her French disdain). *Or rather the bride's interpretation of a star.*

Once assembled, Chef Marnie and the pastry chef had begun working with thin mixes of green, purple, red, and orange icings. Soon the theme revealed itself as the cake was transformed into a towering ombre of the Aurora Borealis. It ranged across the spectrum from the dark sea blue, with green and red reflected off its surface, to the star-laden midnight black sky. They still looked like snowflakes.

Rikka and her camera hadn't missed a moment of the final decoration; it wasn't art, it was mastery.

It had been one of *those* moments. Kate had done her best to fade into the background so that the two chefs took center stage.

Well, not complete mastery, the bride-and-groom cake toppers was tacky at best. The bride's figurine was alarmingly lifelike and an exact match right down to the least ruffle on the bridal dress (*see photo library included in the press packet*). The groom topper might have come off the shelf at any wedding supply shop. His figurine was also a few crucial millimeters shorter than the bride's. The engagement photo (*see included 8" x 10" glossy*) showed him two inches taller despite her heels.

Savannah had insisted however, even after loving the design, that each tier would be separated with a lace trim (*as provided*) dangling into the gaps to mask the Greek columns. Apparently the groom had insisted on them, sourcing them himself. Showing that she had some modicum of taste, Savannah had added the lace. That she'd insisted on using the Pantone Color of the Year, Peach Fuzz. The lace was interwoven with a hot pink to match her wedding dress and bridal rose bouquet respectively, mostly destroying the Aurora Borealis effect. Kate would make sure they highlighted the cake during a pre-lace phase. The columns weren't that hideous...well, perhaps they were.

We have a betting pool for how many kilos of cake will be leftover, Marnie had told them when it was done.

She and Rikka had each kicked in a twenty, though Rikka's estimate had definitely raised Marnie's eyebrows.

You don't know this bride, Marnie had pointed out. *There's no way for the entire guests and crew to eat that much. If she can't cram all the leftovers in my freezers—which she can't because I'm provisioned all the way to Aberdeen in twelve days—she'll have a helicopter fly in to cart it away.*

Rikka had shrugged and stuck with her low number of under five kilos. The fudgy top tier alone weighed that much. *I trust your cake,* Rikka had insisted. *I don't trust the bride.*

At that, Marnie had eyed her thoughtfully.

And now that Kate had met the bride briefly in the kitchen and more painfully during the pre-dinner captain's cocktail party, she wondered if Rikka had the right of it. Savannah Sachs wasn't what she'd expected: blonde, spoiled, beautiful, and an utterly whimsical airhead.

She was brunette and pretty enough to make a lovely bride. It seemed that all women achieved that on their wedding day, though Kate had never come close to testing that theory herself. But Savannah had a frenetic energy and a mind as sharp as Marnie's *maguro* knife. She knew precisely what she wanted, and God help anyone who got in her way. Slender to the point of anorexic, but not—at least according to her. If not, she was one of those impossibly slender women who burned calories even faster than Rikka.

No focus, she'd whispered to Rikka, who'd nodded her agreement.

Rikka fired her energy like a laser at whatever target had captured her attention: camera, computer, or Kate. And Kate knew from personal experience that Rikka's targets never stood a chance. Even Sam Fierro's past as a Marine Recon warrior hadn't saved him. Kate still wondered how Rikka had slipped so effortlessly past his formidable guard.

Kate couldn't think of once he'd even spoke to her.

In contrast, Savannah scattered herself in every direction— as if on a personal mission to control every aspect of a fracturing world.

9

THEIR SHIP HAD LEFT HARBOR DURING DINNER SERVICE, AND THEY were now well out to sea. Kate checked the full horizon around the ship, but there was only water and sky to see. Reykjavik lay out of sight behind them. In another three hours, they'd circle the end of Snæfellsnes Peninsula that reached eighty kilometers to the northwest.

She was out to sea in a way she'd never managed before. Nothing but blue ocean and their cruise ship. No other traffic, not even a stray fisherman.

A glance at her watch made equally little sense; it was past nine o'clock and they were steaming northwest—straight into the sun. It had finally settled toward the horizon, turning the sea into great sheets of blinding sparkles. She'd never traveled so far north, past the latitude of Fairbanks, Alaska, or the bulk of Scandinavia. Just one more big peninsula and they'd reach the Artic Circle.

It was a wonder that Savannah hadn't insisted on having the ceremony at the stroke of twelve in the land of the midnight sun so that she could claim two days as her anniversary. Perhaps she would have if it hadn't meant losing half her audience to their repose. Also, the ship would take two more days to reach Grimsey Island, the only part of Iceland to actually cross the Arctic Circle. And waiting would spoil Savannah's wedding-on-her-birthday plans.

"I love that they called it the Quarterdeck," Rikka whispered as she finished setting up her camera for the wedding.

"Why's that?" Kate should have kept her mouth shut, but it was too late now.

"The Quarterdeck appropriately takes up the aft quarter of the *Octavius* Deck and makes it sound enough like an old-time sailing ship. Can't you just see Ahab and his peg leg pacing about the binnacle—whatever a binnacle was. His ship, the *Pequod,* would be a great name if this ship had another deck."

"Maybe the designers didn't want to invite a visit from the ghost of a great white whale hungry for vengeance."

"Maybe," Rikka conceded. "Maybe."

Facing the rear of the ship, the Butler's Pantry was the last room on the right along the hallway. Inside was a dumbwaiter down to the galley three decks below. The cake had traveled on it, as would future meals for those who wished to dine outside.

Much of the open Quarterdeck had been roofed with a rigid canopy of dark-tinted glass, left open to the sides. The very rear remained uncovered, looking out over the wake spooling aside as they traveled. The weather was fine this evening...night... whatever this was.

Tables and chairs crowded the space, especially with the entire ship's guest list in attendance. She and Rikka had managed to secure a good vantage for the camera by arriving early.

"The cake looks different." Something about the color composition had changed.

"Someone damaged the icing, looks like someone bumped into it. So Marnie turned it around." Rikka had gone in for closeups and garnered the latest news while Kate was chatting with the groom, who everyone else appeared to have forgotten about.

"They should toss whoever touched that cake overboard. Even with the horrid Pantone Peach Fuzz lace, it's a baker's masterpiece."

"I'll contact Sam. He'll come and take care of it."

Kate started to say it was probably best if she left him and his Brooklyn butcher shop in peace, but Rikka's phone was already out. She whispered *Lover Boy* at it, and it auto-dialed. The second ring chopped off half through. Sam didn't say anything, of course; he was never the sort to start a conversation.

"Wedding time, Sam."

"Rikka!" Kate couldn't stop herself.

"What?" Rikka squinted at her.

Sam's silence was eloquent.

She still didn't get it. Kate wondered why it always fell to her to explain things. "Did you mean to propose to Sam over the phone?"

"No! Duh." Then she looked down at the phone, up at Kate, thought about what she'd said, then turned to the phone once more. "Oh, I meant the one aboard ship," she told Sam.

He voiced no surprise, panic, or dismay. A hard man to fluster, Kate was starting to think their odd-couple match might actually make more sense than she'd first thought.

"Here." Rikka did something on the phone's controls too fast for Kate to follow and the camera's feed flashed up on the phone. It was now streaming to Sam.

Kate couldn't imagine why he would want to watch the uncut feed of a society wedding, but he now had no choice. Kate wasn't looking forward to it herself.

The ceremony's brevity was a pleasant surprise though; Savannah had judged her crowd well. With half of them strangers to both the bride and groom, she'd known they'd only stick around as long as it was entertaining.

The ceremony moved along with a smooth alacrity that would neither bore the attendees with onerous duration nor its concision offend any gods who happened to be listening.

Perhaps it was the captain who had set time limits on Savannah's show. Five-five, with her short dark hair just graying at the temples and a smooth Ukrainian accent, Captain Oksana Rudenko managed to cut an imposing figure in her dress uniform. She faded away as soon as the ceremony had completed. Kate made a mental note to interview her later as a master of her own craft. The contrast of the captain's specialty in contrast to Marnie's as a chef in the otherwise common environment of a cruise ship might prove interesting.

The direct segue from the recession of the happy couple— kept decidedly short by the twenty-meter width of the ship—to the cake cutting made Kate think a little better of the bride. Dancing would follow immediately afterward.

A tasteful note in the invitation, *Gifts to support World Central Kitchen* and a QR code, had solved the issue of gift-giving, saving both time and space. For that alone, Kate could forgive Savannah many failings. José Andrés had been on Cooks Network several times promoting his work to feed those in most desperate need: hurricane, wildfire, and war victims. All decommissioned Cooks Network kitchen equipment, too imperfect to use on camera, was delivered directly to WCK at Cooks Network's cost in addition to Kate giving him free ad space whenever he had a new fundraising promo.

After a moment of jostling, which Kate had to assure them she could cut out during the edit (though as the only unchoreographed moment between the couple she might not, it almost bordered on charming—almost), they were poised for the perfect cake-cutting shot. At least the bride was, with some reason. Savannah's wedding dress was a knockout and she knew it. Bret's tux had probably come from the Men's Wearhouse. His handsome face smiling (for reasons that simply couldn't last) over her shoulder was all he needed to be.

His attention wandered briefly to Marnie. She and her sous chef stood in the shadows on the other side of the cake, ready to leap to service after the ceremonial first cut. Their black chef jackets rendered them invisible. Bret made a brushing motion in their direction as if they stood too close for the shot. But Marnie, Rikka, and Kate had run a camera test earlier and she was right where she should be, so she stood fast.

Kate didn't much like the overcomposed image, but it would make good television. She would present it with no comment on her behalf; let others provide their own internal dialogue. Besides, this was only a moment of a two-week cruise with Marnie, not Savannah, as the focus.

And they *were* ridiculously photogenic. Having grown up in the selfie age, they knew the art of posing down to their toes. They even managed to not make it look as over-posed as the hundreds of thousands of selfies that typically annoyed the crap out of her. Perhaps they were genuinely happy in this instant.

The setting didn't hurt either. Turning golden on its slow approach to kiss the horizon, the sun burnished their skin to a rich luster. The contrast of the towering Aurora Borealis cake couldn't have looked better against the background of the sparkling sea. The low golden light even made the lace look almost appropriate as bands of color across the frosting-formed sky.

Maybe the bride did know something of what she was doing. Kate made a mental note to actually read the press packet that the bride had provided.

Marnie had protested about Savannah using the *maguro* knife for the cake cutting. Savannah hadn't merely offered to buy her a new one if there was the least damage; she'd cheated and asked Rikka to name the best *maguro* blade. Rikka's response of, *I've always loved the Tamahagane* had made Marnie's eyes bulge. Savannah hadn't even blinked when Kate informed her that was a six-thousand-dollar knife.

So, she wielded Marnie's fifteen-hundred-dollar knife at her chiffon cake. Savannah was fine-fingered enough for it to look like a long sword in her grasp. Bret's hand beneath hers on the handle didn't show enough to change the effect.

From the camera position at the front of the Quarterdeck and facing aft, the cake was placed near the right-hand rail—with Marie out of shot in the narrow space between the cake and rail. The bride stood to the left side of the cake with the applauding attendees well to the side but visible. The groom stood directly aft of the cake. Behind them lay a few hundred leagues of open ocean with sunlight scattering like God's own glitter.

Kate glanced at the screen that Rikka was using and that she, in turn, was echoing to her phone for Sam. Here, finally, was a good reason to use an 8K camera. Rikka was filming the event with a wide-angle lens but at such high resolution that, during editing, they could zoom in on any detail. If they wanted to, they could fill the screen with the bride or groom's face without overstretching the zoom so much as to make them blurry and pixelated. Yet they could also edit in a wide view of the attendees.

Savannah glanced at Kate, who nodded to reassure the bride they had a good image—something she would have to edit out. Savannah glanced over her shoulder and saw Bret's attention had wandered again to the chefs.

"Bret!" Savannah's harsh whisper was picked up by the microphone they'd wired her with for the ceremony, but would be easy to edit out.

He jerked as if slapped, gave her a nod, and faced the camera.

Then the couple offered a final smile for the camera.

A smooth downward slice; the bride's hand resting over the groom's on the blade.

The angle started fine, but then it shifted.

Savannah and Bret had started with a level cut. They paused ever so briefly partway down. To continue, they angled the blade tip down into the cake to complete the slice.

That's when everything went to hell.

10

KATE'S PRACTICED EYE CAPTURED IT LIKE A FREEZE-FRAME SERIES.

Frame One: the odd knife angle of Savannah and Bret's cut and the depth of the lowest tier. It meant that the tip of the *maguro* had contacted the cake support's bottom plate first. The odd angle also marred the clean line of the dress, which was bound to give Savannah a case of the fits.

Next: a brilliant flash—on the back side of the cake.

Followed by a sonic slap she felt in the center of her chest that made all other sounds inconsequential by comparison.

Then the images began to fracture as the scope of the disaster expanded.

The top two tiers launched upward, punching through one of the overhead tinted-glass panels, with the bridal cake toppers leading the charge.

Marnie and her sous chef caught the primary brunt of the blast. Plastered in an Aurora's worth of icings, chiffon cake, and carrot—the gateau and fudge tiers having left the cake on a vertical rather than horizontal trajectory—were blown back against the railing. They departed the scene with elaborate backflips that appeared almost slow-motion graceful as Kate's mind struggled to keep up.

Bret, the groom, forced to stand around the rear of the cake by the large belled skirt of Savannah's dress—so artfully mimicked in the plastic figurine before it launched aloft—fully caught the force of the cake's explosion. It struck with a body blow to his left side—the one not blocked by Savannah or her massive dress—spinning him like a top as it sent him hurtling down the aft stairway to the deck below.

Savannah remained standing, unharmed, unblemished by flying ganache or whipped brandy-cream frosting.

In slow motion, she lifted the long *maguro* blade from the cake and looked at it with an expression of surprise.

11

NEAR-PERFECT SILENCE REIGNED, BROKEN ONLY BY THE GENTLE sounds of the ship's uninterrupted passage through the waves and the distant thrum of the engines.

It didn't last.

The screams of panic blasted from the crowd as hard as the cake had blasted into Marnie.

Kate looked up in time to see the upper two tiers of the cake, which had shot through the glass ceiling, land one pane aft. They didn't break through despite the weight of the confections, instead sticking for a long moment. All alone and up to her neck in dark fudge, only the bride topper's head remained above the sky-black-and-star-spangled frosting. The groom landed separately on the glass with an absurdly bright *plink* sound that fell into a momentary gap in the screams.

Rikka mumbled something, then aimed the camera to capture the demise of the two upper tiers as they slid off the glass ceiling and down into the sea. Next she swung her camera toward the crowd all trying to cram through the single door to the ship's interior.

"What are you filming?"

"Possible crowd responses. I don't see anyone looking smug or satisfied, but the film might show something."

Kate had been trained by the best in the Secret Service to react to a situation intelligently rather than with emotional panic. Rikka never responded with panic. Not even when Kate had arrested her for her role in laundering hundreds of millions of dollars of counterfeit North Korean currency. Rikka had considered it an amusing side gig. Something to keep her entertained and well compensated while she attended whichever classes intrigued her at MIT. Kate wondered where she'd learned that unflappable calm. Prior to arresting her, Kate knew little of Rikka's past.

But now was not the moment to ask.

She rushed to the rail.

Nothing overboard. No sign of the chefs. Only some cake debris floating far astern in the ship's wake, looking like a smudge upon the bright water. If there were bodies among the debris, they weren't visible in the wake.

She moved to the stairs leading down to the next level, careful to not slip in the splattered cake. Nothing to see of the groom. But she could easily imagine his tumble carrying him over that aft rail and into the frigid Icelandic waters.

Kate spotted help on the way. The old sailor and his four black-clad ninja deckhands launched a small Zodiac from the *Endurance* Deck's rear platform, aft of the indoor-dining room. With someone else seeing to possible rescues, Kate turned back to the mostly empty Quarterdeck. Only three of them remained.

Rikka had left her camera, still perched on its tripod, and stepped over to Savannah. She very carefully extracted the *maguro* blade from Savannah's lax fingers. No comfort for the bride, still frozen in deep shock somewhere beyond panic. Instead, Rikka sighted down the knife blade.

"There's a tiny nick about six inches from the handle; the

edge was immaculate when I sheathed it earlier. Nothing in the cake should have caused that."

Savannah's eyes tracked Rikka's movements, but no other reaction showed.

Rikka slid the blade straight into the cake close above the base layer's support tray.

"Hey!" Kate called to stop her, making Savannah jump slightly.

"Chill. Whatever was gonna go bang went bang already." Lifting the blade upward through the layers of the bottom tier, she hooked something.

Whatever it was, must have been placed between the top two layers of that tier as the cake was initially assembled. Thinking back to the setup, that would fit with one of the breaks they'd taken during the final assembly. Marnie had wanted to check in with her full kitchen staff when they came on shift for dinner service. Or had she been called away? Kate and Rikka had simply followed in her wake. Or had they been requested to follow?

As Rikka dragged the knife free of the mangled tier, a wire broke the surface of the dark blue whipped *sea-foam* brandy-cream frosting.

Rikka wiped a stretch of the wire between pinched thumb and forefinger. She licked them clean. "Wow! Marnie did good. This is seriously *First-Class.*" She stole the bride's favorite phrase.

Still no reaction from Savannah.

As she kept lifting, the wire cut a circular arc around the remains of the tier. Finally clear, it dangled eighteen inches down either side of the knife. Each end of the wire had a thicker shaft about six inches long that ended in a point. One end had a small clamp attached to it and a broken-off lead of wire.

"It's a knitting needle," a breathy voice whispered.

Kate turned to the dazed bride. "I thought knitting needles were straight."

"A circular one is good for sweaters and hats." Savannah spoke as if in a dream, then held out her index fingers about six inches apart. "They also make double pointed ones about this long."

Then she fainted. Dropping to the deck like a falling flower petal, she landed face-first into the cake that had splattered at the groom's feet.

A whole side of her Peach Fuzz dress plowed into the Aurora-colored icing as if it was transforming into a dark night.

The only ones left on the deck were herself, Rikka, and the groom cake topper. At a slight roll of the ship on the sea, the groom topper tumbled from where it had landed on the glass above and fell through the missing panel's space. He landed feetfirst in the cake's remains, leaning forward as if peering over the edge of the cake at his fallen bride.

12

"I GAVE THE BRIDE A MILD SEDATIVE. HER MAID OF HONOR PUT her to bed." The ship's doctor, young enough to be fresh out of his residency, sat in the Captain's Club with a stiff whisky in his grip.

It was straight-up midnight by Kate's watch. Twenty-five minutes past sunset, there was still plenty of twilight to see the man's gray pallor.

For being married a mere two and a half minutes, the bride had been surprisingly docile. Once revived, she hadn't screamed or protested. Her tears had been quiet and appeared heartfelt; more than Kate had expected from her.

"As to the three bodies in our freezer..." He shuddered, then slammed back the whisky.

The captain refilled it without asking or the doctor noticing.

"This ship isn't set up for, nor is her doctor..." he tapped his chest with his glass, stared down at it in surprise, then set it aside without drinking it, "...trained in, autopsies. I'm a GP, General Practitioner. Which makes me a glorified medic, not a forensic pathologist. But my best guess, if it wasn't the hypothermia that killed Marn—" his pallor shifted from gray to sheet white "—that killed *our chefs,*" he said the two words very carefully, "it was their broken backs when they were slammed backward into the railing. The explosion may have collapsed their lungs too. Definitely some broken ribs. The groom's neck broke either on the way down the stairs or as he went overboard."

After that, he collapsed back in his chair, picked up his glass, and slammed back its contents.

"Willem?" The captain nodded to the old salt who was the Zodiac Master responsible for moving people from ship to shore when there was no dock. It made him the ship's safety officer, too. He and his ninjas had also been the ones to haul all three victims from the sea.

Willem so looked the part that Kate wondered if he'd once been a movie actor. Barrel-chested with broad shoulders and a thick gray beard through which a worn Afrikaner accent wandered soft enough that he must have left South Africa's shores decades ago.

"Heard the bang. My boys lit up like bloodhounds, not the sort of sound we're used to be hearing in any way good. One of 'em doing maintenance on the *Endurance* Deck's rear platform spotted that chap in the tux doing a flip over the rail. Barely hit it, he said. Tumbling through air, he went over headfirst and backward like that Fosbury gent flopping over the high jump bar. Said it didn't look like he was doing much by the time he went inta the water. Think Doc got it right at the first, neck gone as he went down the stairs—if he even touched those. Might ha' been the blast hisself that did for him." He even spoke like an old salt.

Then he looked as if he was perhaps attempting a smile somewhere deep in his beard. "Can't say as we tried to rescue any of the cake."

Rikka was the only one who managed a giggle at his joke in the grim meeting.

Kate made the mistake of looking at her.

"Just imagine the bride cake topper setting off on a voyage of her own. She'll ride the Norwegian current, surf the Arctic ice, and journey forth. Perhaps she'll travel all the way to Severny Island in the Russian Artic to, one day, mystify the crap out of a polar bear cub."

Willem definitely smiled behind that beard. Kate would wager he had some great stories, and she looked forward to sitting him down some night over a beer and trading a few, in less trying times.

The captain, untouched by the moment of levity, glanced at the other two members of her crew who'd been called to this conference.

Mr. Charles, the cruise director, raised his hands palm out. "This was Marnie's to-do, I fear. I was ensconced in my cabin filing the boarding reports."

Alli waved a sheaf of papers at them. "Tomorrow's itinerary. With the bridal party out, I was forward on the *Flying Dutchman* Deck distributing copies to the cabins while everyone was down on *Octavius* for the wedding. First I knew of it was when the passengers came screaming back inside." Then she looked at her hand in some surprise. "Still need to get these out."

Captain Rudenko turned to Kate and Rikka, a moment Kate had been dreading. "Aside from a hundred panicked passengers, you two are my best witnesses."

Being true didn't make it any less awkward; they were strangers to this tight-knit crew.

"My boyfriend sent a—" Rikka stumbled to a halt and looked at Kate. "When the hell did my life get so settled that I can call someone my boyfriend without blind panic?"

"Clearly not yet. Focus, Rikka. Dead people."

"Right. Uh-huh. Okay." She took a couple of deep breaths, though appeared no calmer afterward. "I sent a video of the cake before, during, and after to this, uh, guy-I-know-really-well," she rushed that out even faster than she normally talked. "He sent back a diagram of the most likely setup. Those columns that Marnie used to separate the tiers might have been shaped charges."

"What's a shaped charge?" Alli asked.

"Bad news, those," Willem stated with a tone of too much experience. "Ya take a bit of plastique, C-4 and the like. Moldable stuff that, so you play with the shape. If you know what you're about, it'll throw more'n ninety percent of the force one way 'stead of t'other. I remember this once we were setting up a very narrow test but missed the range target. Fifty meters on, we killed a farmer's cow on'ta far side of the fence. Probably shouldn't have carved our unit's number in'ta the face of the C-4 charge. It scorched half-meter-tall numbers in'ta that cow's hide afore it killed him. No chance of saying twasn't us. Damned expensive cow; good beef though."

"That's what my, uh," Rikka struggled for a moment, before gasping out, "*friend* said. Anyone within a couple feet of the wrong direction would catch the brunt of the explosion, but no one else. He's kinda into those sorts of things."

Kate knew that was an understatement. Sam Fierro had served as a US Marine for twenty years, most of that in Marine Force Recon, their stealthiest and most elite team. They had two main missions, reconnaissance and clandestine assault. With all the skills to do the former and switch on a dime to execute the latter.

"I took some close-ups, but I didn't touch the cake other than finding the wire until some pro can get a good look at it."

The captain turned to Kate.

"I didn't see anything except the results: Marnie and her assistant blown straight back, and the groom spinning down the stairs. I do have a US Secret Service background, mostly concerned with taking down counterfeiters," which was how she'd caught Rikka, "and attempting to protect VIPs." Which hadn't gone well at all. No way was Kate going to admit to any expertise with explosives. Offering an opinion on Sam's analysis was like a rookie agent on the Presidential Protection Detail—there was just no point.

The captain nodded. "Well, I have radioed ashore. It is complicated as we are a British company aboard a ship of Bahamian registry, which is cruising in Icelandic waters. But they've promised to send out someone by morning."

"Which will occur in approximately three hours," Mr. Charles noted.

Kate's disorientation only grew worse. She'd never been somewhere that sunrise occurred at three in the morning.

"Perhaps closer to breakfast." The captain then grimaced before turning to her. "Ms. Stark, I know that you are technically traveling as a guest aboard this ship, but I wondered if I might ask a favor."

13

"You so totally fell for it," Rikka teased Kate as they walked into the galley.

"And what was I supposed to do?"

"Let them eat cake!" Rikka declared. Then glanced up toward the Quarterdeck several stories above. "Oh, wait. The cake kinda got blown to pieces."

The only other person in the kitchen was the pastry chef making the morning baked goods—Filipino by his looks. "Who are you lot?" He asked with a big yawn followed by a slug of coffee.

"She," Rikka hooked her thumb at Kate, "is your new executive chef."

"What about Marnie?"

"Where have you been?"

The pastry chef blinked at her slower than a napping cat.

"You slept through it all."

"Part of being a pastry chef. Early to bed, way too early to rise. How did the wedding go last night?"

"A bit of a blow-out."

"So, what? Marnie will be late? She's not due in for another couple hours yet." He fought off another yawn and reached for his coffee again.

Rikka figured it'd be easier to just rip off the bandage. "No way to say this gently. Marnie, her sous chef, and the groom were all murdered last night by an exploding wedding cake."

The chef spit a mouthful of coffee over his rolled-out dough, then tried dabbing it up with the cloth he'd had flipped over his shoulder. "Hey, not funny."

"Not meant to be, but I can riff on that in some amusing ways if that would help. *Three Funerals at a Wedding? The Icing Storm?*"

He stopped in mid-dab and looked up at her very slowly. "You're serious?"

Rikka hit play on the camera and held out her phone.

He leaned in to watch it. "Nice dress. Who'd have thought she'd look so totally hot? I mean, have you sat and talked to the woman? She such a pain in the—"

The explosion ruined the image.

This time he set his coffee mug down in his dough without noticing.

Rikka had time to stow her phone, turn off the camera, and glance at Kate before the man even blinked.

"I, uh, need a moment." His voice wandered aimlessly as if his brain was no longer attached to it. His legs didn't do much better as they carried him out the galley door and into the twilit dining room.

Kate tapped the dough. "It's already getting dry. In a couple more minutes it will form a skin that inhibits the pastry's rise during baking."

"That's so you, Kate." The only way she'd kept her act together last night had been watching Kate's rock steadiness. It was as if even the exploding cake knew not to mess with her. Now she was focused on pastry dough being ten minutes past perfect at the start of a day that, unless Rikka missed her guess, would be rife with ginormous problems.

"Find me Marnie's menu plan."

Rikka nodded and started poking around on one of the computer terminals in the galley. All she found were provisioning lists and meal schedules. So much for databases. Perhaps Marnie had used spreadsheets instead...

"Rikka."

"Uh huh." It had to be here somewhere.

"Look where I'm pointing."

"Uh huh." Then she did. Kate, her fingers now white with a dusting of flour, was pointing at a clipboard hanging beside the computer.

"Wow!" Rikka could only blink at it. "That's so retro." She'd never have thought to look for something like that.

"Fine. I'm Old School."

"So's Chef Marnie, so I guess you're in good company."

"Yes, except she died last night."

"Fussy, fussy." Rikka grabbed the clipboard and began reading. "Brunsviger, rabarberhorn—" Kate squinted at her. "Hey, you've got me. If you don't know, we're lost. The next ones are kanelsnurrer. Are those the cinnamon thingies?"

"Cinnamon-cardamom knots," Kate stared down at the dough, "but I have no idea how to form them." Maybe she wasn't as together as she appeared. That actually made Rikka feel a little better. Having Kate be a little more human felt several steps back from panic that she'd never measure up.

But the stress on her face showed, or perhaps it was the three hours of sleep in the last forty-eight. Whatev—it was freaking Rikka out. She needed her idols to be big and shiny to avoid the pits of despair that opened up around her when she wasn't watching carefully. Sneaky buggers.

So she focused back on the printout. "We need sixty of each and then—"

Kate squeaked. Actually squeaked.

Not good. Very not good.

Rikka tossed the clipboard back onto the chef's tiny desk and they both jumped at the clatter. "Screw it, Kate. Make whatever. After last night, as long as you don't serve them cake for breakfast, they'll be happy."

Kate nodded once, twice, and then her hands began cutting and forming the dough—though Rikka couldn't tell into what. Pastry wasn't exactly her top skill set, but if Kate needed a pastry sous chef, she could become one. If she needed Rikka to fly to the moon by flapping her wings, she'd try.

Poking around the kitchen, she unearthed more dough in the proving drawers, one more lump doing its first rise, and several sets of formed pastries in various stages of their second rise. Then a timer began chiming behind her.

By the time she located the right oven and a pair of oven mitts, the two trays of something small and yummy smelling were on the dark side of golden brown. She pulled those, shuffled them into the walk-in refrigerator to halt their cooking, then slid in two trays of those roll-twist-kanelsnurrer thingies that looked fully risen. Even staring at them, she had no idea how they were formed.

"Find him," Kate didn't look up and her hands didn't slow.

Thankfully he hadn't gone far. The pastry chef had wandered through the dining room and leaned with his forehead against a side-facing window.

Rikka liked sneaking up on people, a skill she'd learned at the orphanage. But he probably didn't need that right now, so she purposely rattled a table hard enough to be heard. He didn't react.

She moved up beside him to watch the sunrise. The ship was still cruising northwest, the three a.m. ball of fire was climbing up over the mountains of Iceland's northwest peninsula.

"She's really dead?" He didn't turn to look at her.

"Yes. Don't go into the front starboard freezer on Deck Zero. You won't like what you find there."

He made no other response. Did he know that he was staring directly at where Marnie had disappeared overboard? Was it chance that landed him precisely here or did it reveal suspicious contemplation of the carnage he had cooked—no, he was the pastry guy—that he'd *baked* up?

"What's your name?"

"Miguel."

"Okay, Miguel. I need you to do something for me."

Nothing.

She reached up to smack the back of his head. She'd meant it to be a light tap to snap him out of it but he'd raised it just enough at the last second that she smacked his forehead back into the glass.

"Hey!" He rubbed his forehead as if she'd run the half-meter of Marnie's *maguro* fish knife through it.

After the events of last night, it struck her as funny. He wouldn't even have a bump, yet he looked as offended as the plastic groom figurine who had been blasted aloft only to descend back into a wedding disaster of epic proportions.

"Why did you do that?"

"Sorry, but I need you to get your act together, Miguel."

"I..." he waved a hand helplessly. "I never told her how I felt about her because she was my executive chef." He collapsed once more into silence and returned to staring aft.

"My best friend is back there in the galley doing your job and it's utterly freaking her out. Now go. Please?"

He glanced at the kitchen, then at her again.

She grabbed his collar and pulled him down to her level from his lofty five-foot-six heights until they were nose to nose. "Go. Now."

He still didn't move.

"Mi-guel..." she ground it out as a threat.

He made a gurgling sound. Oops! She'd grabbed a bit more than his collar. She let go of his throat and he raced off. Whether to get to the galley or to get away from her, she didn't care; he went. She followed close behind.

He'd stopped three steps into the kitchen. "What are those?"

"Chocolate-almond mini croissants," Kate answered. She was surrounded by trays of them.

"That's not the plan for—"

"It is now. Fix it tomorrow."

"But—"

Rikka looked around for the second biggest knife in the kitchen in case he got feisty. The big *maguro* had been locked up by the captain as a piece of evidence.

"Right. Okay. Right." Miguel saved Rikka from escalating to further levels of mayhem by moving to the baking station again without another word.

The scene with Miguel replayed in one way or another for the rest of the morning; it had indeed been strictly Marnie and her sous chef's gig last night. Down in their cabins half below the waterline, her staff had been buffered from the blast and the aftermath. They rose from the ship's depths groggy, ignorant, and innocent. Rikka made sure that the first two conditions didn't last long enough to test Kate's patience.

The morning menu was straightforward. All that was necessary was an extra pair of hands and a bit of organizing. The only sneaky thing Rikka did was make sure that her camera was always aimed at Kate. Because once freed from the pastry, not her specialty, she became the calm force in the center of the kitchen's whirlwind.

During one brief break Rikka whispered to her, "I want to grow up to be just like you."

"You want to be looking for an excuse to smash a fifty-thousand-dollar camera over your best friend's head?"

Rikka reminded herself that: a) Kate missed nothing, and b) that she still couldn't figure out how someone like Kate was her friend. Best friend? Serious dose of *Whoa! For real?* Life was way cool—even with dead people in it.

So why did she have so much trouble believing it could stay this way? Because except these last few years with Kate, her life had been anything but predictable.

Shortly before service began in the dining room, Kate deliberately stood directly in front of the camera—and turned her back on it. Rikka checked her phone—all she could see was the back of Kate's head and a sliver of the stove's vent hood. Kate utterly ignored one of Rikka's finest and most powerful scowls as she called for everyone's attention.

"Before we jump into service, I just wanted to thank everyone for putting the present troubles behind you and leaning into this morning's challenges. We have breakfast service for a hundred and sixty people ready to roll. Once the guests are off ship on today's outings, you'll have some time to grieve and catch up. But we're ready and that's thanks to all of you. Marnie trained up a fine crew. I would just like to add—"

Then Rikka turned and screamed.

14

"Sam!" Rikka raced across the kitchen and threw herself into Sam Fierro's arms.

Kate's pulse didn't recede from faster than Chopin's "Minute Waltz" until she'd ascertained there were no fresh bodies lying about the galley.

As Rikka's waist was little bigger than one of Sam's biceps, he caught her easily, not even rocking back on his heels.

He filled the doorway, doubly with Rikka in his arms.

But Kate could see another face peering over his shoulder. Closing her eyes, taking a slow breath, and then looking again didn't make it go away.

Sam stepped into the galley, not bothering to set Rikka down, because there wasn't really room to do so.

"Hey there, Katydid." The man behind Sam leaned on the door jamb.

Kate opened her mouth, then closed it again. She wasn't a bush cricket but hadn't convinced her twin brother to stop using that nickname since...birth. No chance Paul would change now.

"Uh, sorry about the plane. I remembered the date of your tour, not that you needed it the day before to fly out."

Then she spotted his grimace.

"And you forgot about that too, didn't you?"

"Only a little." He shrugged in that charming way that seemed to make all women forgive his every travesty. "It's here now," he offered as if that made everything okay, "however you pronounce the name of this town."

From the depths of her windowless galley, she'd only been marginally aware of their arrival at the cruise's first port of call along the northern shore of Iceland. And, as she wasn't sure how to pronounce Stykkishólmur either, she kept her mouth shut.

"Stih-kih-shoal-muhr," one of the line cooks said. "Like it's spelled."

"You're hopeless, Stark." Rikka, the one woman other than herself wholly immune to Paul's charms, patted Sam's arm as he set her down.

"Better than you, Pint-size."

Kate held up a hand to stop Rikka's riposte. Once the two of them started, they could go all night—or all day, as it was still morning, and *then* all night. Two hours of sleep last night and none the one before, followed by the last three hours leaning into meal prep, left her buffer severely debuffered.

"I've got a meal service. You two need to get out of the way."

"We've got it, ma'am," Miguel, the pastry chef, spoke up. "And we've already started lunch prep. Dinner is another matter, but that can wait."

"You sure?"

Miguel offered a shrug not all that different from Paul's, but managed to communicate that it was close enough to truth to be okay—not a Paul Stark *fait accompli* shrug no matter the dazzling percentage of fabrication included in any of his statements.

She didn't need to be told twice. Kate scrawled her phone number on the corner of a whiteboard and grabbed a dark-chocolate croissant. Her blood sugar was already belowdecks and she didn't want it to sink overboard as she didn't know how deep the Stykkishólmur harbor might be. She bit the crunchy end off and led her people out of the overcrowded galley.

And square into someone's chest.

The croissant mashed against the man's shirt. The chocolate, still warm, left a large splodge of brown like a stab wound in the middle of his breastbone.

"Good thing it wasn't coffee." In her current state she might have wept over spilled coffee. She desperately needed a caffeine jolt.

He looked down at the large chocolaty smear, then once more at her. His blue-gray eyes studied her intently—his mouth in a hard line. He was worth study in return. He either needed a shave or was one of those guys who knew how good they looked in a two-day beard. Viking-long dark blond hair hung loose down to his shoulders. Her brief moments in Reykjavik before boarding the ship revealed that he wasn't a put-on; many Icelandic men embraced the rugged look very effectively.

Though she'd have noticed him in the crowd last night, you couldn't easily miss the man.

He raised a single eyebrow with no hint of irony nor smile. Serious guy in a worse mood. Well, she could match that—as soon as she found a mug of coffee. Preferably one wrapped around eight hours of sleep.

"Uh, sorry about the shirt. I hope you have a clean one back in your cabin."

"I do not have a cabin."

No cabin meant that he wasn't a passenger. Also, he was all out of age with this crowd, the elderly bird watchers and knitters or the Gen Zers aboard for the wedding. He landed, as she and Rikka did, in the wide gap between.

Which meant... "Local forces or national?"

That earned her a nod of approval for quick thinking despite her current mental disarray. But still no hint of a smile.

"National, such as we have it here in Iceland."

She glanced over her shoulder and saw that Sam was studying the man intently. She looked back at him, "Not merely national forces." Because if he was, Sam would have read that somehow, in the man's posture or attitude, and dismissed him.

He crossed his arms over his chest, thought better of it, and inspected his shirt sleeves. Two new chocolate smudges decorated the insides of his sleeves. He didn't look amused. Stepping over to the cleanup sink, he began sponging at the three brown spots. "SIA," more of a growl than actual speech.

"The Safety Investigation Authority," Rikka unearthed from her encyclopedic depths. "Maritime specialist, I presume."

The man shrugged a yes.

Sam didn't look wholly convinced. But, as Kate knew if she asked he wouldn't answer until he was sure of it, she didn't bother asking.

"I'm Björn," he kept daubing at his chocolate smears, transforming them from dark-chocolate blotches into expanding puddles of milk chocolate. She refused to pay more than passing attention to how dampening his shirt was outlining his impressive musculature.

"Just Björn?"

"We Icelanders aren't big on surnames."

"Just Björn then."

15

THE FIRST TWO OF THE BREAKFAST EARLY BIRDS CAME DOWN THE main staircase, though service was still fifteen minutes away and the dining room's glass doors were still closed. One totted a camera with a fat lens as long as his forearm. Birder. The other sported a lesser camera but an overlarge pair of binoculars. They were comparing pre-breakfast sightings from the harbor.

Kate herded everyone into the public elevator rather than face the incoming tide. It was a tight fit with Sam there, but they made it. She punched the *Octavius* button that looked like a battered square-rigger of old, and ended up sandwiched between Paul and Rikka, forming a temporary demilitarized zone. Or did it?

"What are you doing here, Paul?" Kate glared at her twin.

"Well, Sam texted the pilot—"

Kate winced internally that she hadn't done the same when planning this trip. Even Sam got it right when it came to managing her brother.

"I was just returning from this wonderful—"

"I don't want to hear any sordid details."

"Okay, well, I'll just say that there's a certain Nevada casino that wishes my bank account was smaller and theirs was bigger."

Once again she was wrong about him... Then she caught his smile. No, she'd been right—and she definitely didn't want to hear about what lovely heiress he'd bedded along the way. Or comely dealer at the poker table—he was wealth-impartial when he fell in love, whether for a night or a longer multi-week fling.

"He told the pilot you were in trouble and Sam needed to get to Iceland fast. I had my passport with me, so I came along to help."

Paul was more likely to create a near-death experience for them all rather than being any help. But he always meant well —which was part of the problem. Kate considered her options, but she figured that enough people had already been tossed overboard for this particular trip.

Once they'd all piled out of the elevator, she led them astern toward the Quarterdeck. Rather than garish *CSI: Crime Scene Investigation* tape slashed across the door, a tastefully printed sign announced, *Temporarily Closed – our apologies for the inconvenience.*

And it was locked.

Rikka checked the first door on the side, marked *Pantry – staff only.* It was unlocked. She went through, circled out onto the deck through the pantry's service door, and tugged on the passenger door from the outside. It was still locked.

The Bridge lay at the other end of the deck. Someone there must have a key. But Sam was holding open the door to the pantry for Kate.

Right.

Kate rubbed her eyes. She definitely needed some sleep.

16

SAM USED THE NARROWNESS OF THE PASSAGE INTO THE PANTRY TO his advantage. Holding the door only partway open, he forced Björn to brush against him to squeeze past. Iceland's special police units had turned in all of their weapons ages ago. Yet Björn carried at least two knives, well-hidden, and possibly a sidearm—difficult to be certain without giving himself away, but there was a wear spot on his jeans appropriate for a spare magazine.

He wasn't SIA, the Safety Investigation Authority. Nor was he National Police, who were armed only under very special conditions. No, Björn was something more than that. ICRU? Iceland Crisis Response Unit? That didn't quite fit either. And *why* was a very interesting question.

Once everyone had followed in Rikka's wake, Sam stopped at the threshold from the pantry to the Quarterdeck to assess.

Based on the orientation from his earlier study of the Stykkishólmur harbor map, the sun stood northeast and fifteen degrees above the horizon. He glanced at his watch, made a mental recalibration for latitude and looked back at the sun. Yes, where he'd expect it at seven a.m. local.

The harbor that the *Ice Adventure* had moored in would be very distinct from last night's view of the deep sea. Stykkishólmur couldn't be called more than a small fishing village clustered daintily along one side of the harbor to the ship's starboard. Close to port, a vertical cliff shot up over a hundred meters. Dark rock, neatly shaped in that hexagonal columnar jointing form, made it look as if a giant had tidied the cliff with a massive comb. Above the rocky face, the greenest grass imaginable surrounded a red-painted lighthouse. And, in what he already recognized as an Icelandic trademark, a few white sheep grazed atop those impossible heights.

The deck looked to be in its final post-wedding state, much as he'd seen it on the screen feed that Rikka had provided after last night's explosion. The wedding had given him something amusing to watch as he broke down the side of beef that had arrived that morning, butchering it for his family's Brooklyn shop, Fierro's Meats. Until it had stopped being amusing.

Chairs and tables knocked aside by the abrupt departure of the wedding guests remained askew. Wedding cake spread across the port side and aft portion of the deck from the cake table. Someone had rigged mesh to protect the site from marauding seagulls. Done after the fact by the few smears of icing on the mesh itself. A mound of the shattered cake remained on the table with the groom cake topper lounging back against an outcropping of black frosting heaved up by the explosion to the other side. He appeared far more comfortable than the actual groom's present position would be, crowded into the belowdecks freezer with the two chefs.

He glanced at Kate and Paul. Good to have him finally out of the way. Stonewalling him on the five-hour flight last night had only driven Kate's brother to new heights of chatty affability. There'd been a guy in his assault element of the Marine Corps Maritime Special Purpose Force like that. He never shut up except when they were running deep into unfriendly territory.

Sam never understood people like that, so he made a point of ignoring them. Which had been simple on the flight over. He'd had a buddy send him the ship's full set of plans while he'd been waiting for Paul's return from Vegas, which he'd studied all the way here.

Except now Paul had risen to stand behind Kate and massage her shoulders. Hard to ignore a guy being decent, Kate looked wrecked.

But that didn't stop her. Even in her state, she was inspecting their surroundings with clear eyes.

He watched to see what she focused on in case it became relevant later. Distant: hills and sea. Moderate: sheep-strewn meadows to one side, harbor and town to the other. Near: a slow survey of the entire deck, counterclockwise, finishing with a look at his face. A shrug said she hadn't noted anything unexpected. She was too well trained an observer to exhibit any random behavior that might offer him clues.

Apparently deciding he'd done enough for Kate, Paul again tried to approach the crime scene. But he knew better and made the mistake of casting a furtive glance in Sam's direction before he'd gone three steps. It shouldn't be any surprise that giving his sister a shoulder massage had actually been a ploy to move him out of his seat.

Sam pointed a finger at the center of Paul's chest, then at the chair he'd abandoned beside Kate. When he was slow to move, Kate—without ever needing to see Sam's gesture—grabbed Paul's belt from behind. With a practiced yank, she had him flailing backward to crash land into the chair. Sam knew he could depend on Kate to keep him there.

Rikka swung her camera up as Björn moved in to inspect the cake.

"You will *not* be using any footage of me in your show." Björn faced the camera but didn't make it a question.

Sam carefully didn't look up from the demarcation of the cake-debris perimeter he himself had been approaching. Let Björn find out the hard way that Rikka didn't need a champion, at least not until she landed seriously in the shit.

"Duh!" He knew the patentable eyeroll she'd be using with that tone. "Only man ending up in my personal video library is Sam."

At her answer, Sam had to struggle harder to not react. He remained thankful for every second she came to him, and for every minute she stayed after arriving. He'd stopped being puzzled and settled on grateful. But her *only?* Far more than he expected from such a force-of-nature spirit.

If Björn caught that she hadn't promised anything about any public videos, he gave no sign. Instead he glanced at Kate. "And who's in *your* personal collection?"

Sam shifted his attention farther from the crime scene and more toward the conversation. Kate, rather notoriously, dated few men and never for long. Rikka kept him well apprised of both of the Starks' goings-on. Better than those soap operas his cousin Nadya watched when the front of the butcher shop went quiet.

17

THE QUESTION SURPRISED KATE. IF BJÖRN HAD SO MUCH AS smiled once, it might help, but even Sam smiled more than he did—which was barely this side of never.

If Sam had gone still before, he now turned into a stone. She often rubbed Sam Fierro the wrong way or vice versa. She'd apparently done so for five of the last six years. Not for the crime of letting her Secret Service protectee die, which she still hadn't forgiven herself for, but rather for *quitting* after not sufficiently safeguarding the Vice President-elect's life. The man was a toad who completely deserved the three rounds to the chest his ex-mistress had given him, but it had been Kate's job to make sure that she didn't.

His sudden stillness made no sense.

Had he decided she needed...protecting? Well, to hell with that. Kate needed no one's protection, least of all Sam Fierro's. Especially not from this dour Icelander.

Kate turned to fully face Björn. "Oh, there are so many I would collect given the chance; where do I begin? John, Errol, Sidney—that would be: Wayne, Flynn, and Portier. Do Icelanders truly eschew surnames?"

She ignored the fleeting quirk of Sam's lips that might be a smile precursor.

Björn directly faced her as well, finally a hint of a smile graced those nice lips. And how exhausted was she to be thinking such thoughts.

"What do you do when you're Erik's grandson? Father is already Erikson. Does that make me Eriksonson? Or Eriksondóttir if were a daughter? And then my son? No, I'm Björn, son of Gunnar, son of Erik... Should I keep going?"

"Please don't. It's too early in the morning for such nonsense." Besides, she knew little of her own history before Mom had moved to New York. Somewhere back there, her people had emigrated to Nova Scotia in the pioneer days, but nothing of what happened since. Her grandma had run away from...something. The farm? Or was it Boston? Either way, she too landed in the Big Apple seeking life and love. Few stories and no family Bible or other record had followed her.

Grandpa had conveyed as little baggage from his Bronx youth to his Manhattan life. He hadn't said no when she'd asked if that past included any of the notorious Irish gangs that had once controlled most of the city. But he also hadn't offered any explanation of where the money to start Cooks Network had come from either. She'd finally concluded that it was better not to ask. The other side of the house had crossed from the Scottish Lowlands, leaving their Glaswegian roots behind as well.

Kate waved Björn's attention to the cake.

He shifted in that moment, his focus very intent. His body reflected the change. Now the professional showed through. Coupled with Sam's continued mistrust, she saw more in the change than Björn perhaps intended to show.

He and Sam circled the perimeter of the cake debris, much the worse for a night smeared across the deck. Were they acting like a team or two adversaries competing to see who could spot what first?

Seeing him near Sam, their motions were more in sync than out. An SIA accident investigator might show care and focus, but Björn showed more. Beyond military, he definitely had Special Operations training. She'd keep an eye on him, which wouldn't be a burden with the way he looked.

A loud click from behind her had them all whirling about. Mr. Charles stepped through the now unlocked main door from the *Octavius* Deck's hallway.

"Ms. Stark, will you and your companions be dining here on the Quarterdeck?" As if a crime scene was the most normal place in the world to have breakfast.

She nodded without really considering. He produced menus. Stepping into the pantry, he returned a moment later with five place settings, a large thermos, and five coffee mugs. Kate figured that it would be inappropriate to kiss the distinguished gentleman —but she seriously considered it. Not caring about anything else, she handed him back the menus without inspecting them.

"Enough for five." Personally she was impressed that she could count that high at the moment. She double-checked: Paul, Rikka, Sam, and Björn made four. "Four." Then she remembered herself— "five." She *had* been right the first time.

"Very good, Ms. Stark." He nodded regally and departed.

With her hands wrapped around the warm mug, and the first sip of caffeine threatening to actually elevate her consciousness level a notch or two, she kept an eye on Sam and Björn. Slow. Methodical. When one stopped, so did the other. They would silently confer on one point or another, then move on. Occasionally they'd indicate a spot for Rikka to move in and take a particular closeup shot.

Some of the details that interested them were odd. Sam had a particular interest in the splatter pattern of dark icing on the railing to either side of where Marnie and her sous chef had stood at the moment of the cake's detonation. He even found a tape measure somewhere and took careful measurements.

Björn spent his time checking every single inch—no, she was in Iceland. He checked every *centimeter* of the rearward blast and the stairs that the groom had traversed during his airborne departure.

Others made more sense, like the fake Greek columns that had supported the upper layers. Each measured as long as her forearm. The lower half was round doweling that had been pushed into the bottom tier of the cake to transfer the load of the upper tiers onto the base plate. But the upper half, the exposed sections, were now only one side of a fat Greek column.

They were shaped like a half-cylinder; the other half must have been formed by the C-4 explosive. It had blown in one direction with the plastic half of the Greek column acting as a backing and shaping for the charge.

Sam tapped it with the edge of a butter knife. Not the bright plink of PVC pipe, rather the dead sound of thick-laid carbon-fiber. Held in place by the notable weight of the cake, the force would indeed be highly directable. These were very high-tech columns.

"That doesn't make any sense, Sam. Who has it in for two chefs and a groom?"

He looked as if he was actually about to speak when Rikka came over. "Hey, I just remembered." She pulled the circular wire knitting needle from her camera bag; they'd slipped it into a Ziploc last night.

After inspecting the clamp at one end of the needle wire, Sam and Björn began disassembling the cake bit by bit. They finished, looked at each other, then turned to look over the rail before shaking their heads. Whatever trigger or battery pack had been attached to the other end of that wire had gone into the ocean.

After raiding the pantry for a plastic bin, into which went the knitting needle, columns, several sections of cake individually bagged for chemical testing, and the miniature groom himself, they joined her and Paul at the table. Rikka filmed on last sweep of the area before joining them as well.

A server arrived and had soon placed a sufficient breakfast for ten upon their table. As he was departing, she told him to please let Mr. Charles know that he could send a cleanup crew.

Kate was spreading lingonberry jam on her English muffin, twisting it to create an even coating, when the ship's ninjas arrived.

Twisting her muffin for the last stroke, she watched the ninjas hooking up a fire hose.

Twisting—

"No! Wait!" She shouted as they turned it on.

Turning to look at her, the man holding the nozzle spun, completely soaking one of his companions. His response, in a language she didn't know, sounded plenty foul. His companion turned off the hose. They were all staring at her.

She held up a finger to keep them from acting while she looked down at her companions, frozen in various stages of eating their breakfast.

Paul, apparently forgetting he was in mid-chew, took a deep breath and immediately began choking loudly on his bite of kippered herring. Björn offered Paul a sharp thump on the shoulder as he was reaching for a glass of juice. Instead, he knocked it askew and only Sam's agility saved his breakfast from inundation.

She was losing the ninjas' attention.

"Wait, just a minute." She rose and stepped over beside the disassembled cake to place herself in the way, blocking them from cleaning up. She even raised a hand, palm out toward the ninjas. "Rikka, you said they had to turn the cake at the last minute because of damage to the frosting."

"Right. I did say that. I totally forgot."

"How much?"

"How much what?" But Kate knew it was just a knee-jerk contrariness as Rikka was already reaching for her camera. She had to scroll through the video long enough that Kate's arm was getting tired. Whatever she showed to Sam made him very unhappy. He picked up a handful of the mini-croissants that Kate had formed who knew how many hours ago and came to join her.

18

RIKKA FOLLOWED AND THEY WERE ALL SOON GATHERED ABOUT the devastated base platter for the exploding wedding cake. She hated it when Kate caught key facts that she had missed. As expected of her, Rikka knew she always let people down eventually. But letting her *best* friend down was a pure horror show. Other than Sam, Kate might be her *only* friend, which—

She forced herself to focus on the camera screen, too embarrassed to look up.

Sam eyed the farthest forward that icing had splattered into the railing. Tracking a line from the center of the serving platter, he set one croissant on the edge of the circular sheet. Eyeing the line of icing that had swept the groom overboard but not spattered the bride's dress, he set another roll along that line.

The blast had swept an angle of just ninety degrees.

"Willem said that C-4 explosives were very directional. That's a pretty wide sweep." Rikka watched Sam but it was Björn who answered.

"It can be. It all depends on the setup. Four columns worth

of plastique explosive formed into a very narrow shape would have cut a swath through the guests." He held his arms out and slashed his hands forward, indicating a narrow slice that would have cut down a narrow line of the guests presumably all the way to the far railing. "With a wider spread," he opened his arms to the width of the two marker croissants that still faced the railing, "you'd get a wider killing range. However, the force of the explosives would dissipate far more rapidly, killing those closest but not those farther away."

Sam nodded his agreement, then pointed toward the camera's display.

Rikka rolled the image back and forth frame-by-frame. "This is tricky. Between the low evening light and Marnie's efforts to fix the blemish on the frosting... I think the blemish would have been..." She took a croissant, bit off the end, and set it where the blemish had been. "...about here."

"Which way was the damage originally facing?" Kate's face looked unusually pale.

Rikka had to rewind to before the wedding. Had she even filmed its original location? "Um, I didn't have the camera turned on. Let's see," she closed her eyes to picture the sea rather than the tour buses pulling into the lot to whisk everyone away after breakfast service finished. It had been a long flight, but she'd been so glad to be sitting next to Kate on the plane that she hadn't been able to shut up.

It had been a couple months since they'd hung out together. There certainly hadn't been time during that audition for the *A Brew and a Bite* show. She felt as tired as Kate looked but had been fighting not to show it as a sort of apology to Kate.

She closed her eyes to remember and felt the deck weaving beneath her though they were moored to a dock in the calm inner harbor. Bad idea. She opened them again. Picturing the line of her arrival before the wedding last night, she'd come up to the table about—she shoved hard on Paul's shoulder, sending him skating wildly across the icing and sugar paste splattered on the deck—here. Yes, this was where she'd been last night. She'd helped Marnie and her sous chef turn the damaged section of the icing out of view.

"I was right here. The damage was originally..." she plucked a final croissant from Sam's palm, bit off the end of that one, and set it down on the table, "...here."

Sam slowly spun the serving platter until the two bitten croissants—one marking where the damage had been on the platter at the time of the explosion and the other on the table marking its original orientation—were lined up. Yes, that was exactly where she'd remembered it.

"Uh..." Rikka inspected where the two unbitten croissants marking the angle of the explosion were now aimed. In a haze, she walked over to where she'd put the camera before going to the breakfast table. She'd put it right where she'd had it placed last night.

Kate came to stand beside her, in the same place she had stood during the wedding ceremony.

Together they turned to look at the cake table and the two croissants marking the blast radius if the cake had *not* been turned at the last moment.

"Well, that's not good," Kate whispered softly.

The ninjas were looking down at the platter, then following the intended damage line. Soon everyone was looking at the two of them.

One edge of the destruction zone would have caught her and Kate, probably thrown their dead bodies through the windows of the pantry behind them. The other edge would have meant that the groom would be unharmed and Savannah the bride would now be down in the freezer, an ice popsicle corpse alongside the two of them.

"Kate?"

"Uh-huh?"

"We need to get off this ship. Before something else kills us. Or at least long enough for us to think."

19

"IT'S A WEIRD ONE." LEONA LOOKED HER NORMAL, AWAKE SELF despite the alert that had dragged them into the New York headquarters so early.

"Too early in the morning for weird." Marcus Reynolds wished his coffee mug was a bowl that he could simply plant his face into. Maybe he'd blow bubbles, maybe he'd just soak his brain for a while.

But it was FBI coffee—four a.m. FBI coffee, which meant it had been on the simmer for hours. Though marginally better than Navy coffee, it was probably still strong enough to melt his face off even when dead cold. So, no faceplant. He didn't even take a sip. He merely clutched the warm mug and let the caffeine soak into his palms through the thick ceramic.

Leona had moved in last night. Now they were partners in more ways than one. He'd made it through eight years in the Navy and then five years climbing to Special Agent without ever having his bachelorhood under serious threat before. He didn't think that's what was bothering him. Leona Edwards was the best lover he'd ever had and the best field agent a guy could ask to be assigned with. Though he'd never imagined falling for a powerful and stunning black woman, that was merely a failure of his white-trash background's imagination that had been supplanted by a very nice reality.

No. The reason he hadn't slept a wink during their first night living together was much more visceral. The one thought that had plagued him through the whole night as they spooned together, still echoed in the small hours of the day: *You screw this up, Marcus, and you're gonna be even sadder than this coffee.* He managed to grunt out, "Weird?" to show he was On It.

"Got a very sideways Cooks Network alert."

That snapped him awake far better than even an intravenous jolt of Navy coffee—with the grounds not filtered out. He'd missed why they'd been called in.

They'd put an FBI search flag on any news regarding Kate Stark and Cooks Network. He and Leona were still working through the mounds of blowback from the last two cases they'd had involving Kate. One had uncovered a massive blackmail service that had reached high into corporate, judicial, and even US Congressional circles. The second one had averted an attempt on the President's life by mere seconds and ruined several power brokers from the New York social scene, Congress again, and even the White House.

Their own reputations inside the Bureau hadn't suffered either.

"How sideways?"

"One of Cooks' top videographers took a selfie dive. Snapped her neck falling off a six-story high rock."

"Sounds more stupid than interesting."

"Two minor details."

He eyed Leona, always a joy. A traditionalist, she wore a starched white shirt tailored for her prominent curves. The shoulder harness for her big Glock 17L Long Slide with the MOS sight, holstered alongside those magnificent breasts, only emphasized her fine form. But it was the dark eyes that had finally captured more than his hormones. Leona Edwards was the ultimate in frank, no-nonsense agents—with a sense of humor drier than a gin-only martini.

Knowing him too well, she didn't even look up from her screen, merely did her one-raised-eyebrow thing to tell him he hadn't gotten away with even that brief wandering of his attention to her body.

"Waiting here," he informed her where his attention was now focused.

She was looking down, so it was hard to see, but he was sure her smile would be there. "One, she was found with a long telephoto on her camera. Impossible to take a selfie with it."

"Any scenery where she fell? Maybe paying too much attention to the shoot?"

"Scenery still would be more typically shot with a shorter lens." Now Leona was just messing with him.

"And second?" Because that, of course, would be the telling detail.

"There was an Irish pub in the same small Massachusetts town destroyed three days earlier."

Marcus knew better than to ask and waited her out by risking another sip of his coffee.

"This videographer was there at the time, filming the pilot of a brand-new series for Cooks Network."

He set his mug down very carefully.

She flipped to a new screen. "Three dead. Some sort of an explosion in the brewery."

Marcus considered. "Uh, that's not exactly the sort of place that explodes much."

"Nope."

"Was Ms. Stark there?"

Leona poked around some more. "According to the article about the pub, not even the photographer was there. Just the three fatalities. A couple and the owner. Not much of a reporter." She flipped back to the selfie-death news item. "This other reporter must have called Cooks to obtain the information of the videographer's last assignment. But he didn't connect that the filming had gone bad, simply noted it as the reason the person had been in Gloucester."

Marcus picked up the phone and called the Gloucester cops. It took him under three minutes to get the necessary information. A quick call to Cooks told him the last piece he needed.

He hung up and rose, pulling on his jacket. "All four bodies were accepted by the State Medical Examiner: they're in the Boston morgue. Drive is under four hours."

"Wait, Marcus. How do we justify the Bureau stepping in on this? We need justification before the FBI can go tromping in on the locals, like a multi-state crime."

Now it was his turn to grin knowingly at her. "First, we're just curious." He rose slowly to his feet and stretched, making her wait. "Second, if it turns out to be interesting, we've got a New York photographer dead in Massachusetts. Third," he considered making her wait until they were in the car but she'd figure out the purpose of his second phone call if he gave her more than a few seconds because she was just that sharp, "like the last two times, Kate Stark left the country within hours of the first deaths."

"I thought we trusted her by now?" Leona rose from her chair. "The last two times she was instrumental in the solution, no matter how many fingers pointed at her."

"We do trust her. But we don't have to tell the local cops or our boss, right?"

The smile she sent his way lit him up in more ways than one. Grabbing their jackets, they headed for the door.

20

THEY PASSED A GEOTHERMAL PLANT AS THE TOUR BUS PULLED OUT of town, setting Savannah all a-twitter. Despite the brevity of her marriage, she had neither cowered in her room nor skipped the day's scheduled tour. Red-eyed and twitching at the slightest bang—like the bus doors closing—Rikka was actually impressed that she'd emerged at all.

A few offered their condolences, which she'd accepted politely enough. Most pretended last night hadn't happened, except for a few who assiduously avoided her as if she might be the next to explode. Savannah was polite about the sympathy and decent enough to not bristle at the other two reactions.

Rikka honestly didn't know what to make of her. She and her one bridesmaid—there had apparently been two others, but one had taken desperately sick and the other had stayed home to tend her—stayed close. Sufia Drehmis could have been the blonde version of Savannah. Sufia snapped several quick photos of the plant with her top-of-the-line Nikon camera as if the blocky metal building woven into a nest of massive steam pipes was the most exciting thing in the barren landscape. Actually, it was the only thing aside from grassy slopes dotted with white sheep but...for real?

The day's scheduled bus tour had three main stops—two with history but all three with great birding—and a lot of sightseeing out the window. Once over the high ridge, the volcanic landscape had been formed in convoluted twists by layer upon layer of overlapping lava flows. Those had been covered by centuries of slow-growth moss or lichen that turned it into a mottled carpet of grays and greens over punches of black rock. It grew so slowly that the thickness, or rather the thinness of the lichens apparently indicated the age of each successive flow.

"The abundant geothermal and hydroelectric resources provide all but the most remote Icelander with low-cost heat and power." The tour guide at the front wasn't one of those over-effusive chirpy-bird types that drove Rikka up the wall. She was a pleasant, calm woman who sounded as if she loved a chance to share information about her country.

After the first few miles of the ride, Rikka mostly tuned her out and studied the playback on her camera; there simply hadn't been time before now. Sam leaned in from the seat beside her and watched the small screen as well. They missed many kilometers of purple lupines, jagged lava, and mountains still sporting ice caps, because it was still that chilly in mid-June Iceland. Been here, seen that.

But, for all her vigilance, she spotted only two reactions that didn't wholly fit the events.

Seated beside her, Sam tapped his finger on the groom's face.

"I know. He has an emotional dynamic range of..."

Sam pointed out the window.

Rikka looked and laughed. Because her hands were full of camera, she rested her head on his shoulder for a moment in appreciation. "Okay, even less exciting to watch than the thirtieth kilometer of twenty-year-old lava flows covered in moss. Maybe cool for a geologist or botanist but...yeah, he's worse than that. He doesn't look unhappy but, if thoughts of marriage touched him, he kept his excitement seriously well hidden."

He tapped Savannah's face next. Yep, he'd seen the same two anomalies. It felt weird to be sitting here looking at Savannah, three rows forward and across the bus aisle, and Rikka's video of the star of last night's wedding—until she was upstaged by her own cake.

They watched the whole wedding from the moment of the bride's arrival, ascending the stairs from the deck below like a rising Pantone 13-1023 Peach Fuzz doom, to the final post-cake faint and collapse on the deck.

Sam tapped the pause and stared straight ahead, which probably meant he was watching Savannah as well as everything else going on in and outside the bus. Rikka had learned not to ask what he was thinking. Sam never ventured an opinion until he was a hundred percent certain of his conclusions.

She leaned forward enough to look around Sam's chest at Kate across the aisle. Out! Stone-cold asleep on Paul's shoulder. Her brother looked ridiculously happy about being her pillow. That's why Rikka could never hold a grudge against him for long. He was an utterly ridiculous human, but he loved his twin without constraint or hesitation.

Rikka had never set out to win popularity contests, which had paid her exactly the expected dividends in the orphanage and later at school—she was never popular. By four years old she'd figured out which parts of her brain were smarter than everyone's around her. She'd never even attempted to conform, befriend, and whatever else popular people did. That wasn't her area of smart. Why waste time on skills that weren't a natural fit for her?

Instead, the future Erika Albert (her own play on Albert Einstein, who shared her orphanage-designated birthday) had studied the skills she had, assessed which were strongest—and leaned into them as hard as she could.

It was so obvious that physical contests of strength or attracting boys weren't going to work; not at five-foot-zero with a figure that would only win a beauty contest against a #2 Ticonderoga pencil. But an aging Macintosh SE/30 that had been donated to the orphanage had been conquered by the time kindergarten started—the same year the Internet hosted its first websites. The school's Windows 3.1 machines became her best friend until the day she discovered Torvalds' Linux.

Technology was her superpower and it totally ruled. She'd been the lone-girl geek until she was the lone-woman geek. It rarely made her popular with the boys, who never grew up to become men anyway, at least not like Sam. Her only other real skill, cooking, had a surprising connection to code. Cutting fish required precision and baking was some serious chemistry of its own, yet within those bounds there was immense leeway for creative approaches.

Only one person had ever bested her in either of Rikka's super-strengths, and she did it so often that it would be annoying if Rikka didn't like her so much. No programmer, yet Kate had managed to depose Rikka from her heights atop the Black Hat-hacker kingdom.

And she might have taken over Cooks Network when her parents died, but she was also a world-class chef—not just a skilled cook like Rikka herself. Though Rikka did console herself with cutting a better piece of fish, which had to count for something.

Kate's fitness maintained after six years as a Secret Service agent, having an absolutely killer body, and those crystal blue eyes meant she outclassed Rikka physically in more ways than she wanted to think about.

Worst of all, people liked Kate. Hell, they worshipped her. Kate might be her only friend, but Rikka felt that she worshipped her just as much as her twin brother did. It was a common bond that she would never ever let Paul know.

Actually, she'd done one thing Kate had never done consistently—she had an actual boyfriend. A word that gave her fewer shudders with Sam beside her than it had even last night when the North Atlantic had still separated them. And they'd been together for months and months now, not her normal couple days until they bored the snot out of her.

Rikka looked at Sam just as he turned to her. Somehow reading her dark thoughts, he kissed her atop her head, then ran his hand down her long hair. Just what she'd needed. He always knew.

Huh! What did Savannah Sachs need? Clearly not the rich and recently deceased Bret Calder. But how to figure out what?

She ran the explosion again in slow motion.

The downward slice of the *maguro* tuna blade.

Catching on the knitting needle wire and causing the point to tip downward.

Contact.

A brief whiteout filled the screen as the camera's thirty-five-megapixel sensor overloaded with the sudden light change. Not with one of J. J. Abrams' beloved lens flares that he'd used so famously in the *Star Trek* reboot movies. No, it showed as a solid sheet of white.

By the time the supersaturation of the electronics finally bled off the sensor, allowing it to reveal images again, the two ship's chefs were already gone overboard. Rolling back and forth over the first few frames of visible light, she spotted what may have been the bottoms of the groom's shoes as he disappeared down the flight of the stairs the Bride-in-Peach-Fuzz had so recently ascended.

"I didn't bring my computer," she told Sam. "But there are

methods of recovery I can apply once we're back on the ship. I'll never claw back the bulk of the image or much color information because of the sensor limits. However, I can do a reverse interpolation of noise on each pixel's capture and create partial views."

He shrugged.

"Yeah, I know. Not likely to reveal much we don't know except for three gruesome deaths."

Sam scrolled back to the moment of ignition; for having such big hands, he had a real delicacy of the controls that he had proven on her body time and again. His hand working the camera resting on her lap was...distracting. Very.

He stared at the first flare-up of the explosion. The shape of the blast pattern's formation might be interesting, but it wouldn't tell them anything they didn't already know. He must have agreed as he tapped the camera's power button, leaned back, and closed his eyes.

Right, he wouldn't have slept on the flight last night. Definitely not with Paul nattering away about who knew what. A glance again at Kate revealed that Paul too had succumbed, leaning against the bus window. Even passed out with his jaw hanging slack, he was disgustingly handsome in a pretty-boy sort of way.

She looked up at Sam. Rugged. Like he'd seen the whole world. Half John Wayne, half Harrison Ford, with some Tom Berenger mixed in. *True Grit, Indiana Jones,* and *Platoon.* Why would women ever want a Paul when there were Sams in the world? Well, because there was only one Sam, so all other women had to settle. She managed to resist asking herself why she was the lucky one.

Tipping her own head onto Sam's shoulder, Rikka was jolted off as the bus came to a halt and the doors opened at their first stop.

21

"WHAT HAVE YOU LEARNED?"

Sam hadn't heard Björn's approach until he was three steps behind him, proving his deep fieldcraft training. The drizzle, so thin it was more of a thick mist, didn't mask any footsteps, though he'd still known the Icelander was following him. Easy to see in the glances of those coming from the other direction along the wide trail that led from the parking lot, down through the cliffs, and on toward the sea.

Björn had boarded the bus at the very last second after wandering off to the far end of the ship's quay to make a phone call. He'd ended up with the same view of Sam that Sam had of Savannah, three rows further back and across the aisle. He'd have witnessed them studying the video but been unable to see it.

"Nothing." Rikka sounded utterly disgusted as Björn fell in beside them. "Wedding. Explosion. Three dead. Poof!"

Not that simple, but Sam didn't know what he was missing. His past as a Marine Force Recon now turned butcher didn't exactly shower him with high-society wedding invitations. He rested a hand on her shoulder to keep her from saying anything more.

When she opened her mouth, he squeezed a little harder. She looked up at him and he offered an infinitesimal shake of his head. Her glance aside at Björn said she was about to ignore him. Gods but she was so damn cute. Feisty enough to be a Marine, if she could have herked a pack that weighed as much as she did over twenty kilometers of rough terrain.

He raised his pinkie and nudged her in the soft flesh at the back of her jaw. It turned her head enough to see that Savannah and her bridesmaid Sufia walked ten paces ahead.

Björn frowned as if in confusion. Which was odd, considering—

"Oh." Rikka got it, then whispered to Björn. "That's the bride, ten paces up, flowing brunette hair."

Sam realized that Björn had no reason to know that was the bride. He wasn't there for the wedding. Though Sam had only been paying marginal attention to the feed Rikka sent to his phone until he saw the explosion, he'd been watching closely when the bride had fainted to land in the sprayed icing. And he'd just had the lengthy videos of her on the camera.

He glanced down at Rikka. Erika Albert in a wedding dress. Whoa! Not some frilly giant of a dress like Savannah had chosen, which must have required its own seat on the plane and taken up half her suite on the ship. No, Rikka in an elegant sheath dress. His usual interest in women's clothes was in how fast he could convince them to remove such impediments. But picturing Rikka, not in her traditional black jeans and turtleneck, but in a wedding dress of some rich color to offset her golden coloring? And her dark hair falling long down her back—none of that weird frou-frou up-'do nonsense. Hell of an image. He smiled to himself. It was an image best kept to himself, as it was guaranteed to send Rikka scampering for the horizon.

Picturing her like that with another man? He could feel his fists clenching hard. He had to consciously release them a finger at a time. Picturing himself standing beside her? Yeah, like that was ever going to happen. Life would definitely be better if he stayed focused on what he understood: butchering meat and Marine Recon shit.

He—

Something else had snagged his attention. What was it he'd missed? Rikka was so damn distracting.

Go operational, Marine. Don't be a broke dick. That made him almost smile. Last time he'd used that phrase on a guy, one who had soon left the Marines. Sadly, he'd done it feet first. The dude had grown so blasé after the hundredth or so firefight that he'd thought he was untouchable, and that made him a faulty piece of equipment. Couldn't even remember his name anymore; everyone had called him BD after Sam had tagged him. At least until they called him Dead.

So, what *had* he missed?

He scanned the area. Rikka walked to his right. They'd descended into a narrow rocky cleft. The walls were rough dark lava, offering plenty of hides from any attack from above, and it would also be easy to climb with plenty of ready handholds. The end of the path was now in view and a beach opened wide before them. It was black sand; roughly forty people were spread across the broad reach, twenty-nine of whom he recognized from the bus.

Paul and Kate walked close ahead with Savannah and Sufia holding steady ten paces out.

He could hear six people behind him.

And Björn, to his left...hadn't looked up to identify the bride when Rikka had pointed her out. Hadn't needed to. He'd already recognized her. That was possible, though Sam had kept him in his peripheral vision since they'd boarded the ship together and hadn't seen Björn picking Savannah out of the crowd. She was pretty but unremarkable in her casual attire—hiking boots, designer jeans, and a Yale sweatshirt.

No, Björn didn't merely recognize the bride. He had *not* done something that would be perfectly natural: glancing in her direction as Rikka described her. He'd *intentionally* not glanced her way.

So, Björn had known who she was. Well enough to recognize her back from the other of Savannah's contemporaries who'd come on the cruise. He'd then been so careful to not give any indication of knowing her that he'd given himself away by that very act.

His trust rating on Sam's scale, which hadn't been high to begin with, took an abrupt downward slide. To rank a Ten, you had to be a Marine and not a broken dick of a one. Though, curiously, Rikka and Kate were both higher than a Nine in his estimation. Paul was even stranger. Sam would give him a rating of a Three for reliability, yet he always came through, just never in the way that would be expected...or most useful. But he did come through. Spec Ops buddies might rank an Eight and regular forces—be they grunt, squid, coastie, or fly boy—never passed a Seven.

Five and down you were either unknown or untrustworthy. Civilians weren't on the list unless they did something stupid enough to land on the bottom. He gave them all provisionary Threes until they proved otherwise.

Björn had just slid from a cautious Four to a Two. Perhaps still dangerous, but nearing the bottom of the trust scale. A One should be put down like a rabid hound or used for target practice.

"Look at these."

22

DJÚPALÓNSSANDUR BEACH WAS BEAUTIFUL, MELANCHOLY, AND wholly unpronounceable by foreigners.

Her nap on the bus had only emphasized Kate's exhaustion. When she tipped her head back to watch the circling gulls, terns, gannets, or whatever birds her tablemates had discussed over dinner, her head spun viciously and she almost fell to the black cobbles at the head of the beach. She'd never have made it down to the beach if her hand hadn't been looped around Paul's arm. He told her the tour guide's history lecture on the bus that she'd slept through.

The half-kilometer-wide strand had been a major fishing launch point for centuries. Only two marks remained of so many lives risked and so many lost. The first was unrelated to the old fishing villages, a hundred-and-forty-foot English fishing vessel was wrecked on the beach in a white-out blizzard in 1948—fourteen dead, five survivors. The scattered wreckage still littered the length of the beach and was a protected memorial.

The other mark was a line of four hefty stones of increasing size.

"These are funny, Katydid. Hey, Sam, look at these."

Rikka and Sam joined them with Björn tagging along. Kate didn't know what to make of him yet, but he was so very pretty.

There was a sign, but Paul already seemed to know the story. "These four stones were a test for someone who wanted to be a fisherman. They used rowing skiffs, probably just like the ones your people used in the crossing from Denmark a thousand years ago, Björn."

Even Björn's *smile* was pretty, now that he'd decided to use it. Kate really needed more sleep than thirty minutes on Paul's shoulder. Her normal shields were still passed out cold.

"The little rock," he pointed at a rounded stone no more than a foot across, "was named the Weakling. If that was the best you could lift and set on that rock plinth over there," he waved at a jut of stone that reached a meter above the cobbles, "you ended up cleaning fish and repairing nets with the women."

"Hey!" Rikka reached out to jab Paul in the ribs. Long practice had him dodging aside, which almost took Kate's feet out from under her. Only a quick scramble that sent the sliding cobbles clacking together let her keep her feet.

"The second rock..." Paul found temporary refuge on Kate's other side. Normally she was careful to never end up between the two of them but today wasn't one of those days. "...is called Half-Carrier. It meant you weren't useless. But if too many people could pick up the next rock, Half-Strong, you still didn't get aboard." He indicated the third stone and paused.

"What about that one?" Kate picked up his cue and pointed at the biggest stone, at least a half-meter across. She did it because she knew her brother loved his storytelling. Was that how he wooed so many women, by telling them stories? Kate had never tried that tactic, or any other, to intrigue a potential lover. You met her and that's who she was.

"That one is called Full-Strong. The old stories say that only one sailor ever successfully lifted it and placed it upon the rock plinth." He indicated a small rock platform that stuck up from the pebbly sand.

Paul then bent to lift the smallest one. He tried, rather unsuccessfully, to make it look easy as he carried it to the plinth and back. As he did, Rikka tapped Kate's arm and then nodded behind her. Kate glanced over her shoulder and saw that her own body had blocked the information sign, but Paul's positions to either side of her had placed him perfectly to read out the history of the four stones as if it was his own knowledge. Classic Paul.

He thumped the smallest—Kate checked the sign—twenty-three-kilo rock back onto the gravel. "I'll leave the others for you two gorillas."

Rikka sat on the little one, perhaps to show it who was boss. Kate didn't need to prove anything to anyone and left the stones alone. Björn looked ready to give it a pass but then he noted Sam's watching him.

Sam didn't bother with the second stone that, the sign revealed, weighed over fifty kilos. Instead, he stepped to the third one: Half-Strong. A hundred kilos, two hundred and twenty pounds.

Sam lifted it, showing less strain than Paul had on the smallest, and walked it over the ten steps to set it on the plinth. Björn made an equal show of lifting it off the plinth, walking it back, and dropping it like he was throwing down a gauntlet.

"What is it with men?" Rikka whispered beside her when Kate sat on the second stone. She included a Rikka eye roll. "Total testosterone poisoning. I didn't think Sam was like that."

What Kate couldn't believe was that Björn, who would have the skills to understand what Sam was, still dared to take him on. That took serious guts. A small audience had gathered. Mostly female, she noted.

"Total estrogen poisoning," Kate teased Rikka with a whisper and a nod toward the rapidly thickening crowd.

Before Paul had leaned casually against the sign to block anyone noticing his source of brilliance, she'd spotted the weight of the Full-Strong stone—a hundred and fifty-four kilos, three hundred and forty pounds. And this wasn't a balanced steel bar with weights. This was a rounded, weather-worn behemoth over a half-meter across.

No, Kate decided. Sam was *not* like that. Which meant he had some other agenda going on. Knowing Sam would never reveal his reasoning on, well, anything, Kate worked to puzzle it out herself.

Despite the weather's shift from mist to rain, he pulled off his light jacket and tossed it to Rikka. In jeans and black t-shirt, his hair kept Marine short, he worked his feet into the loose beach material until satisfied with the support there. Squatting, he didn't hesitate. Sam would have already planned every motion ahead of time.

With a clean jerk, he heaved the stone free, driving upward until his legs were straight and he held the stone waist high. Five careful steps to cover ten feet, and he lowered it onto the plinth. His massive physique actually exquisite in the dampening t-shirt. Kate was surprised that none of the riveted women fainted at the sight.

She also wondered how long since the outcropping had felt the weight of the Full-Strong boulder.

Then Sam stepped back, crossed his arms, the muscles still bulging from the exertion, and stared at Björn. He certainly had the full attention of the women in the crowd, and most of the men.

Sam ignored the burst of applause and excited murmurs. He was interested in only one target—Björn.

That's when Kate figured it out. And by the set of Björn's jaw, he did as well. This wasn't a mere contest of strength. This wasn't even some pissing contest over who was the biggest dog.

Björn pulled off his jacket and handed it to Kate before stepping up to the stone. The jacket was thick and warm. In the soft rain, it smelled very male. She hadn't felt chilled until she felt his body heat in her hands.

His lift would be easier than Sam's as the plinth placed the stone at a height where he only had to lift it a few inches before carrying it. He too made certain of his footing, then squatted low. Unlike Sam, he spent some time testing his grip.

Then, in a sharp clean-and-jerk motion, he scooped up the stone and managed to lift it to his chest. His walk back to where the stone had started its rare journey was more a stagger than a walk, twenty small steps to Sam's clean walk, and he dropped rather than lowered it, but he did it.

He then turned to face Sam as he too ignored the crowd's accolades. His look asked a simple question, *Was that enough?*

Sam cricked his neck once in each direction and offered an infinitesimal shrug that didn't say *maybe* but rather *not yet.*

Björn had followed through on the challenge and done credibly. His achievement was causing Sam to reassess something, but he wasn't satisfied yet. A provisional acceptance at best because the Icelander had tried. Had perhaps proved he was willing to go the distance if it became necessary.

All Kate's tired brain could think about as she held open Björn's coat for him was how wonderful he looked. He wasn't a bulging muscle guy...until it was called for. It had looked so very good on him. Kate ignored the niggling inner voice that attested that she was no less estrogen poisoned than the next woman in this crowd.

When he offered his arm to walk her back up the path, she didn't complain.

Though she could feel Sam's watchful gaze boring into her back the whole way up the trail.

23

"So, tell me a tale of Björn, son of Gunnar, son of Erik."
Well, there was no questioning Kate's memory.

Björn's muscles still buzzed like angry bees from lifting Full-Strong; he could only hope that his jacket kept Kate from feeling their twitching where her hand rested in the crook of his elbow. It was so old-fashioned and polite that he did feel something of the gentleman walking with a lady upon his arm.

"I'd rather ask you what the hell Sam was doing just now."

Kate studied him. Those crystalline blue eyes made him wonder if she could see straight into his soul—that was not a comfortable place. He made a point of not looking there even under the most dire of circumstances. After completing raking through the ashes he could only hope to be the sole remnant within, she looked ahead and simply stated, "You'd have to ask him."

"Wonderful. I've clearly made an excellent first impression if you think I'm stupid enough to try that."

That earned him a second look and a dazzling smile. "Not that bad."

Their shared chuckle eased much of the tension in his body.

There was a tangle wrapped up in Bret's death that not even Kveldulf's notorious berserker rage noted in the Icelander Sagas could split asunder into sensible pieces. But perhaps Björn would take a page from Kveldulf's grandson Egill's skills at poetry (aside from his formidable power with sword and axe).

She may have already guessed most of who he was, but he wouldn't be revealing that to some television network icon. Though now he felt an itch worse than heaving that stupid rock around. He knew what Sam was, perhaps not exactly, but close enough. Kate Stark he couldn't pin down at all.

"Well?"

Others were stringing out along the trail. Those who hated the wet mist had long since retreated to the buses. Birders remained on beach and cliff with their binoculars raised no matter the weather conditions. Paul and Rikka walked well ahead, teasing each other mercilessly. And he didn't need to look back to know that Sam trailed behind them, keeping a careful eye.

For now, he'd keep his attention on Kate. "There was a young lad who dreamt of being Kveldulf, the Evening Wolf. Upon his mighty Viking longship, he would set out from the shores of far off Scandinavia and find a great green land. He would see that it was named for ice to keep away the weak and unadventurous. Unlike Greenland that was covered in ice but named in the hopes that others would follow. The lad cared not that some priest actually did the discovering of his Iceland, instead he dreamt of adventure and victory."

Kate squeezed his arm to tell him to keep going.

He'd always preferred Egill's Saga over any other and plunged into the tale. "When he tired of being the Evening Wolf—actually a grouchy old bastard—he would become his grandson Egill. He and his brother Thorolf (my brother's name is really Sam and he became a fisherman) made peace with kings, warred and traded with far-off Celts, and generally enjoyed wonderful lives."

"Did they pillage and capture fair maidens?"

"Maidens? *Andskotans* no! That means *By the Devil*, which is much stronger than it sounds in English. We were seven years old. What self-respecting seven-year-old marauding Viking could possibly want anything to do with girls?" He gave a mock shudder.

And she laughed.

It wasn't a big laugh, just precisely right for the moment and scale of his joke. It didn't start in her chest and rumble forth. Or launch high from the throat. It started with a quick squint of her eyes, a rise of those lovely cheekbones as her smile bloomed to life, and only then finding a voice of its own as if pulled out by that smile and those brilliant eyes.

For the long stroll back to the bus, his sole purpose became spinning the tale in ways that drew out that laugh time after time.

24

Rikka let Kate sleep on Björn's shoulder through the hour-long prime-birding stop. He looked no more put out than Paul had.

The rain had abated, and the sun now punched through massive rents in the clouds. While most rushed out to the cliffs with their binoculars and cameras, the knitters took over a small cafe. There they ordered pots of tea, a Danish pastry each, and began their magic of transforming one-dimensional strings of yarn into three-dimensional sweaters and hats.

Rikka had spent much of that hour considering the topology of the operation performed with nothing but two pointed sticks and a skein of sheep's wool. She also paid attention to what they had to say about the wedding, which was surprisingly little.

Such a lovely bride.

So sad.

Not even a bit of honeymoon.

I'm sure they had plenty of fun before the wedding; that's the norm these days, you know.

The San Francisco Summer of Love in 1967 and Woodstock two years later, honey. They weren't the only ones. Eighty if she was a day and a coif whiter than a snowshoe hare, she offered a mighty wink and a happy chuckle.

By the final stop of the morning, it was simply too much. Rikka grabbed Kate's arm to drag her off the bus, and ended up staring—so wide-eyed that her eyeballs hurt—at the knife-edge hand strike that Kate stopped inches from Rikka's throat.

"I forgot that you wake up dangerous," she managed on a gasp, then glanced at Björn to make sure he was listening, "How many lovers have you killed when all they wanted was wake-up sex?"

"Uh, not *too* many." Kate's sense of humor always woke up before she did, which was awesome before she clamped down on it when fully conscious. Rikka invariably woke up stupid. But she didn't mind waking up stupid around Sam, he always waited until her brain kicked in...or shorted it out with amazing wake-up sex of their own.

Björn blinked rapidly a few times as he digested Kate's remark.

Rikka hauled her up the bus aisle before she could protest. At a quick hand signal, Sam lumbered out of his seat, blocking the Icelander from following them.

"He's too pretty, Kate, I wouldn't trust him."

"I think," Kate yawned hugely as they stepped out into the fresh air, "Sam already has that covered."

"Really?" Sam was still in the bus. Time to put some distance from Björn. "He's always smart about those sorts of things."

Kate nodded, shook herself, and looked about clear-eyed for the first time since this whole mess began. "Where are we?"

"Some place called Budir." It was a barren prominence of rough land by the sea. There were only two buildings: a comfortable looking small hotel and, sitting by itself at the high point, a small, black church. Pitch-black against the richest green that grass had ever been. The clouds above were a wild tangle of shapes and patterns like she'd never seen anywhere in her life.

Kate, perhaps wanting some distance of her own, strolled through a small flock of sheep who regarded them balefully before moving aside. The church's door stood open, and a small placard said that it had first been built here in 1703 out of turf, and that several artifacts of that church still remained in the present wooden one.

They stepped inside and sat together in the back pew. It was surprisingly light with white walls, a vaulted ceiling, and beams painted the same color as the lichens or mosses or whatever they were outside the many windows.

"Picturing you and Sam here?"

"Sure. Can't you see him in a three-piece suit? He'd—" Rikka slapped a hand over her mouth and glared at Kate.

Who offered one of her seraphical smiles.

"That was so nasty!" Rikka mumbled through her fingers. "Total entrapment. I was not thinking that. Not even Sam is ever going to drag this girl to the altar." She carefully didn't look at the front of the church where the tiny altar was wrapped in a simple railing of dark wood.

"Be careful of what you protest too much about." Kate's eyes were sparkling with laughter, typically the only part of her that did, but that was plenty too much.

Rikka kept her hand in place as she shook her head again. No how. No way. Not even to see Sam in a three-piece suit.

"How about you and Björn?"

Rikka had meant it as a redirect, but Kate took the question at face value. And she gazed fearlessly at the altar. Rikka tried... but she still didn't dare. Far too easy to picture Sam there— with some tall, leggy blonde wearing a high-end dress that showed off all the curves Rikka had never developed despite much pitiful begging.

Kate shrugged. "He has a comfortable shoulder to nap on."

"Oh c'mon, Kate. He's as handsome as you are beautiful."

For some reason, *that's* what earned her a surprised look.

"Seriously? Why do you think men always die at your feet?"

And Kate's grimace said that Rikka Albert, the Queen-of-tact, had struck once again. Chefs had a nasty habit of dying around her. Not the ones she took as lovers, because she had impeccable taste in that department—unlike Rikka prior to Sam. But plenty of others. And the one death she'd never forgiven herself for, that Vice President-elect guy.

Once again, Rikka had backed herself into a corner and didn't know what to say.

25

LEONA EDWARDS INSPECTED THE FOUR CORPSES. THE MEDICAL Examiner hadn't tagged them as important, so they'd been in the chiller until Marcus' call that the FBI was on its way.

The harried doc, a slender and very young Indian named Paswan, looked at the four with them.

"Each deceased individual suffered a likely cause of death. Three suffered blunt force trauma, one of whom was either drowned or burned, and one who suffocated. Reports," he waved vaguely at a computer terminal, "say that these three died in a brewery accident. That other one, she took a selfie dive. I do not understand why you think these four are of interest to you."

"Because, Doctor," Marcus stepped in when Leona didn't speak, "your fourth victim was the videographer of the first three deaths. Yet three days separated her demise from theirs."

He jerked upright. That was clearly news to him.

Leona didn't follow as he and Marcus headed to the computer terminal. Instead, she stared down at the first corpse in the row. A black woman, skin tone barely lighter than her own, though she'd gone for that strange bleached-white blonde that some black women did. The man who lay on the third table was white and of a similar age, attire quality, and fitness level to Marcus. Both were tall and slender. The man between them was older and heavier. The woman on the far table was younger and dressed far more casually—the videographer.

Five got you ten that table one and three had been the *couple* mentioned in the article. The black woman and the white man, laid out on the morgue's cold slabs.

She tried not to do it...but couldn't stop herself from looking up at Marcus' back. Her previous partner—professional, not romantic, who'd trained her up from rookie to special agent—had been gunned down as they'd closed in on a notorious hacker in the Bronx. The bastard had slipped their grasp, which had left Leona with a truckload of self-recrimination and a battle tank-sized need for revenge.

Then Kate Stark's assistant, who had once been on the Secret Service's and the FBI's most-wanted lists, had simply handed her the hacker's real name and home address. Leona hadn't known whether to arrest or kiss the woman. In the end, Leona had pretended that Rikka Albert had never revealed her past—a life-debt payment for identifying Jake's killer.

And now she was staring down at the dead couple. White man, black woman. Dead on separate slabs.

Sure, Marcus was knocked over by her body, most men were. No complaints from her and she worked hard to keep up that fitness. But he'd seen past that and, like Jake, made it clear that first and foremost, she was an agent and an asset.

Both she and Marcus were damn good at their jobs. There'd been some training required on the personal side, but he'd learned fast. In fact, once started down a path, he'd shown a sharp imagination. Which made an intriguing contrast with his somewhat dour, beat-cop, public demeanor. That combination had let him slip past her guard until she was willing to live with the first person since senior year at NYU getting her criminology degree, back when conserving rent had been half the reason for being together. More than.

But these two. Black and white. Alive then...dead on a slab.

Marcus turned to her, not a glance at her figure, but straight in the eyes.

He asked something.

All she heard was the roar of the weapon that had executed Jake in that tiny hacker-haven of a Bronx internet cafe.

26

LEONA *CAME TO* IN... "IS THIS A JEWISH DELI?"

"A *New York* deli. We're still in Boston, but they serve pork products, so not Jewish," Marcus sat quietly across the small table from her. "Still, Archie's has the best pastrami sandwich in downtown."

"Why are we..." She waved a hand helplessly at the deli.

Some part of her had stayed functional, Marcus obviously hadn't carried her in here. And as she thought back, she remembered making notes. Observing Marcus speaking with the doctor, even the short drive here. But it was all like it had happened to someone else, someone very far away. Much farther away than—the missing memory slammed in hard enough to almost knock her out of the chair—the corpses on the slabs.

Deep breath. Focus on the present.

The deli faced onto a wide alley, a multi-bay truck loading dock across from them had all of its big steel doors rolled up, but she couldn't tell what they were moving in and out. And she didn't know Boston well enough to have any idea where they sat.

Then she focused on the time itself. "But it's only midmorning."

"Forensics doc wanted some time, and you needed to get out of there. Think of it as brunch. I wasn't sure if it was too early for you to face pastrami, so I ordered an egg salad sandwich as well, and a cherry soda and a root beer. You can have whichever you want."

She inhaled slowly, enjoying the aroma of toasted bread and warm meat rather than the stink of burned cordite and hot blood. Another breath before she could look him in the eye.

"Marcus, I already moved in, you don't have to keep being so damned decent." She leaned forward enough to brush their lips together to show she didn't mean it. Marcus could get mighty literal at the oddest of times. "Split the sandwiches with you, half and half. I'll take the cherry." This was the real world; she'd focus on that.

He'd kept a hold of her hand as she settled back. Right, they weren't in New York and keeping their relationship a secret from the other agents. They'd told the senior agent in charge, because he'd needed to know, but this was the age of cell phones so they still had separate numbers when being called in.

"I've never..." again she waved the other hand a little helplessly. "What did I miss?"

"First, why?"

And there was Marcus the agent; that need to know and understand that drove every good agent she'd ever met. Which also meant he deserved the flat truth. He had to know what had happened so that he could anticipate her actions, or rather inactions, if it ever happened again. Who was she kidding? She should be taken off duty and sent to a Bureau shrink ASAP. PTSD, a black mark on her file for the rest of her career. Oh, never out in the open, but challenging cases and promotions would be quietly assigned elsewhere.

"Black and white, woman and man, on the slab together. I had a flashback to Jake, then a flash forward to—" she couldn't bring herself to finish the sentence.

"To you and me lying there. Yeah, I thought the same, but then I thought, hell, if we gotta go, I'd rather go together than apart. Picture me, trying to hold it together after losing you..." Marcus simply shook his head that he'd never pull it off.

It wasn't a proposal, which was a good thing, but it was about the sweetest thing a guy had ever said to her.

"We'll call that extenuating circumstances. If it happens again, we'll deal with it. But if it hits the fan, I know you'll do what's needed and worry about it afterward." There was no questioning his absolute faith in her. The way he said it, even she believed it.

Which made it about the second sweetest thing a guy ever said to her.

"So," she managed a real breath. Then she confirmed to her inner doubt-demon, which had been screaming since moving in, that latching onto Marcus *had* been a good choice. "So, what did I miss?"

Marcus squeezed her hand one last time before releasing it. Back into agent mode. "After lunch, we return to the Medical Examiner. He'll try to have a preliminary for us. Then I think we need to go up to the pub in Gloucester and see if we think it's an accident or not. I'm already thinking not."

"Why?"

"The three victims from the pub came with a police report. A couple of the eyewitnesses described how the videographer was glued to the presenter's side every step of the way, until suddenly she wasn't."

Leona waited while their sandwiches were delivered. They were properly New York-deli massive, which she appreciated, as the three a.m. wake-up call and the long drive had not included breakfast.

Marcus made a little ceremony of switching the sandwich halves so they each had a half pastrami and a half egg salad.

She ignored the pale yellow of the egg salad contrasting with the black-edged red meat and took a big bite of the pastrami before she could create any more disturbing metaphors. The blast of flavor wiped away any chance of that. It was so simple yet so good: caraway-seed rye, rich brown mustard, and pastrami. No hiding behind sauerkraut or anything else.

"Okay," she managed around a mouthful, "what was in that report?"

27

Kᴀᴛᴇ's ᴘʜᴏɴᴇ ʙᴜᴢᴢᴇᴅ ɪɴ ʜᴇʀ ᴘᴏᴄᴋᴇᴛ ᴅᴜʀɪɴɢ ʟᴜɴᴄʜ. Sʜᴇ grabbed it like a lifeline and excused herself from the dining table up on the Quarterdeck.

Rikka had gone to their cabin to see what she could salvage from the image noise to either side of the explosion. Sam had joined her. Björn had gone off who knew where to confer with whoever had sent him. A glance in the interior dining room revealed Paul charming a whole table of women at least twice his age with tales of unlikely adventures that she'd learned the hard way were all true.

Wanting no part of that, Kate had—foolishly—headed up to lunch on her own after a quick check-in with the galley crew. Marnie had done all of the hard work of provisioning and planning the menu. Dinner service would be the main challenge, and Kate had agreed to come back to help out then.

However, that meant that after she'd gone down the Quarterdeck's buffet line of light-battered fish and chips with a nice side salad and sat at an out-of-the-way table, the wannabees had come buzzing in like a plague of locusts. Their ever-so-polite intent? To get on her show. Rikka would have said, *They wanna harvest your soul.* Which might have been more accurate.

She wasn't sure the last time she'd heard so many disorganized and ill-defined show proposals. Even the colleges and high school television production departments she occasionally visited were better prepared. Those kids also were young enough to not simply assume that, of course, Cooks Network would be glad, no, thrilled to have someone like [insert name here] on one of her shows.

"This is Kate," she hadn't even looked at the caller ID. She did slow down as soon as she realized that she was descending the same stairs that the groom had been blown over less than eighteen hours ago on his journey into the deep blue sea. At least if she went overboard, they were still in the harbor, and she could swim to the pier.

"Hello, Ms. Stark. This is Marcus Reynolds. I have you on speakerphone with Leona Edwards."

But for a quick grab at the railing, Kate might well have gone down the stairs head over heels. "Please tell me this is a social call."

"I wish I could, Ms. Stark. Did you know a Dana Winston?"

Did. "That was more than I wanted to know. How did she die?"

"She apparently did a selfie fall."

"But with the FBI on the case, you don't think that's what happened."

"No, ma'am."

"Cut that out, Marcus." She didn't need a whole dose of formal at this point.

"Cut what out?" he sounded puzzled.

"Kate, Leona here. You have to forgive him; Marcus always gets too serious when there's a case."

"Well, it's a serious case." Marcus' voice growled with annoyance.

"Yes, it is. But—"

Kate interrupted them. "Do I need to be here for this conversation?" She reached the bottom of the steps from the Quarterdeck to just outside the library window. At peak lunch service, nobody was here, so she took it as a temporary refuge and watched the birds soaring about the harbor. Last night's dinner companions would absolutely be able to tell her gull, tern, or whatever by genus, species, habitat, feeding habits, and—

"Sorry, Kate. Just trying to teach my man some manners."

"Your man?"

"Um, my partner. We moved in together yesterday. It's freaking us both out a bit, so let's leave it at that for a moment. Dana Winston was hired to film a Raymond Chandler and Shari Browley at a pub in Gloucester?"

"Yes, in two weeks. We'd have done it sooner, but I had plans out of the country. So we had to delay the shoot."

"Yes, Iceland," Marcus put in. "Very convenient."

Kate sighed. "Are you accusing me of killing one of my camera operators?"

"No, he isn't. Seriously, Marcus, get a grip. It is convenient only in that it allows us to step into a case that would otherwise never come to the FBI's attention. Because they didn't delay the shoot."

Kate closed her eyes. She'd liked Ray and Shari. But now she'd have to have a long talk with them about not messing with a schedule set by the person backing the show.

"An apparent accident at the pub—"

Kate felt the ship pitch beneath her feet, though it remained tied to the pier in the calm harbor. On a gasp, she managed, "More deaths?"

"I'm afraid so, Ms. Stark." Marcus was back. "That makes four."

"No, it makes seven."

"Seven?" Leona and Marcus asked together.

Kate hated coincidences, especially because she didn't much believe in them.

28

Hayden managed not to scream down the line at Björn's report. His office was well-insulated to keep underlings from overhearing secure conversations. But it wasn't wholly soundproof.

One target. One goddamn target, and they'd missed because of a goddamn splotch in the cake's icing? He'd wanted something dramatic in case someone else crossed his path. Just show them the film and let them make their own lifespan choices. This kept getting worse.

He considered recalling his other agent aboard the ship, but even Björn hadn't been told their identity. Issuing a recall would risk blowing their cover.

"A swarm of people are now clustered around Kate Stark, the owner and operator of Cooks Network."

"I know who she is," Hayden snarled back. His wife was passionate about the woman's cooking shows; they watched one most evenings.

"Right, sorry." Björn sounded more cautious than sorry. "I haven't been able to get her alone. Or view the video of what happened."

"The video isn't important. What sort of people?" Hayden half-listened as he tried a few online searches.

"A Eurasian camerawoman, a piece of serious military muscle, and a womanizer she looks very close to but claims to be her twin brother."

Womanizer. Hayden figured that it took one to know one. Björn's greatest weakness as a field agent—he was too damn handsome and, like James Bond, was all too willing to use that. Hayden keyed in a quick search. The only hit was... "He *is* her twin brother, Björn." Nothing on the muscle. No indication of why the woman needed a bodyguard.

He opened up the secure link into a Norwegian mainframe. He wasn't supposed to use this except in an emergency, but losing Bret Calder to an exploding wedding cake counted as one in his opinion. He wasn't supposed to be able to see into the Nine Eyes database at all, as Iceland wasn't one of the nine who shared national security information with one another. But his brother had married the head of the NIS, Norwegian Intelligence Service, and she had opened a private portal for him. No access to the national security side, that she'd kept locked and he didn't want to know, but he could definitely dive deeper here than an online search.

He didn't really expect anything, but Kate Stark's name popped up on his first query. Even a report on her inner circle of three people. He clicked on the face that had to be the muscle and read the brief report there.

"The muscle is, well, shit. Don't tangle with him, Björn. If even half of this decoration list is real...just don't mess with him."

"And if he messes with me?"

Hayden kept scrolling down Sam Fierro's operational background. The Nine Eyes database showed some serious Black Ops that had certainly never made the news. Each one was stamped with the code for successful completion. "You might consider running, very fast."

Björn's derisive snort was ill advised.

Hayden didn't correct him. Let the boy learn the hard way.

"Already figured that out for myself, Hayden."

Okay, Björn had to be damned smart to reach his current position. The brother, the muscle, and the third person…

A Mac Olson, dressed in a hot pink suit with a magenta scarf and matching shoes, was listed as Cooks' studio manager. Below that were another hundred or so names. Must be just the top-tier people. Producers, designers, no name he spotted as being Asian.

"What's the woman's name?"

"Kate. Oh, the camera op. Rikka Albert."

He made a quick search on the name and nothing came up. "No listing that I can find. Must be low-level or a freelancer."

"Could be."

"Björn, do you think someone damaged the cake intentionally, to make them turn it to redirect the explosion at the last moment and take out Bret?"

He wished he hadn't said it, but with Bret Calder dead in the explosion, Björn was now his top asset in the entire team.

Björn was silent for a long time. He'd never been the fastest thinker, but coming up out of intelligence analytics, he was perhaps the deepest one in the department. "If so, it was a very precise calculation. It struck Bret with enough force to blow him overboard, yet it didn't touch the bride beside him. The large bell of her dress kept him at a distance, but not that much of one, as they were cutting the cake together at the time of the incident."

"Not good news. There's someone else operating on that ship. I'll take care of permissions with the tour company. You stay aboard and find out what the hell happened to Bret."

"Any brilliant ideas on that front?"

"You're the man on the spot; you find a way. If that Stark woman has brought in a team—if you can call it that—stick close to her. Maybe they'll stumble on the answer for us."

"Get close to Kate Stark? That is *not* a burden."

"Then stop talking to me and go do it." Hayden hung up the phone. It was only after he did that he considered Björn's tone. He hadn't been willing, he'd been eager. Yet another variable he now had to keep an eye on.

A useless brother, a camera girl, and a piece of muscle? What could they possibly do? Even though it was a thin lead, it was the only one he had at the moment.

No, it wasn't. Gods, he was getting too old for this game, but Bret had been his obvious successor. Could Björn be groomed in any reasonable time frame to take over when Hayden retired from command of *Vikingasveitin*? *That* question didn't sit comfortably.

He sent a message to his deep embedded asset and hoped that they'd have better luck than he expected Björn would.

29

Kate ascended the stairs. The table she'd vacated so abruptly fell dead silent and all turned to look at her eagerly. One of the waiters had cleared her plate, so she offered them a friendly nod and cruised on by. She filled a fresh plate at the buffet and gathered two brownies and a soda before heading inside.

When she entered their suite, exactly as she'd expected, Rikka was still hunched over her computer. She set the plate, soda, and one of the brownies beside her without saying a word before taking the other brownie over to a comfortable chair. Kate knew that Rikka burned calories at a prodigious rate but always forgot to eat when in full-on tech mode.

Sure enough, behind her she heard the shuffling as the first French fries were acquired and consumed. Rikka would barely be conscious of the action, but food was present and calories would be acquired.

Kate slid lower in her chair and watched the sheep grazing atop the now sun-bathed rocky bluff outside her window. At this rate, it would probably be snowing by nightfall; after all, they'd only had three seasons so far today.

Before she reached the end of her own brownie, Rikka dropped into the chair opposite with one of her own. She raised it in a toast before taking a big bite and speaking around it. "I was able to recover about seventy percent of the image by encoding the noise floor of—"

"Don't tell me." Kate knew that techno-speak rabbit hole all too well. "What did you find out?"

Rikka sighed. "Sadly, nothing we didn't already know. They all looked seriously surprised. If I'm any judge, the three of them didn't survive long enough to suffer."

"Well, that's something, I suppose." Kate took a deep breath and wished she was up on that grassy slope with the sheep and that was her biggest worry. But before she could explain about Marcus and Leona's call, Rikka plunged ahead.

"You know what Nine Eyes is?"

"Sounds familiar..." But she couldn't place it. Some new piece of camera gear that Rikka wanted? Or a—

"You've heard of Five Eyes, of course."

Kate's look must have been blanker than she intended as Rikka huffed out her exasperation.

"Seriously? I thought you were a top Secret Service agent."

At least she now had a context of a non-techno-speak topic. Yes, she knew too much about the international intelligence-sharing cooperatives named Five Eyes and Nine Eyes. But Rikka had launched into an explanation and Kate decided to let her have her fun.

"Five Eyes is an intelligence collective of the big English speakers: US, Canada, UK, Australia, and New Zealand. They share all sorts of super top-secret stuff. Nine Eyes adds on our next tier of besties: Denmark, France, Netherlands, and Norway. They get less of the super-top info, but still a lot of cool data. There's also a Fourteen Eyes, but I think that's getting a bit sloppy."

"And this is relevant why?"

"Oh, right," Rikka finished her brownie in two more bites, washed it down with the last of her soda, and plunged ahead. "You just got a ping on your name in the Nine Eyes database."

"And you know this because..."

"I set an alert on your name. Anyone looking into you, anywhere, I wanted to know about that. They also pinged my name."

That jerked Kate's attention away from the sheep. "What did they find?"

Rikka laughed. "You think I let my name show up in any of their databases? No worries, Kate. I've got that covered."

She still didn't like it. Rikka's first run through the Witness Protection Program, properly the Witness Security Program, hadn't proved sufficient. Somehow that first WITSEC cover had been badly blown. She knew it was a risk, but she'd decided to keep Rikka close in her new incarnation. The danger to Rikka was that the two of them had been connected by Kate's initial arrest of one Shirō Usagi six years before—who just happened to look exactly like a marginally younger version of one Rikka Albert. For her second time through the system, Rikka had also followed in close behind the identity change and erased all of the details from her own records. The US Marshals Service, the ones who ran WITSEC, no longer knew she existed. No case officer, no yearly check-in.

Still, Kate didn't like that someone was poking at the name, not that it tied to any prior name her friend had used. She'd told Paul, so that her brother didn't screw that up. Curiously, he proved absolutely trustworthy on the important things, even if he never recalled when she needed their personal jet. She assumed that Sam knew. And two FBI agents. There was also a member of the North Korean Council of Five and his wife, but oddly she could trust them absolutely on this one point. It was more people than she liked.

But if Rikka needed a new identity, they wouldn't be able to remain connected. Kate would lose her closest friend. She didn't have many of those—like a grand total of one—and she didn't know if she could deal with that loss.

"Who was looking?"

"Well, that is a little odd." Rikka began weaving bits of her long hair together. She was never one to sit still. "There's a backdoor into Nine Eyes data through Norway. It was so unexpected that I couldn't trace it before they closed the session. Really well hidden. I set a trap for next time so that I can see who it was, but all they saw about me was a standard *Search String Not Found* system message. I just attached a tracker on that so the next time anyone searches my name in any of their systems, I'll get a full trace as a part of the search failure message."

"Any other hacks I should know about?"

Rikka hesitated, then shook her head. Her slick hair unraveled her bit of weaving. Kate didn't like that hesitation but decided that she had enough worries of her own at present.

"We have a new problem. I got a call from—"

A sharp knock on the door interrupted her.

30

Sam and Paul came into the room, with Kate's brother already speaking. "I booked the two of us into the former groom's suite across the hall. So, we're all set."

"Ick!" Rikka shuddered. "Sleeping in a dead man's room, Stark. You really are one step below a slime mold."

"Hey, someone on the next voyage will be sleeping in there anyway. Bet the tour company doesn't tell them, and they'll sleep there just fine. Who knows, did you ever think *this* could be a dead man's room on some other voyage?"

Rikka pulled up her feet and hugged her knees so that she wasn't touching the floor or the... Then she saw Paul's smile. She *hated* when he slipped past her guard. "That does it, Stark. I was going to give back your Ferrari, but now I never will."

He reached into his pocket and pulled out his keys, waving them at her. She had no idea how he did these things. He was the only one who could find her when she had disappeared into one of her safe houses. Well, he and Kate. Kate had found Rikka under her Shirō Usagi identity and again when Suzi Suzuki blew up in her face. Maybe it was in their DNA.

Paul Stark DNA? Double ick!

Sam gave Paul a nudge into the room, then started to close the door. She knew he'd lean against it because that was how he protected people. Just before it clicked the latch, there was a knock and it swung open a foot—before it met the brick wall she called Sam Fierro.

She could see him nod his head as he counted two, then yanked the door full open and grabbed.

Björn came stumbling into the crowded room, flailing his arms for balance. Only Sam's fistful of his shirt front kept him upright.

"What the hell are you doing here?" Rikka trusted him even less since she'd seen him challenge Sam on the beach.

"I came to see Kate." He brushed at Sam's hands several times before he let go.

"Well, now you've seen her," Rikka waved a hand toward where Kate hadn't moved a muscle. "Goodbye." She gave a nod to Sam.

Sam clamped a hand about Björn's bicep and began walking him backward.

"Stop. Would you just stop for a moment? I'm just trying to find out why the wrong person was killed last night."

In the next frozen moment, Sam stopped pushing and Björn's face passed through several strange transformations as he probably considered how to vacuum his words back up before anyone else heard them.

"Ain't no Time-Turners, buddy-boy," Rikka informed him. "Hermione Granger has the only one."

"Who has what?"

Only Kate holding up a hand kept Rikka from doing more than sputtering. Harry Potter had bypassed Björn somewhere along the way. He sooo wasn't worthy of Kate.

At a nod from Kate, Sam propelled Björn toward one of the beds, giving him a twist so that it caught the back of his knees, and he sat abruptly. Then Sam hung out the Do Not Disturb sign, closed the door, threw the security latch for good measure, and stood in front of it with his arms crossed.

Only the gods above, below, and hovering over Alpha Centauri knew why, but when Sam did that, she wanted to jump him so badly.

"The *wrong* person?" Kate spoke for the first time, her voice dangerously soft. Even Paul didn't dare interrupt that tone.

Björn rested his elbows on his thighs, clasped his hands together, and stared down at them.

When Paul started to speak anyway, Rikka rather enjoyed kicking him sharply on the shin. That had him sitting abruptly on the other twin bed and making *Ooo! Ooo!* noises as he clutched his leg with both hands. Now only Sam remained standing, and his demeanor made it clear he wouldn't be the first to interrupt.

"You, uh, proved it yourself...this morning," Björn made a platter-turning motion. "Someone sabotaged that cake. Either the same person or another one damaged the icing. They caused the cake to be turned a very precise amount, altering the target. Whoever was the intended victim, they weren't the one killed."

Rikka saw Kate glance at Sam. She had never understood what was between them. She knew that they absolutely trusted each other, but they didn't exactly get along. Sam wasn't willing to talk about it. Kate had finally found out that she'd annoyed Sam because she had voluntarily left the Secret Service. But that hadn't fully settled things between them. And she didn't know how to read those looks they exchanged, which was even more annoying.

Kate returned her attention to Björn. "Who are you really?"

That had him sitting up. "And who are you to be asking that? Some television executive with a playboy brother, a bodyguard, and a free-lancer cameraman? You think this is all a game."

"Camerawoman," Rikka put in, but they both ignored her. "Videographer." No reaction to that either. *Right. Shut up, Rikka. This isn't about you.*

Kate had one of those dangerous smiles as she again glanced at Sam, "*Vikingasveitin?*"

Sam nodded.

Björn flinched as if he'd been slapped.

Before Rikka could rise to grab her laptop for a quick search, Kate's next question answered it for her.

"So, what is one of Iceland's elite Special Operations agents from the Viking Squad doing here? This is far more than a wedding gone wrong. Iceland has seen fit to send one of their precious forty-six officers trained in counterterrorism and hostage rescue to investigate. Why this wedding?"

Björn froze for just a moment. Rikka would have missed it if Sam's attention hadn't shifted with a jolt. It meant...

"Who else? I don't think it was Marnie or her sous chef. So, the groom was also *Vikingasveitin.*" Kate didn't ask, she told. "Who was *he* investigating?"

Björn shrugged at that one. "As far as I know, it was just his wedding. Not investigating anyone. And how the hell did you just do that?"

Kate ignored the question and looked at Rikka. "I've been assuming we were the original target. What if we weren't?"

31

He felt the blood drain from his face as he read the news article on his tablet.

Influencer Achieves World Record for Shortest Wedding in History

Someone has beaten the Kuwaiti couple who held the *previous record of being married for a mere three minutes. Their newly wedded bliss ended when the bride stumbled and fell to the floor while departing the judge's chambers. Her new husband called her* Stupid. *She stormed back into the judge's chamber and demanded an immediate annulment, earning her the previous title of Shortest Wedding in History. (Note: Weddings that were tragically bombed during wars were not tabulated for this article as precise timelines could rarely be verified.)*

Last night, with a total duration of precisely a hundred and nineteen seconds, there's a new entry in the record books. Gen Z super-influencer Savannah Sachs' marriage to Icelander Bret Calder aboard the cruise ship Ice Adventure *was blown apart—literally. An exploding wedding cake killed the groom shortly after completing* *his nuptial ceremony to the lovely bride. Savannah was stunning in a voluminous custom-designed Vera Wang for the shipboard ceremony. See the livestream <u>Here.</u>*

This morning on her social media channels, Savannah has expressed her heart-broken sadness but insisted on continuing the rest of her honeymoon cruise as, Bret would never want me to give up on anything.

Authorities are investigating matters aboard ship but have declined to comment on suspects or motives. Videos of the cake cutting catastrophe were posted by numerous people, including the bridesmaid's livestream. Two chefs were also caught up in the explosion.

Some sources are speculating that Savannah arranged it as a publicity stunt—which has been rigorously denied in thousands of posts by her fans. However, it should be noted that the event has added another million followers to her channels in the first twelve hours, with no sign of the rate slackening.

Britney Spears is generally believed to have what is now the third shortest marriage, lasting a mere fifty-five hours before...

HE SKIPPED DOWN TO WHERE THE LINKS TO THE VIDEOS HAD BEEN included in the article.

He clicked and watched each one. Savannah and her husband cutting the cake one moment, a white-out flash, and the groom gone in the next. Panic had ensued and like so many disaster videos, they kept recording as they ran, producing a jumble of—

There! Thank God. He'd light an extra candle the next time he happened to be in a church. In one frame of the third video, he saw Savannah still standing. Still alive before the ruined cake. For some reason, she held a long sword. An odd choice, but his niece had always found ways to play to the audience, even as a little girl.

By the fifth video, there wasn't anything new to see: ever-so-careful perfect pose, cutting, explosion, panic.

He was going to find whoever had turned Savannah's cake into a bomb and tear them apart. Not limb by limb, but joint by joint—literally. He was going to wield agonizing retribution on those responsible in ways that hadn't been seen since the Winter Hill Gang had killed off the entire McLaughlin Gang in one brief bloody war for the control of Boston's underworld.

He was reaching to close the final video when it caught two people standing well off to the side. A stout tripod supporting a pro-grade video camera, similar to the one that Dana Winston had carried to her death when she *fell* off Tablet Rock in that Gloucester park.

Pausing the jumbled video, he zoomed in, tilting his head to view them right-side up.

No.

It was impossible.

But there they were.

At least Kate Stark. Her position masked whoever stood by the camera, but enough showed to see it was someone small. Someone the size of Kate's assistant.

And, damn it all to bloody hell, they'd survived!

32

Paul's knowing smile said he was about to dispense some idiot wisdom, probably even more Paul-like than usual, so Rikka kicked his other shin as she crossed to the desk to snag one of her laptops. He was still occupied making *Ooo! Ooo!* noises by the time she'd returned to her chair and booted up.

Accessing her videos of the cake cutting, she ran them through projection software to convert the 2D camera data into a 3D image. Then she rotated that until she had a from-above view of the deck's layout and everyone's positions.

"Sam, what's the lethal radius reach of that explosive?"

He crossed from the locked door to squat by her chair. Resting a comforting hand on her shoulder, which fought against the chill of how close death had brushed by this time, he traced a finger of his other hand in an arcing line that centered on the cake.

"So, Savannah, Kate, and I would be dead, but even the closest of the watching passengers were far enough back to only be injured."

Sam's nod affirmed the fact, then waggled a hand to show that was only the most-likely scenario.

She turned to Kate. "What that means is that there are only the three of us as a possible target in the cake's original orientation."

"Who have you pissed off lately, Rikka?"

Rikka paused. There was... But that was ridiculous. "No one lately."

Kate's look said she wasn't buying it.

"Honestly," she raised the three fingers of a Girl Scout salute, not that she'd ever been one. There'd been a whole group of them at the orphanage, but they'd wanted no more to do with the outsider computer whiz than a young Betsy Franklin had wanted to do with them—back when that was Rikka's assigned name. Franklin was the orphanage's name, fine. But who named a Japanese kid Betsy?

Kate waited.

"Long ago." She glanced about the room. The others knew she'd been through WITSEC, though only Kate knew she'd been through it twice. But Björn wouldn't know. "Before," was all she said. Before her second passage through the Witness Security Program.

Kate's nod accepted that, but said it was going to be a hot topic the next time they were alone together. Rikka would make sure to sweep wherever they met carefully for bugs first. She didn't mind the crawly ones much, but the listening ones freaked her out worse than a herd of spiders. The suite, with five people in it, became claustrophobic, making it hard to breathe.

Kate shrugged. "Well, if anyone is hunting me, I don't know about it. Björn?"

He jerked as if he'd been stuck with a cattle prod.

"What can you tell us about Savannah that might make her the original target?"

"Nothing."

Kate gave him one of her don't-piss-me-off looks. Even Rikka rarely messed with those.

"Honestly. Savannah Sachs, twenty-eight-year-old, wealthy at a seriously obscene scale."

Paul burst out laughing. "Oh, buddy. You just put your foot in it with my sister on that one."

Björn scowled up at Paul, and it was Rikka's turn to laugh.

"Didn't do your homework very well, did you, Mr. Viking?"

33

IF BJÖRN SURVIVED THIS, HE WAS GOING TO CHOKE THE OLD MAN
until he turned blue. Typical Hayden to send him into the field
with too little information.

He looked up at Sam Fierro. *Stoney* didn't begin to describe
the look he sent back. Perhaps fulminating. Former military, at
least Björn assumed it was former. Again Hayden hadn't
specified, merely warning him to avoid the man. Get close to
Kate Stark yet avoid her bodyguard, while trapped on a ninety-
meter-long ship. Right. Sure. Whatever you say, boss.

A mere staff videographer wasn't a likely companion for
Kate Stark, but he'd seen how close they were. And if she was
just a staffer, how could she get away with kicking Kate's
brother?

Well, at least the pretty-boy actually was her brother, so he
had no competition there.

That left only the greatest enigma of them all, Kate Stark.
He'd pretty thoroughly convinced himself that she was as
innocent as she claimed—yet she represented more anomalies
that one person should ever have.

Kate had some level of training that he knew nothing about.

TV executives didn't wake up throwing a picture-perfect knife-hand strike—or be able to stop it ten centimeters from crushing Rikka Albert's windpipe. A hundred and eighty centimeters tall and not a millimeter of it out of place.

Situation, think about the situation—and think fast. Sam's patience was stretching thinner by the second.

Kate and Rikka, if they hadn't been the ones to damage the icing and turn the cake, would have been victims, not suspects. Sam and Paul had flown in after the fact.

Conclusions? Paul Stark couldn't be the bumbling yet charming fool that he presented so flawlessly. Sam Fierro was much more than a bodyguard just as Rikka Albert was far more than a staffer. And, though he'd never met a television studio executive before, he bet that there were no others like Kate Stark.

"Who *are* you people?"

Rikka laughed.

Paul had stopped rubbing his shins and was dusting at his slacks to make sure Rikka's kick had left no mark.

Sam remained with his heels planted on the carpet, so no attack was imminent. Björn hated to acknowledge that if one came, he didn't stand a chance. Even if he managed to land the first blow, it wouldn't end well for him. He'd seen that on the beach. Moving that stone took everything he had but not everything Sam had.

That left Kate Stark. The obvious leader. So, following Hayden's advice, he ignored the others and focused on her.

"Seriously. You do understand how much of an anomaly your team represents, right?"

Those blue-blue eyes studied him for long enough that he was desperate to turn away but, at the same time, couldn't. "Let's turn that question around. *Vikingasveitin—the Viking Squad.* What are you really doing here?"

"How do you even know about us?"

Kate merely smiled. The amusement didn't reach her eyes this time. This wasn't the lovely woman who had slept on his shoulder, creating a dozen hot fantasies. She was as much something *other* as he was.

He had to give some answers, the question was how many could he safely offer? Start slow and see where it went. He turned to face Kate once more. "I received a call last night that said Bret Calder, one of our top operatives, had been killed in an explosion. I was sent to investigate, determine the source of and reason for the attack, and take care of the perpetrator."

Sam shifted up on his toes, no more than that. Björn, who'd never felt claustrophobia now felt the crushing weight of it wrap around him like a boa constrictor.

Kate raised one eyebrow but didn't look aside, so neither did he. "Arrest, if possible, terminate if necessary." She didn't make it a question.

Who the hell was she?

"Your current suspects," she demanded his list.

Björn waved his hand about at her and Rikka. "Nothing personal. No known motive. But who else had such access to the cake? The two chefs provided by the ship would never have turned their own weapon upon themselves."

Rikka Albert's fine fingers were bunched into a fist he could fit in the palm of his hand.

Kate remained unmoving.

He waited her out.

"Really, Björn? You must expand your thinking."

"Okay, so who do you suspect?"

Kate didn't answer, instead tipping her head to Rikka.

The little woman spoke fast. "First, you even think of accusing Kate and I'll have Sam beat you to a pulp and then I will personally toss you into one of your volcanoes—alive! You'll feel every instant while becoming part of the Mid-Atlantic Ridge with your molecules slowly being stretched apart as half of you goes west and half of you goes east for the next couple hundred million years. Or I could just erase you and see how you deal with that."

"Erase me? Like I'm a drawing on a white board?"

"Yeah, first I'd—"

"Suspects, Rikka," Kate cut her off, saving him from laughing in Rikka's face.

"Right," she blew out a hard breath. "We were called away from the cake assembly three separate times, down to the galley. Any of the staff chefs would have known our movements. The ship's Bridge lies at the opposite end of the same deck. The captain and senior officers could easily travel between the two unobserved. The back stairs to the deck below also would have allowed easy access to any of the passengers or crew. Bret Calder certainly knew explosives if he was *Vikingasveitin*. Perhaps he planted them to off us or his bride, then someone else turned the cake. Savannah...huh." Rikka cleared the 3D projection from her laptop screen.

No one spoke while she worked the keyboard faster than anyone he'd ever seen. They all simply watched her and waited. From the time Björn actually thought to check his watch until she finished and pushed the lid closed, seven full minutes later, no one here had fidgeted, except him. Paul was the only one who had moved, shifting to the head of the bed where he leaned back against the headboard and began cruising through his phone messages.

"Sorry, she's such a social media queen that I had to build a couple routines to analyze it all. Typical for her generation, she has a lot of climate change and other activism topics. Less fashion than our generation would expect, about average for a wealthy Gen Zoomer. But that's not the interesting bit." And she shut up.

Björn tried to read her smile...but couldn't. "So, what the hell is the interesting bit?"

Her smile shifted into a sneer of pure contempt. "You don't know a thing about patience, do you, Mr. Björn-the-last-nameless?"

As his antipathy for the little woman increased exponentially, he noticed that Kate and Sam were waiting quietly. One deep breath. Two. Three. It barely helped.

"You'll learn," Kate said softly before turning to Rikka. "What's the interesting bit?"

"Didn't I just ask that?"

Rikka stuck her tongue out at him. "You aren't Kate." Then rose from her chair, turned it so that she was directly facing Kate, then sat down again.

"You know about your great-grandfather Stark being in the White Hand, of course."

34

THE BODIES HAD BEEN LESS REVEALING THAN MARCUS HAD hoped.

"The three who died in the brewery, ah, incident," Dr. Paswan chose his words carefully, "died from three separate causes. Mr. Mike O'Connor was either boiled or drowned. Actually, he was both boiled *and* drowned, but I can't determine which factor took precedence. The female victim, while showing indications of second and third-degree burns to her front, was killed by blunt force trauma to the back of her head and torso. I would hypothesize that she was flung backward by a most fiery explosion. The second male, Mr. Ray Chandler, died from cerebral hypoxia."

"Hypoxia? Like he suffocated at high altitude?" That made no sense at all.

The Medical Examiner pulled back the sheet covering the corpse, thankfully only enough to reveal one arm before he lifted the limp hand. "Cyanosis, blue-tinted skin at the extremities due to lack of blood oxygenation. He inhaled some liquid. But only enough to impede his further oxygenation, not enough to explain a fatal degree of asphyxiation."

"What about the fourth body?" Leona showed none of the early signs of trouble. Her jaw remained tightly clenched, but she'd carefully followed the ME's explanations, making notes in her small pad. He loved that retro part of her. She was the smart one of their team who knew the answers by the time he'd fully formed the question.

"Oh, she was dead before she fell."

Marcus spun to look at him. "Say what?"

"She exhibited several compound fractures from her fall, where broken bones pierced the dermal envelope, the skin. Each of these exhibited minimal blood loss, despite one severing a femoral artery." He pointed at a clear bucket filled with a dark red liquid.

Marcus checked in on Leona, who merely grimaced and looked away as quickly as he had.

"Her body still retained eight pints of blood. For a woman of her age, weight, and general fitness, I would estimate that her normal blood supply would have been below ten pints, therefore minimal blood loss. I also find it unlikely that she would break her legs and an arm as well as the suffering of a cervical fracture. That combination of damage seems most unlikely from a simple fall."

"Murdered?" he asked.

"Someone snapped her neck and dumped her off the rock," Leona spoke and the ME nodded his agreement.

Marcus scanned around until he spotted the victims' personal effects boxes. He checked the number on the toe tag, then stepped over to the one with the matching number and the name Dana Winston. It was by far the fullest of the four.

Leona stopped him with a gesture. "Let's review the others first, so that we don't miss anything critical."

Thorough. The woman was very thorough, both in the field and in his bed. He wasn't sure which he appreciated more. Marcus sorted through the other boxes quickly.

Mike O'Connor. Wallet, keys, clothes. Nothing else.

Ray Chandler. The same plus an engagement ring still in the box.

He exchanged a look with Leona. They were nowhere near that; they'd had the conversation enough to know. But —shit!

Shari Browley. The same minus the ring but plus a tablet computer that powered-on when he tapped it.

"Locked." He turned it over to Leona.

She took it and walked over to Shari's body on the table. Pulling back the sheet, she waved over the ME. "Would you please hold open one of her eyes?"

He reached out a blue-gloved hand and she aimed the tablet's camera at the woman's face.

Then Leona checked the screen. "That did it. Thank you, Doctor."

She was tapping through the screens as she returned to Marcus' side. "Nothing much. A detailed schedule. Nine signed appearance releases to allow their images to be used. Something called a shot sheet," which she opened. "It includes a detailed schedule, one item of which was noted as *Back of House – Brewery Tour.* Thirty minutes had been allotted for that with no other note."

She made notes on her pad as Marcus turned his attention to the last bin, trying to keep his smile to himself.

"What?" Leona asked without looking up.

"I'd still like to know how you can tell what I'm thinking before you look at me."

He could feel the invisible smile in reply.

"Shock, not PTSD. We're never going to be worried about you going blank again."

She stopped, glanced at the corpses, then back to his face. The smile of relief that she aimed his way was radiant. It half-tempted him to steal the engagement ring from Ray's belongings, even if they had only just moved in together last night.

She inserted a password for herself before returning the tablet to the proper effects bin.

Last of all, Dana Winston. Wallet, keys, and a knapsack filled with camera equipment. The camera itself had a cracked lens but looked otherwise intact.

"Do you recognize this stuff?"

"You're the techy one on this team, Leona. How about you?"

"Some, but not enough to know if anything is missing."

Marcus pulled out his phone. "Well, at least we know who to ask."

35

KATE KNEW NOTHING ABOUT A WHITE HAND ANYTHING, LET alone her great-grandfather being a part of it. To make her point, she raised her own hand, twisted it back and forth to look at each side carefully before holding it out to Rikka in question.

The eye-roll response made her smile. Then Rikka giggled when she understood that Kate had caught her being the straight person. Usually that was Kate's own role, but on rare occasions—very rare—she could trip up her friend.

The nice moment was blasted apart by the ringing of Kate's phone. She winced when she saw Marcus' number but answered anyway.

"Who's dead now?"

Björn's head jerked up so fast.

"Same count here. There?" Marcus asked.

"Same."

"That's good...I guess." She could hear Marcus wince at his own words. "We have a question for Ms. Albert."

"What kind of question? You're on speaker with an unknown in the room."

Rikka was leaning way back, as if the phone was going to bite her.

Björn scowled.

Kate whispered to him, "You *are,* so deal with it."

He didn't look any happier, but he kept quiet.

"A camera question."

Rikka leaned in. "Cool. I know about those. What's up?"

"We've recovered Dana Winston's equipment pack and camera. We need to know if there is anything relevant here. I'm turning on my camera."

Kate accepted the change to a video call.

Rikka flipped open her laptop and the image appeared on the room's big screen television seconds later.

Kate supposed it was a good thing that she didn't know enough about phone security to be scared how easily Rikka had done that. If Björn recognized the move of a top hacker, he offered no sign of it.

"Spread everything out on the counter," Rikka instructed.

Kate watched one of Marcus' hands and Leona's two darker ones rapidly lay out the gear; Marcus' other hand would be holding his phone aloft.

"A Kinefinity Terra 6K?" Rikka looked over at her own Red V-Raptor XL 8K and felt a desperate need to hug Kate. She'd never noticed that other Cooks Network videographers wielded an eight-thousand-dollar camera body and hers cost five times that. "Is that just for me?" she whispered and nodded toward the Raptor.

Kate shrugged easily. "You seemed to like it."

Rikka could only nod fiercely. Not just for the camera, but that Kate's thoughtfulness ran deeper than the Grand Canyon. Heck, deeper than the Mariana Trench, and that was seriously deep.

"Uh," she focused once more on Marcus' image just so she didn't start bawling in public. "Camera body. Canon EOS backup body with a short zoom mounted just in case the Kinefinity crashes. Two spare batteries with charger. An okay set of lenses." The twelve-hundred-millimeter monster that had so impressed the birders at the table cost twenty grand, more than Dana's entire network-provided kit. "That does it, Kate. I'm throwing over Sam. I'm going to marry you and have your babies."

"Okay."

She risked a glance to see if Kate was joking. Dammit! Kate's humor surprised her every time. She was half-tempted to suggest a wedding date just to see what Kate would do with it. But weddings were a dangerous topic at the moment.

Back to the phone view. "A... Huh, I don't see them. Marcus... Never mind, just keep your phone steady. Leona, do you see any memory cards? Good camera packs have a hundred little cubbies. They'd be as fat as a couple credit cards but a little narrower and lumpy. For Kinefinity, they're shaped like a seven-square game piece for Tetris."

Kate assumed that meant something in a non-Kate world.

The hands on-screen dug around in various pockets and came up with two of them, both still shrink-wrapped.

"Okay, on the left side of the camera, press the SSD button, then flip open the little door that runs vertically along the side."

Leona hit the release and flicked it open.

"Oh, crumbs!" Rikka looked at Kate. "I'm so sorry. There's no recording media. Definitely not a selfie death. She couldn't take a picture of her toes without those. Someone else has the cards."

36

HE NEEDED TO THINK.

There were two places he liked to do that. The Plough and Stars in Cambridge, Mass., was the best Irish pub this side of the big water. Oh, a few others had better ratings, but this one had been a neighborhood place for over sixty-five years. Dark wood, a long bar, high ceilings from which hung giant stars. A man could sit with a pint of draft Guiness, lamb stew or fish and chips, and lose himself in the nightly bands. It was a fine place to stop thinking—let his subconscious do its thing—and forget about the world hurrying by just outside the windows.

It also had the advantage of never having been a part of Irish Pubs, Inc.

Father had brought him here the day he'd turned twenty-one. They'd sat at the bar facing the old oxen-dragged plough mounted above the mirror-backed array of liquor. *You never mess with this one, lad. This here is a refuge. If they're ever in trouble, you pay off their debt. No questions. Anonymous. You just pay it and walk on. You hear me, boy?*

Other than a few tight years during the pandemic, they were too popular to need any help. Even then they were enough of an institution that an envelope of just a hundred grand left beside the cash register had more than covered their shortfall. Too honest for their own good, they'd posted notices for a month about that *lost envelope* before the police had declared it was theirs to keep. They'd probably declared it as tip income and paid taxes on it. Saps.

But today he needed to start thinking. It was also still midmorning, too early for a pint. Instead, he walked out to the middle of the Harvard Bridge. He let his stride shorten just enough to pace out three steps per Smoot.

In 1958, a decade before The Plough and Stars opened and he himself was born, Oliver Smoot's fraternity had measured the bridge over the Charles River from MIT to Boston by laying him on the pavement three hundred and sixty-four-point-four times. He sometimes wondered how they'd judged the final point-four of a Smoot to make the full span—head-to-belly or feet-to-balls. Every tenth Smoot was still numbered on the pavement; the paint restored by MIT students each year. When the highway department had replaced the sidewalks, they creased the concrete every Smoot, five-foot-seven rather than the typical six-foot spacing.

Over the middle of the Charles, standing on the one hundred and eighty-two-point-twoth Smoot—and its notorious *Halfway to Hell* marker with an arrow pointing at MIT—he turned to lean on the rail and face the northeast.

Behind him, two lanes of traffic rumbled by. The occasional e-bike or scooter whizzed along the bike lane like an annoying mosquito. Even the occasional rhythmic beat of an actual human-powered bicycle rolled by.

When he was sure no one was watching, he let the two Kinefinity memory cards Dana had handed to him, moments before her demise, drop into the dark water and join the other...detritus he'd dropped there over the years. At least that was done.

Between this bridge and Massachusetts Bay lay Boston's North End, the *USS Constitution,* and Logan Airport. Beyond that, far beyond that, across most of the North Atlantic, lay Iceland. The incoming tide brought the smell of the sea. Was it the same scent that Kate Stark and her assistant now took in with each breath?

He wanted them both—one who deserved a highly painful death, and Stark for being her friend. He'd had a man shadowing Stark ever since he saw the news article about the G-7 meeting. *Chef Saves the President.* Big news, two-inch letters on the front page of everywhere. He'd flipped through the article, not really caring, until he saw the last picture. A prime shot of the kitchen crew working diligently. Kate Stark in the foreground, a lot of working chefs farther down the line. And slightly blurred in the background...

He'd known her as Suzi Suzuki and celebrated the news of her death; even verified the death certificate. Though barely half in the shot and unnamed in the caption, he knew her instantly. She was alive. He'd determined she wasn't an employee at the G-7's meeting hotel, but rather a companion of Kate Stark. He didn't know her name but, against all odds, he'd found a dead woman.

So he'd hired a man to watch Kate Stark, except he never reported that the two women were together. At least not until that film shoot at the Pig 'N' Whistle. He had a contact there, who'd witnessed everything and had overheard about the upcoming filming in Gloucester. In a slightly panicked phone call, he pretended to be the bar owner Mike O'Connor. *I just want to confirm the schedule and everyone's name and contact number. You know, in case anything goes wrong.* That had led him to the videographer. She'd had secrets, big bad ruin-your-life kind of ones.

He'd told her what to do: one small wire cut to disable the Close Valve button, one broken-off pencil jammed in a pressure relief valve, and one push of the Open Valve button to start the overpressure of the Brite tank. He hadn't mentioned the catastrophe it would cause—or how much worse the reality had been than even his plan. He'd worked with Mike when IPI was financing the launch of the Twin Lights Pub; Mike had been a good guy. It was a pity that sometimes the course of business caused collateral damage.

And yet he'd missed his target. Ray and Shari had jumped the schedule, shutting out Stark and her nameless assistant.

He'd lost track of them again...until that article about the exploding wedding cake that had almost killed his niece.

Even the memory of how close that came to killing Savannah had him clamping the railing so hard in his fists that he was surprised he didn't rip it off the bridge structure itself. That someone else had a serious hate-on for those two—no big surprise—had nearly gotten his niece killed was beyond tolerance.

Deep breaths.

Ocean air.

The cool breeze that wandered close over the Charles River on warm days.

Keep breathing.

It didn't help. He might be old-school, but his father had taught him this business. Sure, he'd been the one to take it mostly legit—mostly corporate structures and creative financing now—but he missed the simpler times when all he needed was a bit of muscle. He'd eradicated people, and their families, for far milder offenses than attacking his niece.

She was his only heir, even if she didn't know it yet. By the time Father had been his age, he'd been seven years dead by a stroke. Shot four times in the chest during a mob brawl had done for his grandfather in turn at the same age. He knew he was living on borrowed time.

He'd found no sign this time of Suzi Suzuki or whatever she

was calling herself now, but Kate Stark had been there for the explosion and a small woman had been running that camera. Yes, for the next eleven days he would know where to find them, together on that ship. Now to decide how to best go about making sure the woman didn't try to blackmail him again—ever.

37

THEY WERE DEEP IN DINNER PREP BEFORE KATE REMEMBERED. "What was that thing you said?"

"Which thing?" Rikka carried a sheet pan of crab-stuffed mushroom caps from prep to the ovens. The gentle sway of the boat was an aspect of shipboard cooking she'd never considered. Extra attention was needed to not chop of fingers, oven doors were latched open before reaching inside, and agile feet kept trays of mushrooms headed where they were intended.

With no primary meat course, she'd sent Sam to go off and do whatever he did for fun. Ignore Paul, humble Björn, or lay about on the deck working on his tan. That last idea almost made her smile. More likely he'd be out climbing a vertical rock face or swimming five kilometers in the frigid waters to keep in shape. The treadmill and weights in her office were plenty enough for her.

Eleven of the surviving twelve kitchen staff were head-down on their own tasks—pastry was already done for the day. The noise—no conversation was possible from more than an arm's length. Ladles clanged in soup tureens, releasing clouds of a sweet-corn clam chowder. Three different chopping boards resounded from the rapid vivisection of produce for two types of salad. The sharp snap of a torch announced the sugar glazing of the pound cakes to accompany the honey-sweetened four-berry topping for desserts.

Kate raised her hand to Rikka as if examining both sides.

"Oh, that thing," Rikka leaned in close enough to be heard. "That will take some explaining."

"Fine, get over here and help me stuff the manicotti while you explain it."

"Sure, just one more tray of mushrooms." She made quick work of that, then joined Kate. "You know about the White Hand, of course." She took up a piping bag of smoked salmon-spinach-ricotta filling and began stuffing the tubes.

"No." Kate began piping reindeer and ricotta as her half of tonight's surf-and-turf manicotti.

"The Irish mob in New York? Where your paternal great-grandpa made his fortune during Prohibition? Well, out in the Bronx, but still New York."

"He did? No. Maybe…" What did she know? It was only her heritage.

"Duh! It's not there in the FBI's or Secret Service databases, but I was able to put it together after some serious digging." Rikka finished her half faster than should be humanly possible and turned her attention to the chanterelle sauce for the topping.

Kate kept piping her reindeer filling into the large pasta tubes. If Rikka said it was *serious* digging, that meant that no mere mortal could have put the pieces together. But she also didn't doubt Rikka's skills at finding out things like that.

"On your ma's side of the house, your g-ma was the one with the money but in Boston rather than New York. She was Scottish, but way deep in the McLaughlin mob, Boston's big

Irish gang of the 1950s. Like in that movie *The Untouchables*, you know Capone's accountant George?"

She didn't, so she kept her mouth shut.

"That's what she did. There was a big gang war in the 1960s that wiped them out. With no one alive who *owned* the money, it looks like your g-ma was left holding the bag, kinda literally. Suddenly seriously wealthy, with untraceable funds, she moved to Manhattan and got married. Their descendants, your mom and dad, met at the opera—probably why they always had season tickets—like it was the first date every time." Rikka stared up at the ceiling for a moment. "Yeah, that fits and it's seriously sweet. No wonder you turned out so cool. Do you think they knew about their parents' and grandparents' mob pasts? You gonna finish those?"

Kate looked down at her hands, one frozen around a single tube of manicotti; a manicot? The other barely keeping a hold on the piping bag. "Did they know...*what?*"

Rikka extracted the prep work from Kate's limp fingers and set about finishing the turf portion of the dish. "Sure. Scads of mob money a couple generations back. Don't take it personally, Kate. They've been clean ever since, not so much as a shady 1040 tax form. Made their money from illegal booze on one side with gambling and loansharking on the other, which in US history is cleaner than most. Would you rather it was slave money or cotton money, which was slave money anyway, or shipping money, which was slave *and* cotton money, or—"

"I get the idea." Kate should take the money and—she didn't know what. Her parents would be in their seventies now if they still lived. Her grandparents, on both sides, had been... lovely. She wanted to deny it, but Rikka's explanation fit a few of her memories a little too well for comfortable denial. "They, uh, never talked about their pasts."

"Still puts you ahead of me," Rikka finished the last one. Then she set it in the tray and poured the sauce over it. Kate wouldn't have heard the next part if not for a brief lull in the galley's mayhem. "I didn't even have parents. Dumped me off at the orphanage without so much as a name. Don't even know if they were the ones who did that."

Kate waited until Rikka had finished with the sauce and set the pan into the cleanup sink. Once Rikka's hands were free, Kate wrapped her in a hug.

Rikka froze stiffer than a celery stalk. "What? You taking me up on my offer?"

Kate wanted to laugh. "No, I'm not going to marry you. But I know so little of your past. I'm sorry it was so awful. As a friend, I should have asked more. I profiled you back into your mid-teens, but never got any further."

Rikka didn't relax, but she did tentatively return the embrace. "It generally sucked. I might not have told you if you'd asked. And I'm surprised you found even that—I erased my youth and started over a couple times."

Kate pushed her back but didn't let her go. "I'm not gonna think less of you for your past."

Rikka studied her carefully from most of a foot lower. "You sure?"

"Hey, I already arrested you once for money laundering. You done anything worse than that lately?"

Rikka tentatively returned the smile. "Not lately."

"So, don't and we're good. I'll check on the salmon quiche and you go do something useful."

She nodded fiercely, making her long ponytail flutter behind her like, well, a pony's. She might have even sniffled. "If I ever change my mind about men, you better watch out."

Kate laughed. "I think as long as you keep Sam around, I'll have nothing to worry about."

Rikka raced away to check on her grilled mushroom caps.

Kate knew that Clifford would have a good eye on the quiche. Instead, she poured herself a cup of tea and sat at

Marnie's small desk. She pretended to review the schedule for tomorrow, but neither her eyes nor her mind would focus.

Had she been the intended victim of last night's murder? An unknown mob past, newly risen? Someone seeking vengeance for crimes over a half-century gone? Until recently she'd been little known outside of culinary and Secret Service circles. She had so little time to participate in front of the camera that even fans of Cooks Network might not know her name.

Younger, more ambitious chefs—like poor Ray and Shari—wanted to push ahead faster than she could manage. They'd probably been so eager to impress her that they'd done the Gloucester filming on their own. Hard to blame them; she'd once had that level of ambition. What had that ambition felt like? Her ambitions now were for steady growth and quiet evenings. Was that a sign she needed to ease her control of programming even more than she already had and leave the ambition to others?

Off topic, Kate. Focus. Work the problem.

She'd slammed into global recognition after saving President Kennelly's life several months ago. If she needed proof, network viewership had risen eighty-seven percent during the week following the G-7 exposé with a carryover nineteen percent year-over-year viewership increase in each month since. On shows she hosted, an initial hundred-and-seven percent increase had only dwindled to a sixty-nine percent increase.

While it indicated a more engaged viewership, she hated that it must include a ghoul factor. People hoping to witness yet another chef dying on one of her shows. Lately there'd been plenty of news on that too. All external—she'd refused marketing's pleas to play that up.

Even if Rikka said that no government agencies had made the connection of her family's past to her present, it didn't mean the Irish mob hadn't. Was there even an Irish mob out there anymore? She'd have to ask Rikka.

It was time to prep for the start of meal service. With the opening of the Quarterdeck and the afternoon turning so fine after the gray Icelandic-mist morning, there would be dining both inside on this deck and three levels above them via the dumbwaiter. She'd never done a split service like that before and decided to head aloft to check on the setup.

She hoped the fresh air would help her think.

38

WHEN SHE ARRIVED ON THE QUARTERDECK, KATE WAS RELIEVED to confirm that there remained no sign of the wedding cake, exploded or not. Not so much as a damp spot on the decking where the detritus had been washed overboard. Even the pane of glass that had been blown out of the canopy by the abrupt departure of the upper two tiers and the bride topper had been replaced. She managed her first full breath in hours and her shoulders dropped from around her ears to level with her jaw; they'd be a long time yet getting back to normal.

The morning's rain clouds had shredded into long streamers across the sky. It looked as if God had reached down and raked her fingers through them, releasing great slashes of sunlight to glitter upon the sea and bathe the deck in unexpected warmth.

"They say in Iceland that there are four seasons every day of the year."

Kate had noticed the two servers setting up tables and dishware for the buffet line; they didn't look to need anyone's help. She hadn't noticed the people sitting at the table placed far enough under the deck canopy to have it block the wind but not the low sun—knitters.

"Clara. We shared the first-night dinner. Are you and Ambassador Kevin enjoying your cruise?" There was an open seat, so she sat for the first time in hours.

"You mean last night, dear?"

"Last night?" Kate managed no more than a confused mumble. "Sorry, it's been a busy night and day."

"Is it true that you're cooking for us?"

They had the full attention of the other six knitters seated around the table. Four kept knitting without glancing down at what they were doing. The other two watched their knitting but glanced up to watch the goings-on. Each was working on something different, though most were still in too early a stage for her inexperienced eye to identify what the project was.

"Yes. I've been helping out until they can locate a real chef."

One of the women scoffed. "I've watched all your shows, Ms. Stark. You have nothing to prove to this girl." *This girl* was in the deep end of her sixties if she was a day.

"I've never cooked on a ship before."

"I've never *knit* on a ship before, but Sister," she nodded toward a woman who looked almost as unlike her as Rikka did from Kate, "said we had to see Iceland before we kicked, so here we are. But we're still knitting. Can't stop us." Then she offered a wink before hooking a U-shaped plastic loop into her knitting, making three more stitches, then doing something quick that removed the loop and left a lump in the knitting.

"It's called a cable," Clara told her.

That clue allowed Kate to see what the woman was working on. "A cable-knit sweater. I've never seen one being made before."

"Now you have."

"Now I have." She sat back and listened to the soft clicking of needles and the call of gulls circling above. The servers had moved on to arranging the dessert and ice cream station. No hurry, no sense of panic. One picked up an intercom phone, answered a question, listened, and hung up before crossing to them.

Kate considered hiding under the table but forced herself to hold strong in her position and brace for the attack.

"Ms. Stark. A Ms. Rikka asked me to let you know that dinner prep is continuing on schedule."

Kate looked at him askance. "And?"

"She suggested that you find a *certain gentleman* and enjoy yourself." He was clearly puzzled by his own statement.

Kate wasn't. "Uh, thank you. I'll be right here for a bit if anyone needs me."

He nodded and returned to his setup.

"A gentleman?" Clara asked with a smile.

"My assistant has a somewhat fanciful view of the world."

"Is he handsome?"

Kate's exhaustion ran deep enough that she answered. "Very."

"Then why are you sitting here with us?"

"Refuge?" she wasn't sure anymore.

Clara accepted that without asking from what, which she deeply appreciated. "Do you knit?"

There was more of a flurry about the table when Kate admitted that she didn't than at any prior comment.

Clara lifted a bag that had been sitting beneath her chair—a intricate black-and-yellow pattern that was part bumblebee and wholly vibrant African. Kate peeked and saw that, while all of the other knitters' bags were unique, none of them boasted half the panache of Clara's. From it she extracted three balls of yarn: a muted tangerine, a brown-mustard gold, and a rich royal blue. She peered at Kate's face over the top of all three.

"The blue." She put the tangerine and gold away as the other knitters nodded. She continued digging around in her bag. "It's easier to learn on straight needles, but those are hard to carry through airport security anymore. We'll start you on a long circular needle, which you can pretend are two separate straight needles."

Kate felt a sudden chill. She glanced aloft, but the sun still shone down upon them through the torn clouds.

Clara unrolled a cloth pouch, the type she herself might have stored a set of knives in if it was made of leather. It was lines with little pockets, most filled with sets of needles. "That's odd. Where are my four-millimeter circulars? Oh, I must be getting old. To, uh, save weight, I left those home. I don't need them for my current project, you see."

The chill up her spine turned to ice, like the ice accumulating around the three corpses down in the belowdecks' freezer.

39

She was exactly where Rikka had said he'd find her. Björn climbed the rear stairs up to the Quarterdeck and could only admire the woman sitting on the opposite side of the deck in the shining sun. Pure class and a real stunner to look at.

Because Hayden had given him so damn little to go on, and clearly wasn't in the mood to give any more, he'd set out to learn what he could on his own. He'd spent the last few hours in the library researching. He'd sat in a corner chair with two walls to his back. That way at least no one could read his screen over his shoulder. And if there was a hacker somewhere on the boat, his VPN should stop them.

Rikka Albert showed up nowhere. She'd created a grand total of zero news. He supposed there were people who did that with their lives. As a videographer, she'd need some good computer skills, but it didn't mean she had to be very noteworthy. Computers and social media weren't his areas. Tactical counterterrorism scenarios, weapons, battle planning —those were the areas where few could match him.

Sam Fierro had a digital footprint Björn understood. Minimal, other than a butcher shop and twenty years as a US

Marine. Beyond that, his research taught him a lot about the USMC and very little about the man.

If he'd merely been in the Corps, there'd have been a few bios when he did an event or changed ships or done anything of note. And there was no question that whatever the man had done, it would be worthy of notice. No one, but no one in the *Vikingasveitin* had ever outlifted him. Yet this Marine had used lifting techniques that Björn had never seen and almost split a gut trying to match.

But the key proof was that his anemic records went from showing a steady climb for a new man—followed by nothing. A PO Box address that had to be a simple forwarding stop. No rank information, no news, no nothing. He'd turned into a ghost, then come out the other end with a twenty-year honorable service citation and the very impressive rank of sergeant major. That had Special Operations written all over it. Whether MARSOC, MEU(SOC), or Recon he had no way to tell, but perhaps Hayden had been right in telling him to treat the man with extreme caution. That he was a butcher would connect him with Kate and the little Asian American as his girlfriend might explain his presence but...yeah, caution.

Compared to those two, Paul Stark's exploits were everywhere, mostly in publications like the *National Enquirer* and *The Daily Mail.* It would be easier to map who he *hadn't* been romantically linked to than the other way round. He topped a number of Most Eligible Bachelor lists and showed no signs of relinquishing his title.

And there was no sharper contrast than his twin sister. Former US Secret Service and owner / operator of the world's Number One television network on cooking. She'd taken Cooks into the stratosphere of the top twenty networks globally.

People died around her, including a Vice President-elect she was guarding. But she'd also saved the American

President's life—after three days as head chef at a G-7 meeting. He wondered if there was anything she couldn't do.

Though for all that vaunted background, she hadn't so much as glanced in his direction as he stood at the top of the Quarterdeck's stairs. Her skills must have gone stale. He'd certainly have noticed her, couldn't have missed her from an entire ship's length away. She simply stood out that much.

Yet when he went to take a step forward, she ever so slightly raised a hand and made a fist—at an angle only he would see. *Freeze.* Not a suggestion, but she managed to instill the military hand sign with all the force of a general's command. He froze, but still she didn't turn. Okay, at least her observation skills remained intact.

The woman facing Kate stopped, blinked twice, then closed her bag. "I must be mistaken. I suppose I'm getting forgetful."

Another of the women reached into her knitting bag and pulled out a needle. "Here, Clara, Kate can use mine to learn."

Use them for what? Björn was glad he had stopped moving at Kate's command, or he'd have tripped on his own surprise. The woman held out a circular needle identical to the one Kate had showed him this morning, encased in an evidence bag.

Then the woman's eyes drifted past Kate's shoulder to him. "Oh my, he *is* handsome. I don't think she'll be much interested in knitting, Clara."

All of the women, except Kate, turned to look at him. Every one of them were older than his mamma, but their assessing smiles certainly weren't.

"Clara, could I ask you a question in private?" Kate asked as if nothing was out of the ordinary.

"Is it about the young man?" Clara's merry whisper carried to him easily as he closed the distance to the table.

"Please," Kate kept her voice soft.

"Well, of course, dear." She rose to her feet.

"And bring your knitting bag."

"I always do." Clara didn't so much as arch an eyebrow before gathering it up, tucking her current project into the bag, and following.

Kate didn't wave him off. He'd have ignored the signal if she had, but had to bite back the slight disappointment that he wasn't going to hear Kate's answers to the questions the knitter was sure to ask. He trailed the two women off the Quarterdeck and into the ship.

40

KATE SAW THAT THE FIRST OF THE FOODSTUFFS WERE COMING into the pantry on the dumbwaiter, so that space was off limits for a quiet conversation. The next was the Hotel Manager's office, but Mr. Charles was holding a meeting there with a number of the tour staff.

Patting her pockets revealed no keycard; she could picture it lying on the desk in her suite. Rikka's would be in her back pocket but, with the start of meal service, fetching it would be going into the fray, not leaving it behind.

Already people were drifting into the halls and into the stairwells heading to dinner. At the far end of their hall, she could see the door to the Bridge. The ship had a simple sign there. If the sign was green, passengers were welcome to knock and ask for a tour. Red, please stay away. It was red, as they'd be leaving port and cruising during the meal service.

Out of ideas, she led Clara upstairs to the *Flying Dutchman* deck with Björn trailing behind. Forward past the various suites, they exited out onto the top forward viewing platform. It did offer a quiet place. Lounge chairs, a high plexiglass wall to block the wind forward, and aft a stairway up to another level that revealed a bewildering array of radar and communication antennas.

She stopped at a lounger, white plastic frame with a cover that matched the yarn Clara had held up. "Would you mind emptying your knitting bag on this?"

"Whatever for?" But, after a studying Kate's expression, Clara began to do so, saving Kate from making up a reason.

Björn stood to one side, his arms crossed over his chest. As if he was trying to imitate Sam's earlier guarding of the suite door. He looked very good doing it.

While Clara emptied the bag, the sheer cliff of volcanic rock began moving backward. A few of the sheep grazing on the hilltop watched as the *Ice Adventure* reversed slowly out of the port before returning to their nibbling the lush grass. Far less complacent, birds soared aloft off cliffside nests and yelled at the ship in protest for threatening their young.

Once more they were heading out to sea. She did her best to ignore the inevitable metaphor.

Kate saw, with chagrin, that Clara extracted her room key from a side pocket and set it atop the now empty bag. Better than she'd done with forgetting her own key.

Clara had the contents spread out on the lounger's cushion. The three large balls of yarn that she'd seen before. A small ruler, round-nosed scissors, and a small tin of sweets, which Clara had opened to reveal it contained two fat darning needles, a dozen tiny brass rings, one of those cable U-loops, and other small items. Beyond that a cloth case filled with a wide array of knitting needles, both double-pointed and neatly coiled circular ones. Finally, the current project with several small balls of yarn and a dozen or so rows of knitting on a much thinner version of the circular needle they'd found in the cake. An intricate Fair Isle pattern was already emerging.

"That's my Shetland Wool Week hat."

Kate's expression must have revealed her utter lack of knowledge.

"Five hundred of us, mostly women, travel to Lerwick in the Shetland Islands each September for Wool Week. Each year they release a free hat design and everyone knits one, in their own colors. I decided on lupine purple and gray-green lichen this year in honor of this trip to Iceland. I'm going to make the very top with this for the sky." She tapped a ball of blue yarn that did indeed match the sky above.

"And your, what did you call it, four-millimeter circular needle definitely isn't here?"

Clara waved a hand at the knitter's array. "No. As I said, I left it at home. My hat is on two-point-seven-fives to create the delicate pattern. I knew when I packed that I didn't need the fours."

Except Kate hadn't watched the hand wave, instead she'd watched Clara's face. No hint that she'd been caught out, but something wasn't ringing true despite that.

Björn's expression, initially puzzled, had cleared and he was watching them intently. He was smart enough to realize what she was after. Except, by the angle of his head, he'd been watching the hand wave, not Clara's face.

Kate kept her disappointment to herself. Disappointed in lack of corroboration or that he wasn't as skilled as she hoped? Then she considered his training: military, not Secret Service. He would naturally focus on the action, not the individual. She would give him a pass this time.

"Perhaps you brought it and then it was mislaid?"

"I can't imagine how." If she was a liar, she was a very skilled one. Except for that one brief slip.

Clear of the dock and the abrupt headland, the ship spun lazily about its axis until it was pointed out to sea.

"Do you always have your bag with you?"

"Oh yes, you never know when you have to wait somewhere and a bit of knitting passes the time much more pleasantly."

Kate knew she'd already crossed several lines of pushy propriety, and yet Clara hadn't pushed back. "I'm sorry, but I have one more question. Might someone have extracted the needle without your knowledge?"

"As a hypothetical, if I'd brought them with me, I suppose it is possible."

"Thank you."

"Now might I pose a question of my own? Why are you so interested in the needle that is sitting by my chair at home?"

Kate could swear there was a half-truth there somewhere.

Björn was once again watching Clara repack her knitting bag as if that's what was important.

"I fear that I'm not at liberty to discuss that at this time. I really appreciate your help. And I may take you up on your offer for a knitting lesson later."

Clara offered a bright smile that didn't wholly reach her eyes. "I will look forward to that."

After she was gone, Kate stared forward. The village of Stykkishólmur fell astern. A haze on the north horizon marked the long peninsula they would spend much of the evening and well-lit night circling.

Björn moved up to stand beside her. "Too bright to see the Aurora. But in the winter, the sky shines with it for hour upon hour."

"I think I saw enough of the Aurora last night in the cake design." Kate had always wanted to see the display, but far less now than before last night.

After a time, Björn asked softly, "Did you see her hands?"

"Her hands?" Kate couldn't find the energy to turn and face him.

"As she was putting everything away? The last thing she did was pat each set of needles down into the pocket, I suppose to make sure they were well seated. She made the slightest extra gesture, as if habit had her tucking away doublechecking one more set of those wire-needle things that wasn't there."

Kate slowly turned to look at him. Björn *had* been observant, simply with different skills than her own. That meant—

"There you are!" Rikka popped up at her elbow with no warning, facing Björn. "Did you kiss her yet?"

Kate felt the heat rise to her cheeks as Björn glanced at her before slowly shaking his head.

"Oh, my God. You two really do match, you're as slow as she is. Come on," Rikka tugged at her elbow. "You don't want to miss the dinner you made. I have it on good authority that the manicotti is excellent tonight."

Kate let herself be led.

Björn didn't follow.

41

"Did you get her in bed yet?" That was Hayden's idea of how to answer the phone and simultaneously move himself to the very top of Björn's beat-the-shit-out-of list.

"She's not like that." Rikka was right, he should have kissed her while he had the chance. Björn could feel the heat rising to his face. Not like Kate Stark's lovely blush but rather the searing heat of fury. Beating on the *Vikingasveitin's* commander might not be a good career move, but he was very tempted.

"Like I care. That's your specialty."

Björn's desire to smash Hayden into a pulp grew until he half-feared he'd snap his phone in his fist. "I'm more than some goddamn gigolo."

Hayden's scoff moved him from Björn's pound-to-a-pulp category to top candidate for permanent removal from the world of the living. The way Kate had handled Clara made it clear—at least to him—that he needed to treat Kate as a fellow investigator and not a suspect.

"Besides," he did his best to keep his voice steady, "we were busy chasing a new lead—together."

"Well, that's something. What did you find?"

"Some lady lost her knitting needle; the exact type of needle Kate found in the wedding cake as part of the trigger."

There was a long silence.

"It's possible that someone lifted it, but it seems more likely that she's involved somehow."

"What? Some old biddy is your top suspect as a bomber? Get a grip. Keep on the Stark woman." Hayden ordered.

Deciding Hayden was either wrong or playing his own game and lying, Björn had no problem with that assignment. And, he wouldn't be so slow to act the next time he and Kate were alone together.

Hayden continued. "Another team has questioned and cleared the two bridesmaids who didn't come. But it means that their suite isn't occupied. You're now in Room 601, directly across from the bride's suite. Do *not* get tangled up with the bride instead of Stark, but don't let her out of your sight either."

He hung up.

The man always did like the last word.

Savannah had a wild energy that might be fun to dive into, he'd certainly enjoyed that sort of ride in the past. But Kate Stark, ten years older, displayed a rock-steady demeanor that was incredibly sexy.

The one odd thing—okay, one of the many odd things in the conversation—Björn had never told Hayden that the knitter missing her needle was old. It confirmed there was another operator aboard, but not *Vikingasveitin* or he'd have recognized them. Perhaps one of the servers on the Quarterdeck?

He smacked his forehead. Clara! It had to be the knitter. But that didn't fit either. Had she been helping Bret, or had she been the one to kill him?

What goddamned game was Hayden playing behind the scenes?

42

KATE MAY HAVE ACTUALLY FALLEN ASLEEP AT THE DINNER TABLE. If she hadn't, she didn't remember anything after the half-glass of wine she had with the Surf and Turf Manicotti.

She did remember a big man with an arm around her waist escorting her to her suite—and being disappointed when she focused and saw that he was Sam and not Björn.

Her next memory was waking up and blinking at the window. It was light around the edges of the black-out curtain, which told her nothing about the time this close to the Arctic Circle in mid-June.

Five a.m. She'd slept ten hours, which felt like only half enough but counted as a major coup. However, her internal chef's clock had gone off. Rikka was already gone, so Kate hurried through a shower and raced down to the Galley.

Rikka was there with Miguel the pastry chef. Two more prep chefs strolled in close behind her and headed straight to the espresso machine. She let them have first dibs and crossed to Rikka.

"We doing okay?"

"Rockin' it, Kate."

Kate pulled her into a sideways hug long enough to kiss her atop the head. "You're the best, Rikka."

"You're only saying that because I let you sleep in." Though her voice completely gave away her emotions.

Kate played along, "Caught me. I'll pitch in as soon as I get some caffeine."

Rikka turned back to rolling out crusts for the individual breakfast quiches.

They were two women, far too used to being alone.

Which turned her thoughts to Björn as thoroughly as if that had been Rikka's plan all along. If not for that moment of desperate searching, Kate might have convinced herself of that. No, that wasn't Rikka's style. Her manipulations trended much more to the blatant. Kate had lost all power of speech when Rikka had blasted Björn with *Did you kiss her yet?* as a greeting. That matched her style.

Women alone.

Clara and her missing knitting needle. Would forensics find Clara's fingerprints on the needle, if any were recoverable? Björn had sent all the evidence off to the lab before the ship had left Stykkishólmur. Thankfully, the bodies had been removed from her freezer as well.

Her freezer? They'd better find a replacement soon. It had been barely thirty-six hours. But, if this crisis lasted the same again, she'd be certifiable.

43

KATE MADE A POINT OF CIRCULATING THROUGH THE DINING ROOM several times during service until she spotted Clara and Kevin Bragason breakfasting at one of the tables for two. They didn't sit in silence as she'd seen other couples do; they conversed and appeared glad to be sharing a meal together. Last night at dinner, she had noted that Clara had returned to her knitting group on the Quarterdeck while Kevin presumably dined down here with fellow birders. Or fellow diplomats, Rikka mentioned that there were several on board.

"Good morning. I wanted to thank you again for your time yesterday; I hope that you're both enjoying your breakfast."

Kevin stared at her blankly for a moment, then laughed. "You are very formidable in your chef's jacket, Ms. Stark, I didn't recognize you at first."

Clara simply nodded her good morning.

"Dressing as a chef is my secret disguise." Kate told Kevin as she noted that Clara's knitting bag was tucked under her chair. Had she missed some key item when inspecting its contents last night? Had she verified that the bag had indeed been emptied? Not that she could recall, though it had looked that way.

What was she missing?

"Well, your secret is out. This salmon quiche is incredible."

Clara raised her fresh-made sourdough bagel with a thick schmear of salmon cream cheese in a complimentary fashion.

She nodded her acknowledgment and moved on none the wiser.

There was something she'd missed; Kate was sure of it.

She made a point of stopping at several other tables, including the one with Savannah and Sufia. Two days later and people were still avoiding the woman, typically leaving her bridesmaid as the only one willing to dine or sit with her.

This morning they chatted quite unannoyingly about the upcoming outing, though the topic soon turned to what Kate was learning was Savannah's favorite topic—the geothermal plants of Iceland. Kate soon begged off for kitchen duties, though with the service tailing off, the load had shifted from her shoulders to the clean-up crew's.

Savannah was more pleasant than the first impression she gave—or the second or third—but still nicer.

Clara was more...slippery.

Kate knew that she possessed no skill for dealing with slippery. But she knew someone who did.

44

"YOU WANT ME TO WHAT?"

"You heard me."

Paul *had* heard Kate's request, hard not to as they sat shoulder-to-shoulder on the Zodiac transiting them from the ship to the shore of Vigur Island. What he couldn't do was believe it.

Two boats were ahead of them, running to the rocky beach. A low house, a big barn, and a small windmill were all there was to see ashore.

"You really want my help? That isn't like you at all, Kate."

"There's something going on and I can't see it."

"No sneaky-jeans." An old tease from their childhood when she asked how he always got away with things and she always got caught. He'd been wearing jeans and she'd been in a little-girl dress. He'd plucked at his clothes and claimed it was his sneaky-jeans.

The next time their parents caught her during one of his escapades, she'd been wearing jeans. When she'd complained that they hadn't worked, he hadn't been the least surprised.

Even at six years old, Kate had always been the straight shooter. She couldn't lie with a straight face and always plunged directly at things rather than finding the back door or an open window of opportunity around the side.

"She loves her husband, so do not mess with that."

"Right, no seducing older women." He could only smile at her eye roll. If he wasn't hanging on because of the rough surf, he'd have hugged her. "You're just so...Kate. There's no other way to say it. You are *so* you that it's almost unbelievable. I'm on it."

Then he laughed in her face when a blast of spray slapped the back of his rain hood and soaked Kate's face.

"No sneaky-jeans at all."

She sighed because she absolutely knew it was true.

He'd spent all day yesterday enjoying himself but felt at loose ends. That feeling was happening more and more of late. He didn't like it.

During yesterday's outings to the beaches and old church, he'd cozied up to the long, leggy tour leader—Alli was lovely—though he'd made no move yet. In her own way, she was as daunting as Kate. Eighteen years on the expedition ships, working her way up to Tour Leader. She'd traveled from McMurdo Sound in Antarctica to Svalbard, which lay eight hundred miles closer to the North Pole than even Iceland. She counted countries the same way the most peripatetic of the RVing Americans counted states.

In the afternoon, he'd toured the ship. Not merely the passenger spaces and the Bridge, but he had finagled a private tour down through the crew and machine spaces. His Filipino was weak and, while the ship ninjas' English wasn't bad, their Spanish was better. He'd sat with them for an hour trading dirty jokes—a type of joke that always sounded better in Spanish anyway.

After dinner, instead of working the bar, he'd borrowed a couple of birding books from the library and given himself a crash course on the ship's main topic of conversation. He'd never been a birder, but absorbing trivia about what interested others was his forte. Studying Iceland set the baseline, but he spent more time learning breeds common in other places he'd traveled. The trick was to find where they'd *never* been and then show his supposed expertise where they were less likely to trip him up. Worked every time—except when it failed spectacularly, which was all part of the game.

This morning, they'd donned their life jackets after breakfast and trooped down to the lounge. From there, the staff released groups of ten passengers at a time into the Zodiacs. Down the steps to the stern boat deck. Hand his daypack to one of the ninjas, "*Gracias,* Arturo." Let Alli and Willem, the head boat-hand—who really had the best stories, and the dirtiest jokes once you got him started—each clasp forearms with him. Down one step, other foot on the rubber side of the boat as the swell lifted it, and a quick step onto the flooring as the swell continued on by and the Zodiac dropped below the ship's deck. Sit on the inflated pontoon side and slide out of the way. "*Gracias,* Sandro," as he took his pack from the ninja working their Zodiac and tucked it between his feet.

He'd coaxed Kate out of her kitchen. A trick barely managed even though lunch had two main meat entrees and Sam had agreed to handle those with Rikka taking the lead.

"You need to get out more, Katydid."

"I need to sleep more, Paul. And stop being in places where chefs get killed."

"Yeah, I have some ideas about that." He grinned as they held on as the bow of the boat beached onto the rocky shore. "Make fewer enemies."

She didn't appear to appreciate the joke, maybe because he'd only half-meant it as one.

"Ask yourself who were they trying to off during the last two big debacles?" He left her with that thought before stepping off the boat and using the little step stool thoughtfully placed off the bow. This really was a fine way to travel.

45

KATE SAT FROZEN UNTIL THEY HAD TO SHOO HER OFF THE ZODIAC. The first time something like this had happened, the North Koreans had been targeting her and Rikka. The second time at the G-7, she'd been the only one in the crosshairs. Maybe this time she could blame it on Rikka. That would be at least a partial relief.

What if they really were the targets and not someone else?

She staggered up the beach, peeled off her numbered life jacket, and dropped it on the pile with the others from the *Octavius* Deck.

Having missed last night's preview lecture on today's activities, she looked around for someone to follow. Someone other than Clara and Kevin Bragason.

She could only watch in amazement as Paul latched onto one of the anomalies, a Gen Z wedding guest who carried a large set of birding binoculars. A lovely brunette fifteen years his junior, who just happened to be standing next to Clara and Kevin. Before Kate could look away, he was already chatting up all three of them. Even after all these years, she still couldn't see how he did that.

And by his gestures at the sky, they might even all be talking about birds. To the best of her knowledge, Paul could barely tell a pigeon from a robin.

As she looked elsewhere, another Zodiac came ashore and Björn soon stood at her side.

"Good morning, Kate." It was a very nice smile; she did her best at returning it.

"Hi. Do you know what's happening here? I missed last night's lecture."

"With the hours you keep, why am I not surprised? Sure, I'll be your guide. You look great this morning."

"Compared to last night?"

"You looked a mess." His smile didn't abate.

She didn't enjoy being called a mess. But, on the plus side, he had been watching her. It wasn't clear if she remained as one of his suspects. However, knowing that she was innocent, she decided to take his notice as a compliment.

He dumped his own vest-in-bag beside the ones that Savannah and Sufia had just placed on the *Flying Dutchman* pile.

"Moving up in the world."

He laughed. "You ought to see the room, it's great. Second best on the ship after Savannah's bridal suite. If I ever meet the two bridesmaids who didn't show and saved me sleeping next to the bilge pump, I will gladly kiss their feet. Only open suite, and the boss wants me to stay aboard until we solve what happened to Bret. Room was paid for, so the tour company didn't complain."

"That and being from the Viking Squad might have swung a bit of weight in your favor." Kate knew that she too couldn't stand to leave until she solved this. "So, Guide, guide me."

Another boat crunched up onto the dark gray rounded cobbles. Birds were...everywhere. The arriving boats barely spooked them aside on the beach.

"The crow-sized black guys with the white wing patch and thin beaks making all the racket here along the beach are black guillemots. Juveniles out of the nest, but not yet ready to go anywhere. But they aren't one of the three main attractions here. There are a lot of Arctic terns, who you'll meet shortly. Also many puffins, who are even cuter in real life than in pictures, and, the real reason there are people here: masses of Eider ducks."

"Eider ducks."

"Yes," he took her hand and hooked it on his elbow, then pointed at the waves where hundreds of artistically black-and-white ducks floated and dove in the surf. "The common eider. The couple and their seven-year-old son who live here make their living with a small souvenir shop, the smallest post office in Iceland, and harvesting the eider down."

"Harvesting..." Kate swallowed hard.

"No killing. Methods are far more humane in the modern day. They gather the down from the nests that the ducks pluck themselves for lining. The humans change it out with a bit of straw, no complaints from the ducks. Either way it insulates and is softer than the rocks."

"Oh." Kate studied him with a side look. "Well, Björn with no last name, you are rather disorienting."

"Too much at once?"

"No," Kate decided. "No. But I'm no longer used to military-grade concision of speech. For the last six years, I've worked with artists, chefs, and other creatives. They're the worst, *Hello, I'm a Creative*, with a capital C, of course. *I have a thousand ideas and I'm going to pursue them all at once.* Typically to the exclusion of pursuing any of them well."

"What about Sam Fierro?" His tone took on a sharp, competitive edge.

"Sam isn't exactly the chatty type." She managed to keep

her smile to herself because she didn't want to be the only one who felt off balance.

Björn's grimace said Sam was keeping him plenty out of kilter.

At a call from Alli, those nearest to her gathered in a clump. "Twenty people in a group. We're going to take a one-mile loop walk around the island. We'll move slowly enough to allow pictures. A few pointers. First, stay on the trail. If you wander off, you could cave in a puffin's burrow and crush their sole yearly egg. Yes, they will be nesting practically below your feet. Second, make sure you take a pole, you'll see why." Her smile invited them to enjoy the joke.

From a bucket, they each selected a meter-long stick with a small plastic flag stapled to the top. Kate's efforts to spot some meaning in the different colors, red, blue, and yellow, failed utterly. She kept waiting to be sorted, like drawing colored knives to separate a competition into cooking teams. When that didn't happen, she figured that just maybe they were simply different colors and she needed to get a life. Sure, as soon as people stopped trying to kill her.

Alli led them to the edge of the field beyond the lone house and behind the barn. "Past here, you'll want to hold your sticks well above your heads like an umbrella." She demonstrated holding the stick so that it stuck a good arm's length above her head.

"There's no *umbra*," Kate complained to Björn.

He laughed at her joke, which earned him a lot of points. "Hardly any shadow at all from the little flag," he agreed, acknowledging the Latin root of the name. He might think of her as a key suspect in Bret Calder's death, but that wasn't stopping her from liking him.

They were at the lead of the group, close behind Alli as they trooped past a stone wall and onto a narrow path through deep meadow grasses.

When something slapped her stick straight downward, she almost dropped it in surprise. Looking up, she saw a robin-sized (after going on a serious diet) bird, white with pointy wings and a black head, hovering close above the stick. It struck again, landing a sharp rap on the stick with its orange beak.

All down the line, birds were attacking the tops of people's sticks.

Alli spoke loudly enough to be easily heard over the *Tonk! Tonk! Tonk!* of successive stick strikes. "They don't like us transiting their breeding grounds. As potential predators, they attack the highest point to drive us off. This habit, in turn, makes it safer for the puffin and common eiders to nest here. Keep your stick aloft or they'll strike the top of your head and, trust the voice of experience, that hurts."

After a few hundred meters, they transited from the meadow to an ocean cliff environment.

"You can lower your sticks for now, though you'll want them later in the walk. Watch the cliffs and cove."

At that instant, a foot-tall puffin, in his black-and-white tuxedo proper enough for a major New York fundraiser, landed not three meters away. Its bright orange and clown-big beak was clamped over a cluster of small fish. Stumbling like a drunk, he disappeared into a hole that must indeed come close beside their path.

Before she could be sorry not to get a better look at it, three more landed and another appeared from a different burrow and took off. The cove had hundreds, perhaps thousands on the water and many more zooming close over the water's surface.

From this vantage, she could also see the tour group that had proceeded them walking over the central ridge of the small island. Paul and his brunette of the moment were still closely attached to Clara and Kevin. She sent a mental thank you his way.

"So, Kate, is this a good time to ask what the hell Rikka's comment meant?"

She turned back to Björn and couldn't ignore the parallels. Just as Paul was hoping to get information from Clara, Björn wanted to interrogate her. My, wasn't *that* disappointing. "What comment?"

"I watched the recording of the wedding finally."

"And?"

"Rikka's comment."

"That's not helping me."

"She said, *I win.*"

Kate concentrated on the surface of the trail, though it was even enough to require only the occasional glance. "When did she say that?"

"The moment after the cake blew up and all three people died. Before she just happened to find the wire knitting needle embedded in the cake."

It was the first time that he'd sounded even remotely like what he was, an investigator into Bret Calder's death. She supposed that she deserved that. Letting herself get comfortable around the man. Especially a member of the *Vikingasveitin.*

"I have no idea. You'd have to ask her."

They were most of the way around the island, she'd barely noticed the ducks or the second, smaller tern colony, before he spoke again. "I'm sorry, but I had to ask."

Well, at least he was aware of having utterly killed a nice moment. That was more than most men managed.

46

"WHAT DID YOU MEAN?" KATE HADN'T BEEN ABLE TO FACE sitting with anyone at lunch. She'd grabbed a hamburger and a plate of fries before retreating to the cabin. In a token gesture to a healthy diet, she'd grabbed a bunch of grapes on her way past the dessert table. It had been adorned with a wide variety of lovely cheeses that normally would have caused her to linger.

Rikka, apparently done with the lunch prep, had spotted her slipping down the hall toward their suite and followed her. Sam, of course, moved as close behind as Rikka's shadow. Paul, lounging in his suite across the hall with the door open followed them in.

"What did I mean when?" Rikka stole a couple of Kate's fries.

When Paul reached out to do the same, she slapped his hand away, though not hard. "Get your own. We're fifty feet from the lunch line on the Quarterdeck. And grab me a soda too."

Paul complained bitterly as Rikka asked for the same lunch as Kate. Sam simply held up two fingers, and Paul left the room.

"When?" Rikka asked as she ate another French fry that Kate never saw her take.

"After Marnie's death. After the cake exploded."

Rikka knitted her brows, then booted up her laptop and played the recording of the explosion on the big screen TV —again.

Kate was so sick of watching people die on screen. This time Rikka turned up the volume and it was even more painfully real as the thunder of the explosion slapped into the suite. Oddly it brought back the memory sweet smells of flash-caramelized sugar.

It was Rikka's partially restored image, which she hadn't seen yet. When the cake blew apart, the image didn't simply white out. Marnie and her sous chef had been too close to the cake to observe anything more of their deaths. But now she could see that the blast hadn't caught Bret Calder squarely in the chest. The edge of the explosion was so well defined that it had slammed into half his body and spun him cruelly aside as it sent him tumbling away. Slightly nauseating was the fact that his head didn't make the turn as quickly; he ended up looking over his shoulder a bit too literally. At least that explained the broken neck.

In the half-second before he disappeared—

"Run that back. There. Freeze that frame. Zoom in on his face." Kate studied his face. "He looks—"

A loud knock, which sounded more like a kick on the door. When Sam opened it, there was Paul, hands full with two plates of food.

"Paul, can you go find—"

Björn stepped in behind him carrying two more. He handed his second plate to Sam as Paul handed his to Rikka. He fished her soda out of a pocket and handed it over.

"Damn, he looks surprised as hell." Paul and Björn said almost in unison as they looked at the screen.

That's what she wanted Björn's opinion on. Bret Calder didn't look surprised; he looked shocked. Yet another detail he wasn't around to explain. She was building up a whole list of questions she'd like to ask him.

"Okay, Rikka, go back to full screen and let it run."

Rikka took a massive bite of her burger and did so. By the time the white-out of the bright explosion ended, both Brett and the chefs were nowhere to be seen.

The camera swung up to focus on the top tiers of the cake as they landed on the top of the canopy they'd broken through. Rikka grinned as she tapped a key to zoom in on the bride topper; it looked forlorn, sunk neck deep in frosting before it slid overboard.

Then, very distinctly, so loud it could have only been her or Rikka standing close by the camera, *I win.* And Kate knew it wasn't her own voice.

"Mumph," Rikka mumbled around a mouthful as she paused the playback. "I'f w'd."

"Chew, then try again."

"I did win," she managed once her mouth was clear.

"Win what?"

"The pool."

Kate looked at the others. Even Sam shrugged, unusual for him to offer an opinion on anything.

"What..." And then Kate remembered and couldn't help laughing.

"I know, right?" Rikka laughed with her.

Kate tried to stop, but it was hard.

"Only you. Rikka. Would think of. That. At that moment." Was all she managed between bouts of laughter—way too near the hysterical side of the scale for her liking.

47

"So, that cake was craaaazy too big for the number of people, but the bride had specified every last millimeter of it." Rikka happily explained to the others around another mouthful of burger, small enough this time to be understood. "Marnie was running a pool on the weight of cake remaining after the ceremony. I figured that the bride would toss the leftovers over the rail in a fit of pique at how little was consumed. So, I wagered under five kilos left. Even she wouldn't throw out the top tier for the one-year anniversary. I was right but for all the wrong reasons."

She stole another of Kate's French fries just because she could, as she considered.

"I'd guess my winnings are still in Marnie's pocket. Can't say that I thought to check after they recovered her body."

Kate gave her *that* look. She could tease Kate every time, but never once had Rikka slipped anything by her.

"Okay, I thought of it, but couldn't bring myself to go picking the pockets of the dead." She hated being decent. There had to be at least three hundred dollars lost there.

Kate turned to Björn. "Satisfied?" Her voice had a harsh

edge that appeared to surprise Björn as much as it surprised Rikka. She'd been so sure they were getting sweet on each other.

He nodded solemnly, then mouthed a silent, *Sorry.*

"Well, that's something you don't see every day," Rikka whispered for Kate's ears alone as she went to steal another French fry. Except Kate was out, so Rikka shifted a generous handful from her own plate to Kate's. Then she stole one.

"Did you find out anything, Paul?"

Rikka almost knocked Kate's plate to the floor as she twisted to look at her, then Paul. "Wait! You trusted your brother with something? Now we're all screwed."

Paul growled. Another point scored for Rikka Albert, minus a kazillion and one for Paul Stark. "I found out plenty, Pint-size. What did you do? Oh, you made a half-decent burger. No, wait, I bet Sam was the one who did that."

That hurt. Yes, he was right, Sam had done that and it just might be the best burger she'd ever had. Right up there with one from Guy Fieri's Flavortown in Vegas. She'd spent the entire morning freaking without Kate in the kitchen. No way was she ready to run a whole kitchen, but she'd done it to get Kate out in the world.

She'd made it through the prep and service solely by channeling every ounce of inner-Kate that she could muster, and she was wrecked worse than a three-day hacking streak from pulling it off. Kate panicking over, well, *anything* simply didn't have a place in Rikka World. Perhaps she was being naïve, but she was sticking with her beliefs that the world had to spin around somebody and that Kate was as good a candidate as anyone.

Her only solace had been a chance to kick Björn's ass when she found him still aboard and not planning to join the morning's shore expedition. He'd rushed onto the very next boat after she was done with him.

"Paul," Kate said softly, cutting off the next round of the bout. Which was just as well, Rikka wasn't up for much at this point.

One last growl before he turned to Kate. "Actually, I did. Clara knew the groom, Bret Calder, rather well."

Björn's head popped up at that. "Who?"

"One of the knitters," Rikka made it a scoff, deciding that Björn would make almost as good a target as Paul.

He ignored her and turned to Kate. "The one you questioned yesterday up on the viewing platform? Really?"

"Wait! You questioned Clara and didn't tell me?" Rikka turned to glare at Kate, but she was staring out the window. The ship had left the island. Rocking lightly on the crossing sea, it was working its way out of the deep fjord where Vigur Island was tucked. All she'd seen of it was a low lump of green out the window and a little line of Zodiacs racing back and forth between the ship and the beach.

"When we boarded... A few people had gathered about the groom..." Kate seemed to be worrying away at a memory. "I had assumed it was pity for how Savannah had so completely overshadowed him..." She spun back to face the room. "But one of them was from the older crowd. She carried a gold-black-aquamarine knitting bag. Paul, could you go find Clara and ask her to join us?"

"But not her husband Kevin?"

"No, not Kevin."

Rikka couldn't resist asking just loudly enough for Paul to overhear as he stepped out of the room. "You mean your brother actually did something right?"

Her timing was good; the automatic door closer swung it shut before he could snarl at her. And another Paul-point in the bank.

48

Clara braced herself outside the door to Kate Stark's suite as Paul knocked. She should have been more careful when talking with him on Vigur Island. Despite all her training, she still couldn't recall quite how he'd done what he'd done. Unearthed her connection to the groom.

"You are very skilled, Mr. Stark."

He offered a brilliant smile and a slight bow that appeared sincere.

The massive man who opened the door must be Sam Fierro. She understood what his service record meant. Clara had hoped to be facing only Kate, but that didn't look to be the case.

It was getting less and less likely that she could keep any control of this situation.

He moved aside and she spotted the mysterious Rikka Albert, a woman with no discernable past, and Kate Stark sitting at the room's desk. Only after she stepped into the room did she spot the final occupant. She covered her surprise, but a glance at Kate said that she hadn't done it quickly enough.

"Are you also *Vikingasveitin,* Clara?"

Björn spun to look at her.

"No, dear." She offered Kate a nod of acknowledgement. "ISIS."

"We'll assume that you mean the Icelandic Security and Intelligence Service and not the Islamic State."

"That would be a safe assumption."

"Please, sit." Kate waved her toward the sofa.

It allowed her a moment to assess the situation.

Sam guarding the door said there would be no rapid exit.

Paul Stark possessed surprising skills, but she wondered if they extended beyond his immense ability to charm. She suspected that, with the proper training, he could become formidable.

Rikka Albert might appear to be no more than Kate's assistant. But Clara had seen her absolute calm after the cake explosion; that took some kind of training. She also sat before an extremely high-end laptop, which wasn't running an interface Clara recognized. A quick scan showed that Ms. Albert's side of the bed was a technologist's playground. So, Kate Stark had a pet hacker.

And a glance at Kate again stated that she'd revealed far more than she intended. She nodded her head in like recognizing like and folded her hands on her knitting bag knowing the next move wasn't hers to make. She didn't need to wait long, not when facing a mind like Kate's.

"Did you give Bret your circular needle? Or is needles more appropriate?"

"People are split. The singular and the plural are both accepted."

Kate nodded her thanks. "Did you give Bret your circular needle or did you plant it in the cake yourself?"

Clara couldn't ignore Björn's gape of shock and turned to him. "It seems that Hayden likes playing two ends against the middle. I was assisting Bret but was told to maintain my low profile upon your arrival."

"Are you okay with me ripping off his arms next time I see him?"

Clara actually smiled. "With my full support." She turned once more to Kate. "I supplied him with the needle as well as the small clamps and so forth." She reached into her bag and pulled out her cough drop tin of small knitting supplies, rattling it briefly before tucking it away. "He arranged for the customized support columns, and batteries are readily available."

Sam Fierro made some gesture she missed.

Kate barely glanced his way before returning her attention to Clara. "You failed to mention the detonators for the columns. They...ah, were easily disguised as additional circular needles. A round shaft of metal attached to a wire."

As no safe route remained, Clara hoped that absolute honesty would pay off. It was the only thing that ever worked in the most desperate situations. But what sort of person was Kate Stark? She supposed that she was about to find out. "An M6 detonator is almost identical in size and shape to the head of a six-millimeter circular needle. I provided him with two of those as well. But they aren't a standard part of my kit so I didn't make the mistake of *missing* them."

"Hold it," Björn interrupted. "Bret set up the bomb that killed him. Why would he do that?"

Kate's smile said that she too was well aware of Björn's blind spots. "No. He had a different target. Rikka, play your 3D analysis of the cake's turn."

In seconds Clara was watching a remarkable overhead representation of the wedding. The cake, the key people, and the first ranks of the guests were all there in exquisite detail with few gaps. She'd very much like to chat with the young woman about how she'd rendered the backs of objects and people, then realized she'd be unlikely to understand much of the answer. Still, it was fascinating.

"This is the original event," Rikka ran the video ahead. The image was a little jumpy, but Clara suspected that could be ascribed to the laptop's limitations rather than the programmer's.

The explosion ran much as she remembered. "What I don't understand is how that happened. Bret was very skilled with explosives; he'd never have made such a mistake."

"That's because the cake was turned at the last moment. Rikka, run the simulation for the cake's original orientation."

Clara watched the raising of the long knife. The awkward angle of Savannah's arm as she reached well behind her to keep her hand on the groom's. The cut. That much was the same.

The direction of explosion was completely different.

Rikka hit Pause.

The blast image swept over the bride, except for where her hand rested over Bret's. *That* was the precision Clara expected from a *Vikingasveitin* operative. Then she looked at the rest of the image and saw that Kate and Rikka were well within the damage zone in both angle and radius.

"Oh."

"You can see why I've been concerned about the intended target."

Clara absolutely could.

49

KATE HAD WATCHED ENOUGH REPEATS OF THE VIDEO TO KNOW precisely what was happening when Clara saw each element of it. Her face showed a distinct satisfaction at the accuracy of the simulated second explosion, but surprise at the end of it. As if she was approving of Savannah's demise, but been surprised by Kate and Rikka's presence in the blast zone.

Kate struggled not to show the wave of relief that swept through her. For once, she and Rikka had simply been in the wrong place at the wrong time. Perhaps the same was true of the Gloucester pub disaster? That would be a true relief and she sent a quick prayer to anyone listening that Marcus and Leona's findings revealed precisely that.

"I suppose Bret couldn't have anticipated our final camera position until everything was assembled. So, if we weren't the target, why was Savannah?"

"Bret was trying to kill his own bride?" Björn blurted out. "Then why did he marry her in the first place?"

Kate could see Clara trying to decide how to answer that and shook her head slightly.

Clara's grimace included a fair portion of a smile. "Your

departure from the Secret Service must have been a great loss of skills to them."

A rumbling growl of agreement from where Sam still guarded the door added to Clara's smile.

Kate ignored Björn's shock. Though not entirely. She was a little pleased that he liked her without having done deep research on her. He'd bumbled on her wealth and now her past —his surprise both times unmistakable. A man who liked her for being herself counted as a very pleasant surprise. Time to deal with that later.

She kept her attention on Clara. "I'm assuming you have an answer to Björn's first query."

Clara's look said she did. "I'm sure you have noted Savannah's fascination with Iceland's geothermal plants."

Kate resisted the surprised blink, managing to turn it into a nod of acknowledgment.

"It is her intent to purchase them. All of them. Except for petrol for our vehicles and boats, Iceland is almost wholly energy independent. That is because of our harvesting geothermal and hydro energy. Wind remains a negligible factor. The majority of our geothermal operations are held by three companies, all privately held by Icelanders. Shall I say, we don't exactly trust an American heiress' motives."

"As an American heiress myself, I can hardly blame you." Kate wondered what dirty past Savannah's money had. Perhaps she was as unaware as Kate had been.

"Bret was sent to befriend her, to gently persuade her that there were easier targets. Savannah remained determined. At which time certain, ah, powers decided that only one solution remained."

"Murder?" Björn nearly exploded himself.

Knowing too much of statecraft, Kate felt little surprise. "Why marry her first?"

Clara sighed. "His initial plan was to marry her for her

money and, once he had access, to lose it, thereby rendering her powerless in a carefully ill-conceived scheme. But she was moving too aggressively toward acquisition and had kept her funds shielded. He agreed to the wedding in order to stay close to her until another solution could be found. He was not in favor of, I fear there is no way to say this delicately, permanently removing Ms. Sachs."

"He didn't approve...yet he set it up anyway." Again Kate studied the view out the window. Once again, nothing but the perfect horizontal slice where blue sea met blue sky. The next anything beyond her window in that direction would be the Arctic Ice.

"Rikka, replay the original film from the end of the ceremony and through the cake cutting." She didn't need to turn from the window to watch it, instead she listened.

The first kiss as a wedded couple. The short recession across the width of the deck to hearty rounds of applause. The pause of happy chatter as the bride and groom repositioned themselves for the cutting. The slick sound of the bridesmaid Sufia extracting the *maguro* blade from its sheath. After handing off the blade to Savannah and the sheath to Marnie, she made sure Savannah's dress was arranged perfectly before retreating and raising her phone to record the moment.

The awkward silence as everyone turned to watch the cutting.

Savannah's final check-in with Kate that everything was perfect.

At the same time, Bret glancing toward Marnie and the sous chef. He waved a hand as if to shoo them aside. His attention was *not* toward the camera, the cake, or his bride.

"Freeze it!" Kate spun her chair around to face the big screen. Everyone else had been watching it raptly. "Back up five frames. No...six. There."

She hadn't seen it on the screen, she'd noticed it during the ceremony itself. "What is that expression, Bret?" she asked the dead man. He was grimacing in Marnie's direction as Savannah took his hand and he turned away from the chefs.

"Regret," Paul turned to her. "I, uh, would know that one anywhere, Katydid. I probably owe you about a thousand apologies for the stunts I've pulled over the years."

He did. And, being her brother, she knew there would be more in the future. But... "We'll let that one apology cover it, Paul. Thank you, apology accepted."

"What does Bret regret? And why would he look at Marnie?" Clara asked the dead man in turn.

"Holy frosting, Batman!" Rikka's eyes had gone wide. Then she faced Kate. "At least we now know who damaged the cake."

"We do?" Kate asked.

"Duh!"

50

Rikka bit her tongue hard enough to hurt but it didn't take back the *Duh!*

"Why do you put up with me, Kate?"

"Because you offered to marry me yesterday afternoon."

Rikka managed a laugh and let it go. Kate's dry humor *was* funny when she let it out.

One deep breath. Two. She didn't dare risk a third because Paul might figure it out and then he'd steal her thunder.

"Bret did it. He must have changed his mind at the last minute. Look at his hand," she pointed at the screen. "Not the one on the knife, the one around Savannah's waist. He didn't have to do that."

His right hand was wrapped there as if it belonged. As if he was trying to hold her close despite the distance forced upon them by her voluminous dress.

"Bret damaged the cake to force the turn. Then the explosion would blow harmlessly overboard, like some sort of prank cake. His grimace and gestures to her said that he hadn't counted on where Marnie had taken up station between the cake and the railing."

"But he wasn't willing to stop what was about to happen because she was there." Björn practically whined.

"He was trapped," Clara observed. "He couldn't stop what was about to happen without revealing his hand in the whole thing. If he wanted to stay with Savannah, he had to play it through; though he miscalculated the amount of the turn."

"Or he was as cold-blooded a bastard as he looked," Kate watched Clara as she spoke.

Clara's slight shrug said that maybe he had been. No one seemed to be missing him much.

Björn nodded. "Sounds about right. He could charm the pants off...uh, sorry. But he was damn good with women." He glanced over his shoulder, "Up in your league, Paul, but not very nice about it afterward."

Rikka laughed aloud, but not at Paul's look of chagrin.

Kate raised an eyebrow at her as others scowled.

"Any bets on the real date of Bret Calder's birthday?"

Kate almost smiled. "Any day but his wedding day. He'd been a plant all the way back a year ago when he happened to sit at the next table over from Savannah in Las Vegas."

"Bingo!" Rikka nodded fiercely.

Kate made a winding motion with a twirl of her finger. She kept it up until Rikka had stopped being so pleased with herself and scrolled to the moment immediately after the explosion. There Kate signaled for a stop.

"I still don't get why he's so surprised here." Björn shook his head. "I mean he knew the explosion was coming, right?"

No one answered. Rikka didn't have a clue.

"He's shocked. At himself," Kate finally explained. "He'd misjudged the position of the damage he made to the icing to force Marnie to turn the cake. In his last moment, he knew that he'd screwed up by about fifteen degrees and he wasn't going to get to spend the rest of his life with Savannah."

Rikka studied the image and decided that Kate was exactly

right. On orders, with Clara's assistance, a *Vikingasveitin* operative had managed to kill two chefs and himself. Tried, convicted, and executed by his own hand.

51

"*What?*" Hayden was as friendly as ever.

Björn and Clara had retreated to his cabin's balcony on the uppermost deck to make the call. The Arctic Ocean stretched north to the horizon.

"I'm here—with Clara."

He supposed that the stony silence was all the apology he'd get from Hayden for putting Clara aboard without informing him.

"Bret killed himself."

"He...what?"

Björn wanted to give Hayden a dose of his own medicine by not answering, but his commander was also *Vikingasveitin*. Who knew what retribution he could unleash if his foul mood turned even worse than normal. He could feel the chill of the Arctic ice pack even though it lay far over the horizon of the restless sea.

Thankfully, Clara rescued him before he could get himself assigned to a *hákarl* farm, fermenting shark meat for a living. He couldn't stand the stuff, most people couldn't. Just because it was a holdover from some seriously desperate Vikings didn't mean it should be the damned national dish.

"Bret Calder changed his mind at the last moment. Rather than terminating the subject, he appears to have decided to go through with the marriage—long term. At the last moment he damaged the cake, forcing the chefs to turn the damaged section to the rear. By a miscalculation on his part, he was caught in the blast, as were the two chefs. He accidentally killed himself."

"May he burn in his own urine! By Satan, why would he spare her?"

"Indications are that he fell in love with her."

"That wasn't the goddamn assignment."

Clara didn't answer and Björn figured keeping his own mouth shut was the best course of action. His assignment was done. It meant he'd be pulled off the ship. A pity as he'd be sorry to leave Kate Stark behind.

Hayden finally spoke. "We still haven't dealt with Savannah Sachs. See that she falls overboard or something." And he hung up.

"Is she really planning to buy up all of our geothermal energy production companies?"

Clara shrugged. "Hayden is convinced of that."

Björn's specialty was counterterrorism. He didn't want any part of an assassination squad; that was more Bret's type of operation. And even Bret had ultimately decided not to follow through. Oddly, he knew that if he did murder Savannah, it would hugely disappoint Kate Stark. He didn't like that either.

He rubbed his forehead as if he could massage the mental jumble inside into some sense of clarity. "What if we find out whether or not that's what she's really up to first?"

Clara frowned at the sea before leaning over to pat his hand. "Björn, I think I have been in the business for too long. I remember the Cod Wars against the British invasion of our fishing grounds. I had an uncle who almost died on the *Týr* fifty years ago, which is why I joined the intelligence service. You do not carry those memories and prejudices. You are a good boy. Remember that."

Björn mostly tried to remember that he wasn't twelve.

52

LEONA MOVED WELL DOWN THE BAR TO TAKE THE CALL BECAUSE Marcus was busy interviewing the third and fourth of the witnesses they'd been able to track down. He sat with a couple regulars at the far end who made a real Mutt and Jeff crew. One was tall, broad-shouldered, on the balding side of handsome. The other, short with a white beard, revealed thinning salt-and-pepper hair mostly gone to salt past his ball cap pulled low. The cap said *Fasolt and Fafner Contractors, fees negotiable* on the front. On the back it said *Seattle Opera,* which Marcus claimed explained the joke, but it didn't explain anything to her.

"Hi, Kate. Count still the same here."

"Same here, too. We've solved ours. Ugly, but nothing to do with us. How are you doing?"

"At the pub. A major wreck in back, which is sad; it's a nice-looking place. Cozy. Good place for a pint."

"I could be convinced to take it over and retire there."

"Could do worse." She could almost see herself and Marcus doing just that...but not quite. "We're interviewing some of the regulars who were here as happy-client interviewees on the day of. Their shooting timeline is following the notes we found on Shari Browley's computer. She was one organized lady."

"Crap." Kate didn't put any real energy behind it. Instead she sounded weary and resigned.

"Sorry."

"Me too. That team had the spark, that indefinable thing that works so well."

Leona smiled to herself in the mirror behind the bar. That's what made Marcus so damn attractive. They were both hard-driven agents but so were most who worked in the big-city offices like New York. But when they were together, everything just worked so much better.

Marcus called out from the far end of the bar. "Those cases in the car. Could you grab the smaller camera?"

Leona headed out the door; they'd taken over possession of the property cases from the Medical Examiner. "Hold on, Kate. We may need Rikka's help again. Is she around?"

"Right here." The sound quality changed as Kate went to speakerphone. "Just the two of us in our suite, trying desperately to find the energy to go cook dinner."

"*Cook* dinner?" Leona asked, mostly to fill the time as she grabbed the camera bag and headed back inside. "You are a wonder, Ms. Stark." She made it light and funny, but Kate didn't appear to be in a laughing mood. Back inside, she extracted the camera and held it out to Marcus. "Okay, here it is."

"I don't know what to do with this thing."

The bearded guy hiding under his ball cap held out his hand. After flicking a few switches, he glanced at the bottom of the camera. Popping open a door, he pulled out the battery, selected a spare from the case, and slid it back in. This time the camera powered up. He fooled around a little more, nodded to himself, pressed a button, and set it on the counter with the lens aimed away. The display on the back was visible to all of them.

"Hi, Kate, still there? We have footage on the smaller camera. It looks as if..." Leona looked around the bar and spotted where the Cooks' videographer must have been standing behind the bar and adjacent to the waitress station. "... Dana Winston filmed the back room through a display window beside the bar. You know, one of those places where patrons can peek into the brewery and—Holy shit!"

"What?" Kate and Rikka called out in unison.

Leona couldn't answer. One of the massive stainless-steel tanks had exploded. Within seconds, a giant CO_2 bottle was ricocheting about the room. In rapid succession, it kneecapped the bar owner, broke a pipe that released a gout of flame to take out Shari, and then Ray stood alone. He wavered for a long moment before collapsing out of sight. The video ended.

"Couldn't see any of that from where we're sitting," the bigger guy looked ready to puke. "We heard the awful banging. The camera lady stood over there, so she had an angle we couldn't see. When the banging stopped, she waited a few seconds, then simply walked out."

Mr. Ball Cap nodded in silent agreement.

Leona moved away while Marcus began doing his friendly commiseration thing with them...then began extracting every detail the two guys might not have realized they'd seen.

"I'll send the video to you, Rikka." Leona had seen far worse deaths. At least these three had been abrupt. Brutal but abrupt. "I don't know if it tells us anything new until we get a better look at it."

53

AFTER DINNER SERVICE FINISHED, KATE SAT OUT ON THE Quarterdeck alone. It had emptied with the cool evening, but the ship was steaming east so the lowering western sun, and the warm blanket one of the stewards had wrapped about her shoulders, kept her comfortable enough. She sat in a turned chair with her feet propped on the rear rail. The stairs down which Bret Calder had been catapulted by his own explosive descended close to her right.

Without turning she knew it was Rikka who had settled beside her. She'd made no sound on her approach; simply not there, then there. She'd have at least *felt* Sam's presence. Sure enough, legs in black jeans, and black high-top Converse were soon propped alongside hers against the rear railing. The shoelaces were Aurora Borealis colors, but that was too obvious.

"Sixties tie dye?"

"Aurora Borealis." It wasn't like Rikka to be so obvious. It should have been the coronation colors of some Zulu king in 1703 or a Fourier transform of a rainbow.

Kate looked to see if she was okay and spotted the laptop Rikka had brought with her. "No more videos, just tell me."

"Leona was right, not a whole lot there. The takedown was ugly. What's interesting is that you can see the pub owner hitting the proper control to release the over-pressure in one of his big tanks. Tapping a meter, hitting the release a couple more times, and looking up at the pressure relief valve. The safety valve didn't pop even though the pressure kept climbing. I called Marcus and Leona to check. Someone, we're guessing the dead videographer, had cut the wire to the safety control switch and broken off a pencil inside the pressure relief valve to block it. Really simple stuff, so—poof!" Rikka fountained her fingers upward. "Or actually—poof!" Her fingers mocked a sideways explosion rather than a vertical one. "Explosion passed right through where Shari had been standing seconds before. Right where we'd have been if we were there."

Kate closed her eyes against the sun shining off the rolling sea, a bright runway in their wake.

"I'm thinking about that pub. How would you feel about going into business with me there? Take it over, just run a quiet pub in a small town."

"Two Gals Irish Pub and Brothel."

"Brothel?" Kate opened her eyes to look at Rikka.

"Okay, maybe not until we're both like really old. Two Gals Irish Pub, Retirement Home, and Brothel. Video stores are totally passé, but we could make it a used bookstore as well. Or Two Retired Gals Brothel, Bait, and Bookshop. That has a better ring to it, and we'd get some hunky fisherman to help us wile away the years."

Kate turned back to the shining sea. "I was just thinking of a pub."

"That would work too, I guess. Would it be okay if I brought Sam? Though I don't know about him ever leaving Brooklyn.

His butcher shop goes back generations, like all the way back to the Mayflower or the Stone Age or something."

"If you don't get that he'd follow you anywhere, you don't understand that man."

"He'd...what?" It started as a shout but ended in a whisper.

"Seriously, Rikka. You've got something with him that women like me can only dream about."

"A guy with muscles?"

Kate twisted her head to look at Rikka again.

"Okay! Okay!" She held up her hands in protest. "Don't give me the Kate Stark evil eye. Paul is the only person I know immune to that. Anyone with an ounce of common sense would sell their life's belongings and move to a one-person hermitage in somewhere like Minnesota or, even worse, Florida, after being hit with a KS-double-E."

KS-double-E? She liked the sound of that. Actually, no. It sounded silly in her own head. Like so many other things, it only made sense when Rikka was actually saying it. Kate couldn't resist asking, "And Sam?"

"Don't talk to me about Sam that way. I'd panic and run."

"We're in the middle of the Arctic Ocean."

"Okay, I'd panic and swim. Except I really, really hate cold water. There's something else weird."

"Weirder than you being in love with Sam?" Rikka's strangling noise made Kate feel much better.

"No!" she declared when she recovered her breath. "Just kinda weird about that Gloucester pub. You know about IPI, of course. According to Shari's running show notes on her tablet, they bankrolled the pub in Gloucester."

"They who?"

"IPI. Weren't you listening?"

She was but it wasn't making any sense. "I can't say that I've made a study of Irish pub finances."

"Well, you should. Remember all that stuff I told you about

White Hand and the McLaughlin mob being part of your family tree?"

Pulling the blanket tight around her shoulders no longer blocked the evening chill. Not trusting herself to speak, she managed a single nod.

"Well, the modern Irish mob moved into the sponsoring-pubs business. The plan was they set you up and then take a chunk of your gross income—forever. They financed that pub in Gloucester, Massachusetts. The Irish mob is now called IPI, Irish Pubs, Inc."

Kate pulled the blanket over her head.

"There was more on that camera's memory card than just the video."

"Do *not* tell me." She wasn't coming out from under her blanket again—ever.

"It's audio only. Dana ran her camera and recorded the guy who bribed her to ruin the pub. It's kinda creepy."

"Please don't," Kate whispered from inside her woolen cocoon.

"No names, but she recorded her own murder. Marcus and Leona are working on finding a voice match."

54

He sat high on Grimsey Island with high-power binoculars. He would look no different than any other birder who traveled here. When his flight had landed an hour ago, the little green-and-white cruise ship was already anchored a couple hundred yards outside the harbor. No one aboard had ventured out yet, other than a few early morning birders roaming her decks.

By the time they unloaded the Zodiacs from their stack on the top deck, he was freezing. The Arctic Circle actually crossed the north tip of the island. His phone insisted it was an unusually warm day—five whole degrees above freezing with clouds moving in and threatening a heavy mist. At least he could see everything, there wasn't a single tree on the island to block the view and it didn't take many buildings to house the population of sixty.

Scrubland grass, a small airport, and a puddle almost too small to call a lake. And thousands of birds. He'd planned to shift farther from the walking trails, but the little bastards had attacked and shredded the hood of his parka before he'd escaped them. To imagine that he'd thought they were cute with their pointed wings, shining white bodies, and black skull caps. But that was before they'd tried to punch holes in his head.

There, the first Zodiac was pulling away from the ship. He watched them through the binoculars. Some were heavily bundled up, but he inspected each face carefully.

No one he knew.

Nor on the next boat.

He was going to die here, frozen in place on this godforsaken island that lay twenty-five miles north of Iceland. There were only five Irish pubs in the whole country and they were all on the far side of the main island. Instead of being in one of those, he was sitting out here with joints stiffening up with age when he should be handing off control of IPI. He'd kill for a full Irish breakfast and a pot of strong-brewed tea by the same name.

That made him smile. Kill? Not yet. He was only scouting today. Mostly because he couldn't think of any way to arrange an accident here. But he couldn't wait, he'd had to see with his own eyes that he'd finally found her.

The fourth boat had a face he hadn't expected. Savannah sat front and center, his niece's lovely face aimed straight into the wind, actively surveying all that lay before her. She looked so like his sister at that age, it was unnerving. He'd almost forgotten she was on this cruise, even though the death of her fiancé was what had brought Kate Stark's current location to light.

She was an interesting girl. Savannah had the cutthroat instincts to become his heir when he was ready to let go of Irish Pubs, Inc. And Savannah was his only blood kin, but he'd never been able to arouse her interest in the financing of Irish Pubs—at least not the legitimate side he'd told her about. So far, he'd kept the other aspects of the business to himself.

His sister Ashli and brother-in-law Tommy had gone down ugly while Savannah was a freshman at Yale. He'd managed to keep it out of the news because there were some things his niece didn't need to know about her parents. But like so many people of her generation, she was all het up on climate change and saving the environment rather than her heritage.

She had inherited a bloody fortune because he, Ashli, and Tommy had been equal partners and they'd built IPI into a major powerhouse. Not the kind of bloody it had been in the old days of Whitey Bulger and Punchy McLaughlin, but not exactly clean either. He'd made sure Savannah stayed clean— and unaware. He ran the corporation and let her reap her share of the benefits. With all the tax shelters he'd structured in, there was plenty to go around.

Savannah was a sensible girl. Whenever they did meet, she spoke of investing rather than just living a billionairess lifestyle she could easily afford. He approved of that and mostly stayed out of her way. Though, claiming he was prone to seasickness, he'd turned down the wedding invitation. Not that she'd asked him to give her away in Tommy's stead as she should have. *No one is* giving *me, a grown woman, away like some possession.* Her call.

Then he did forget all about his niece.

Second from the stern in the same Zodiac sat Kate Stark, her face instantly recognizable. And the person beside her was invisible in a parka but looked to be half Stark's size.

Finally!

55

Once they all beached, Alli split them into two groups. "First group: the local walkers who want to wander into the small shop-cafe and stroll the cliffs to watch the puffins fly in. Second group: the long hikers up for an easy but fast out-and-back walk to reach the Arctic Circle marker."

Kate glanced at Rikka to see which she'd prefer, but she'd disappeared so far inside her parka that there was little sign of her. She'd been atypically quiet since their talk last night. She never should have said what she had about Rikka and Sam's relationship. It was none of her business and it had definitely freaked out her friend.

"Due to a wobble of the Earth's axis induced by the moon," Alli continued, "the Arctic Circle presently moves north across Grimsey Island about fifteen meters each year. For the first three hundred years, markers were placed on the island each century. A decade ago, they made a three-meter, nine-ton concrete sphere that is rolled north each year to mark the circle's position. In another twenty years, no part of the island will be in the land of the midnight sun. Then they plan to roll the sphere off the north shore and into the ocean."

Kate tentatively stepped over to the Arctic Circle hike group and Rikka followed. She waved off the three guys, hoping that a bit of gal time might help. Kate did notice that the three of them fell in together and, by some unspoken agreement (even on Paul's part), they followed a hundred meters behind.

Finally understanding that, for once, she'd have to put in the first word, she spoke softly. "Look, Rikka, I'm sorry what I said about Sam. But you shouldn't let it freak you out, because you're wonderful together."

The parka hood twisted one way, then another, finally turning enough toward Kate that she could see Rikka from nose to chin. "That's not what's freaking me out. I mean it is, but that's just normal freak out for me. I do that, don't I? I wish I was always steady and sure about everything the way you are, but that's not the way I'm wired."

Kate barely resisted a loud scoff. She only managed because Rikka was hurting about something, and this was about her friend and not her.

"I've never been in a relationship that lasted more than a few weeks. But Sam and I have been together for months and months. That's seriously weird for me. I've never trusted anyone for that long except you."

"You don't trust Sam?"

"Are you kidding me? Hundred percent trust. He doesn't know any other way to be, does he? It's that he's trusting *me* that so screwed up."

"Aren't you trustworthy?"

"No!" Rikka's shout was loud and bitter enough that others in the group looked their way. Those ahead then hurried their pace a bit to create a gap. The two friends were soon walking in a bubble in the midst of the thirty people who'd opted for the longer walk to reach the actual Arctic Circle.

"I thought you left all that behind after we ran you through the Witness Protection Program," Kate kept her voice down to a whisper on that fact.

"I did," Rikka's voice matched hers. Then fifty meters later she whispered, as if talking to herself, "after the second time."

Last night's chill was back, a far deeper chill than the cold mist soaking her face and her hair below the woolen cap she'd pulled on. "What did you do, Albert?"

A slight movement of the parka might indicate a shrug by the woman buried somewhere inside it.

Kate grabbed her arm and dragged her aside from the group. They stopped in the shin-high grass until the rest of the walkers had moved by. The three men stopped where they were well back of the crowd. The only other person was a lone birder sitting up the slope, close enough to an Arctic Tern nesting meadow that they were constantly soaring and swooping behind him, but not close enough to make them attack. Though he did look a little tattered with bits of white stuffing pulled partly out of his dark blue parka's hood.

Alone enough to speak without the risk of being overheard, she turned Rikka to face her and dragged back the hood to expose her face. "Tell me. I can't help you if I don't know what the heck you did."

"You'd help me?" Rikka looked ready to cry, though Kate couldn't tell if it was panic or relief.

"Haven't I always?"

Rikka looked everywhere except at her before answering. "Whoa! You're right. I'm not sure what to do with that any more than I am with Sam."

"I get that your past sucked, Rikka. But you're my best friend, kind of my only real one. Setting aside Sam and Paul, everyone else wants something from me...money, a job, instant fame, something. Even Marcus and Leona like the reputation they're gaining inside the FBI by working on the crime portfolios I inadvertently uncover."

"I bet now that Bret's murder turned out to be unintended suicide, the main thing Björn wants from you is sex."

"Probably, but off topic." Kate knew that but still hadn't decided how she felt about it. "Bottom line, Rikka, we've got to stick together or we're both lost."

Her arms were suddenly full of Rikka Albert, and they simply held each other close.

"Okay," Rikka nodded to herself as she stepped back. "Okay. Let's catch up with the group." And they stepped back to the trail and picked up their pace.

Kate was about to shake her when Rikka held up a hand to stop her.

"No, don't pry. That would just make me feel even worse for not telling you sooner." She took a deep breath and huffed it out. "While I was being Suzi Suzuki during my first passage through WITSEC, I got bored. Missed doing the dirty hack, riding through the data like I was a cyberpunk cowgirl heroine in a William Gibson novel that I always dreamt of being. I was sick of pretending I was little miss goody two-shoes college girl."

"Who did you hack, Rikka?"

"Well, I figured I used to be a bad girl, until you caught me as Shirō Usagi working for that Chinese Tong in Boston. So, what if Suzi Suzuki kept to her a-little-too-sweet name and only hacked bad people?"

Kate nodded that it made a certain kind of sense. She didn't say anything though, knowing how easily Rikka sidetracked onto new topics.

"It went fine at first. Everything went to charities or got invested in interesting startups. Nothing traceable to me, of course. Charitable organizations that only existed long enough to make the investment before disappearing again, kinda thing. Well, I skimmed a tiny bit for an awesome collection of the very best kitchen toys. You'd have liked my setup. Too bad you never got to see it before I had to leave it all behind on no notice."

Kate actually preferred a fine knife and large cutting board to most kitchen machines. Enough of a traditionalist at home that she kneaded her bread by hand, using a sourdough starter she'd started years before during a trip to Fire Island. No question but Rikka's kitchen would have been a land of technologic wonder.

"Well, I, uh, I...overreached." She mumbled the last word.

"You? How did you do that?" The FBI had confirmed that Rikka was still one of the world's top hackers when Marcus and Leona had by chance traced her to Kate's side.

"I'm not really sure. Overconfident, obv. But I'm never sloppy. He was a nasty piece of work and I uncovered a chunk of it. I went for blackmail, trying to drive him out of his business instead of just taking his money and making him start over from scratch. I never told you how my WITSEC identity got blown when you had to come rescue me."

Yet another failure on her part to not show more interest in her friend's past. She'd heard that Suzi Suzuki's Witness Protection cover was blown and rushed in to extract her. She'd helped set her up the Rikka Albert identity but never asked why Suzi's cover had failed. No, she had. Hadn't she? Had Rikka evaded? Kate had been too lost in her parents' recent deaths to remember one way or the other.

"The whole thing backfired. The guy was bad, but he was also powerful. I did some poking around; he had ties all the way back to the Chinese Tong that hired me. I didn't have a rule against meeting people then and I'm sure those guys could describe me too well from the prison cells you put them in. He managed to blast through the WITSEC system—bribed the hell out of a US Marshal. Or threatened her family. Or...I don't know what, but it worked. With my Suzi Suzuki cover blown,

I'd probably be dead now if you hadn't showed up. If I never said thanks, Thanks!"

That sounded more like the Rikka she knew; five years late might well be early for Rikka. "You're welcome."

"Anyway, Mr. Bad News?"

Kate risked a careful, "Uh-huh."

"He's the head of the Irish mob for everything north of Philadelphia."

Kate stumbled on the flat trail and would have fallen to the dirt if Rikka hadn't steadied her. "IPI?"

"IPI," Rikka confirmed. "I just connected the pieces last night."

"Is he after you—or me?" Kate asked once she was sure of her footing on the otherwise smooth trail.

Rikka shrugged. "I don't know. I'm really, really, like super-really sorry, Kate. But my name doesn't exist anywhere, I make sure of that. Which means that he saw a photo or something of us together. My guess? He'd coming after you to find me."

"And then what?"

Kate didn't even know why she asked. This was the modern Irish mob. She'd tangled with plenty of major gangs during her early days in the Secret Service both before and after she'd caught Rikka and turned her state's evidence. If Irish Pubs, Inc. ran everything north of Philly, they were huge. Which meant they were hugely powerful. They'd punched through the WITSEC shield once to find Rikka. They'd have no compunction about killing her to get to Rikka for once and for all.

Kate knew one thing for certain. Once they reached the Arctic Circle marker ball, she could measurably increase her life expectancy if she just rolled herself off the northern end of Grimsey Island and tried swimming across the Arctic Ocean.

56

Shortly before reaching the *Orbis et Globus* Arctic Circle marker, Kate waved that it was okay for them to catch up.

When Sam reached Rikka's side, she simply turned into his arms and latched onto him. He lay his cheek on her damp hair and breathed her in.

"I'm okay," she mumbled into his chest. "I'm okay. Just don't give up on me, Sam. Okay? Promise?"

In answer he held her tighter and her nod, sliding her slick hair along his cheek, said that was all the response she required. It was also the closest to a promise that she'd ever made to him in turn. He did wonder if she understood that.

When she announced *Wedding time, Sam!* while calling him from Savannah's ceremony, he absolutely lost the ability to speak. He'd had to consciously remember how to breathe. Then, of course, her being Rikka, she'd launched into some explanation that she'd meant Savannah's wedding and, of course, he'd know that. He had. But it didn't stop her from knocking the breath out of him first.

"There's something Kate said I had to tell you."

A small herd of buff-colored Icelandic horses trotted over to inspect the group. He kept his smile to himself as one arrived close behind Rikka and snuffled at her hair with a blast of warm breath. As expected, when confronted by any critter bigger than a domestic house cat, Rikka yelped and launched herself.

He'd anticipated the motion and shifted his nose aside before she impacted it with the top of her head. Instead, he caught her against him with one arm around her waist. With the other, he pet the horse's nose.

"Don't do that," she told the horse even as she tentatively reached out to brush at its nose. "Otherwise, glue factory for you, buddy. Bitchin' 'do." Indeed, the horse's long mane was as multi-toned as a high-end California bleach job.

Sam noted that it wasn't any taller than Rikka but had the heavy bones and musculature of a draft horse. Tough and hardy. Must be to survive the winters here for the last thousand years since the Vikings brought them over.

Once he set her down, he saw that she topped the horse's withers by just one hand, a bare four inches taller.

She led him aside from both the other hikers and the horses. Then she explained all about the Irish mob and why they were after her.

At his glare, she held up a hand with three fingers raised. "I was never a Scout, but Scout's honor, I've run a hundred percent clean since Kate saved me a second time. I'd never do anything to mess her up. Though it looks like my past may have. I think the Irish mob will hunt her down in order to find me."

Twenty years in the Marines had taught him to never react from his emotions. What he *wanted* to do was scream. To blast her with his rage. Why the hell had she just made him promise to never give up on her? So that he didn't simply kill her for betraying everyone's trust? How goddamn twisted was that?

But that was his emotional response.

The first thing his training made him do was make a slow scan of everyone in the vicinity. He recognized each person presently at the big gray ball that marked the Arctic Circle as coming from their ship.

Thinking back along the path they'd walked to reach here, he'd identified seven locals and three birders who weren't on this cruise. One of whom had watched their group intently as they moved past. A lookout. No, scout. No...they'd already found her; except he knew Rikka was a shadow, barely existing in modern society with a digital footprint probably smaller than most newborn babies. Which meant they'd found her through Kate.

He'd let Kate worry about Kate for the moment. She could handle herself better than almost anyone he knew, Marine Corps or not.

For now, he was going to keep Rikka alive until he calmed down enough to create a rational plan of action. It made him a target as well, but hopefully that meant he could see the attack before it arrived.

He pointed at Rikka, then pointed close by his left side, making it clear she should be at his left heel so that he'd always know where she was. He had to keep her close, but he couldn't stand to touch her at the moment. Sam certainly didn't trust himself enough to speak.

On the walk back to the boat, he did note that the one solo bird watcher had flown away like one of his birds. Perhaps literally. The plane he'd watched land while eating breakfast had headed aloft as they stood at the concrete marker. He glanced at his watch. A scheduled two-hour turnaround. Long way to come for a two-hour bird watch, sitting in the middle of the island.

Sam eyed the spot he'd sat. It would be hard to pick a *less* likely place to watch birds. Yet...he scanned around...it was convenient to the airport and an ideal position to unobtrusively watch the comings and goings from the *Ice Adventure.*

He considered telling Rikka, but there was no way he could speak to her right now without yelling at her. And reacting with emotions could get a Spec Ops warrior killed, so he kept his mouth shut.

57

CHATTING WITH BJÖRN ON THE RETURN WALK, KATE APPRECIATED that he was as bad at flirting as she was. It let them just talk and, under any less trying circumstances, he'd have made her laugh any number of times. He told her stories of Iceland, of the Sagas, and of how a young boy really had tried to follow in a legend's footsteps until it led him to join *Vikingasveitin.*

But she didn't miss Sam checking his watch. Not a glance; but actually studying it. Next he glanced toward the airport, then scanned a wide arc, one that started where the tattered bird watcher had sat and ended at the ship.

Last night's chill returned ten-fold, and she didn't think it was the heavy mist now making her hair lay chill against her neck. Nor the slow drip that had formed to slide down her spine at unexpected intervals.

Had that been a mob scout? Had she stood that close to a potential shooter, yet none of her instincts had kicked in? Unlikely. Handguns were illegal here, rifles and shotguns severely restricted. When the largest land predator was an Arctic fox, not much bigger than a large house cat, major sidearms were not called for. The rare polar bear who drifted over from Greenland aboard an ice floe once every five to ten years were dealt with by the authorities, if they survived the journey at all.

Anyone aboard ship would have already had plenty of opportunity to attack her or Rikka already, making them an unlikely threat vector.

Sam caught her repeating the inspection he'd just been making, probably reaching the same conclusions. He offered the slightest nod, which Kate returned with Rikka none the wiser. She watched as he varied his gait so that his position constantly shifted—now a little in the lead, now trailing by a half step—to place himself between Rikka and any unknowns who passed their group.

She also noted that he didn't once touch her. After a few attempts to engage Sam, Rikka had gotten the message and retreated once more into her parka. Kate almost felt sorry for her, but the large target painted on the center of Kate's own chest had to remain her primary focus.

Kate studied Björn sidelong. If her escort had noticed anything out of the ordinary, he gave no sign. Of course, he wouldn't know that she and Rikka were potential targets of a force much more dangerous than an exploding wedding cake.

She liked him. And he was so very pretty. But he didn't make her feel notably safer.

Such was her lot. Not everyone got a Sam. Even now, as furious as Kate had ever seen him, he still protected Rikka with his own body.

58

Hrísey Island was another of those remotely idyllic places, now that the ephemeral sun had emerged once more. Paul supposed that the *potential,* yeah right, of forty bird species there and a couple million bright purple lupines did it for some people. He really did not see the draw. The silence echoed strangely in such places as if it was trying to stretch him thin like the last scrapings of caviar insufficient for the final piece of toast.

Cicely, the leggy brunette he'd used to get close to Clara the secret agent on Vigur Island. He wasn't sure he'd ever met a real secret agent before, which was seriously cool. Cicely, however, had proved to have the same number of brain cells as long legs. Unless you wanted to live and breathe social media, which bored him worse than cheap peanut butter.

He'd bagged out on the Hrísey shore excursion, rattling around the ship but finding no distractions. The ninjas were running the Zodiacs back and forth for the shorebird hikes. The kitchen crew had it down and only bothered Kate for the heavy dinner prep. The others had gone ashore, dragging even Björn with them.

When he hit the top deck viewing platform for lack of anywhere better to be, he spotted Savannah. She was stretched out on a lounger. In the bright sun and the wrap-around wind barrier, it was very pleasantly warm. She'd shed her jacket, which had masked a very nice figure landing just on the fuller side of athletic. She'd pulled her long dark hair back from its big curls into a tight ponytail, which showed off her broad Irish features and strong eyebrows. Not bad at all to look at—and as clearly bored out of her skull as he was.

"Where's your pal?" He hadn't seen her without her one loyal bridesmaid for the entire trip.

"She's a pushover for wildflowers," Savannah flapped a hand toward shore.

"Care for some company?" She didn't strike him as the sort where the right move was to go ahead and lie down on the nearby lounger *as* he asked.

Again the wave of the hand, this time granting him passage.

He'd often enjoyed consoling widows, though he'd never tried to intrigue one a mere two days after a murdered beau. Actually, there had been Andrea on the Amalfi coast of Italy that one time. Their fling had ended rather abruptly when the police broke into his room to arrest her for actually committing the murder. A pity, as she'd been doing a fine job of proving she was a lioness in the bedroom.

She'd then tried to hang the whole thing on him. Kate had flown in, did her nosing-through-the-facts thing, then had a single meeting with the woman. She'd admitted to the deed and he'd been freed within the hour.

They now knew that Savannah was an innocent, so that made her somewhat safer—if he didn't count various secret arms of the Icelandic government trying to kill her off. Her aloof attitude since the death of her fiancé also made her an intriguing mystery. Paul always liked unraveling mysteries.

He thought through how best to approach her. Bets were

odds-on that she was sick of talking about anything to do with dead husbands, weddings, and cakes. She'd become bored with island hopping. She'd come ashore at Grimsey but hadn't bothered to join the group doing the long walk to look at a gray concrete ball sitting on the grass. Instead, she'd taken an early Zodiac back to the ship. He'd liked the horses and teasing Björn about his interest in Kate but even that had run stale.

Paul recognized many of the bird species now and could talk about them intelligently enough to pass. But he'd run that game to the limit as well. Those gals with the big binoculars and the guys with those cannon-long lenses mystified him— neither of which Savannah had wielded.

On the verge of launching into their shared Irish heritage, he remembered watching her on the bus ride.

"What's with you and those geothermal plants?"

She sat up halfway to get a good look at him as a smile shot wide across her face. That boosted her from merely attractive to lovely.

59

BJÖRN ENTERED THE DINING ROOM TWO STEPS BEHIND KATE; SHE had an amazing walk that was a pleasure to follow. Rikka beside her ranked severely cute but wasn't his type, especially not with her massive boyfriend lurking about. Kate stumbled to a halt as she stared off to the side. He had to lean forward past the door jamb to see what had so caught her attention.

It was her twin brother, Paul, sitting at a table looking very, very...happy. Not smug, the way Björn might have felt this morning if he hadn't lost track of Kate after dinner last night, but happy. Beside Paul, Savannah had her head thrown back in laughter. That, too, was new.

"Do we dare?" He overheard Kate whispering to Rikka. Then winced as if sorry she'd asked the question. There'd been some strange tension between them after the trip out to the Arctic Circle, but he couldn't unravel why.

"Oh, we can't miss this show." Rikka tried to make her tone light, but barely managed it.

As they moved forward, Kate turned her head and tipped it just enough to give him permission to follow. Neither one had turned, yet they both somehow knew he was there.

Rikka hesitated for one step, letting Kate draw ahead, before she whispered to him, "You shouldn't stare so hard at her butt, no matter how good it is."

"But it *is* so very fine."

And instead of the elbow to the gut he'd prepared to block, she looked up at him. "You're speaking to me?"

"What? I'm not allowed to?"

Then her gaze tracked over his shoulder and all he saw was sadness before she hurried after her friend.

Björn turned his head very slowly. Sam Fierro stood mere centimeters behind him—way inside his personal space without his situational awareness warning him. By only the thinnest of margins, his training kept him from leaping out of his skin. "How do you do that?"

Sam flashed a millisecond-long smile that made no attempt to venture anywhere near his eyes, then waved a hand for him to continue to the six-seat table. Kate and Rikka had sat directly across from Paul and Savannah, leaving the seats at either end open. Sam sat down at the end between Kate and Savannah, which left him between Rikka and Paul.

That arrangement made it impossible for him to start a private conversation with Savannah and find out what her real intentions were.

Instead, all he could do was sit and brood over what the hell was going on. Paul and Savannah were both from immense privilege, they matched like a Glock and its holster. He supposed that Sam and Rikka matched as well—neither of them seemed to have much in the way of means, or much of a past for that matter, but both consistently followed where Kate led.

But what the hell was a woman of Kate's standing doing with him?

He wasn't stupid; her interest shone as clear and obvious as he expected his own did. Okay, so why did *he*? Because she was an interesting, attractive woman with the best laugh a boy had ever dreamt of—even if he hadn't been able to tease it out during yesterday's walk. Based on what he'd seen of how others reacted to her, all wanting to cozy to the great Kate Stark (who he'd never heard of until two days ago), just might put him in a unique position with liking the woman without her reputation proceeding her.

If that was his main attraction to her, he could live with that. Maybe if they—

Björn cursed himself when he heard the word geothermal go by. Paul was in the midst of something that Björn should *not* have missed. He and Savannah were leaning forward, talking very earnestly with Kate about geothermal energy.

Oh shit. *Two* billionaires hot for Iceland's energy supply? Hayden was going to tell him to kill both. Great way to get Kate in bed? *Sorry that I had to kill your brother, but how about it?*

"You know they've done boreholes, deep ones, and hit temperatures of four hundred and even six hundred degrees Celsius," Savannah punched a finger down enthusiastically, practically spearing her last piece of toast. "In America, we drilled down, found some strong thermal gradients, then abandoned the projects."

"What if we could tap that?" Paul's words practically overran hers. "Talk about green energy. Can you imagine that kind of plant tapped into Yellowstone and pumping out gigawatts in every direction? It reminded me of this time I was in Taiwan with—" he glanced at Savannah, "a, uh, marine scientist."

Savannah rolled her eyes at him and laughed.

"Anyway, we had—"

Björn's phone rang. He kicked it to voicemail, then spotted Hayden's name on the display. It rang again. It could be a death sentence for him if he didn't answer.

With a curse, he silenced the ring to not annoy others and

abandoned the table. He hurried out of the dining room. There were people on the stairs, in the corridor. No outside doors at this level and his own room was five stories above. He hurried along until, at the bow of the ship, he found the one-room hospital. Empty. He went in, closed and locked the door, and answered the third call.

Too angry to trust himself, he hit speaker and dropped it in the center of the padded patient bed so that he could deal with Hayden without giving in to smashing his phone to shards.

"Is she dead yet?"

"By hell, may the trolls take all your friends!"

That shut up Hayden for a moment; there weren't many worse curses in Icelandic.

"I was sitting at breakfast with her and—"

"Poison. You know how to use that."

"—and she and Paul Stark were talking about how to take our tech—"

"Shoot them both."

"—to America."

Björn let the silence stretch. He'd learned that much from watching Sam Fierro operate.

Then the door opened. No knock. No sharp snap of a card key releasing the lock. The locked door simply opened silently and Sam Fierro was standing at the threshold with his arms crossed. There as if his mere thought had conjured the man.

"I still want them both dead," Hayden announced his brain-addled decision.

Sam merely raised his eyebrows. He stepped into the room and let the door swing shut behind him. Then settling on the balls of his feet ready for action, with his arms crossed, he did his *I'm-a-stone-wielding-giant* act.

Björn took a careful breath and kept an eye on Sam as he continued speaking to Hayden. "That's because you're an idiot. Someone needs to pry you out of your chair and bury you, you old fossil." Then he punched the Disconnect icon hard enough he might have sprained his finger.

"Satisfied?" He faced Sam.

Nothing.

"Bret Calder's original assignment was to kill Savannah Sachs before she could buy up our geothermal power companies. Wait, you already knew that. My commander..." he nodded toward the phone "...considers that a still-open mission."

More nothing. Björn began to wonder if he'd walk out of this room or end up on the bed in desperate need of the ship doctor's services. Hopefully he wouldn't finish the morning in the same freezer where Bret had spent the first night of his married life. That thought had him planting his feet and balling his fists. If he was going down, he wasn't going down easy.

"I thought to find out what she really intended before passing judgment. I was just about there when my commander called. He's not the sort of man that is safe to make wait."

Björn could actually hear Sam's neck vertebrae crack as he tipped his head one way and then the other.

Sam stepped forward until only the bed separated them. He looked down long enough to read Hayden's name still displayed there, then he punched the phone with one of his massive fists. One clean shot, driving the phone deep into the padding, and it snapped like kindling despite the hardened Gorilla Glass front. Even the titanium chassis warped badly as the electronics inside crackled like a breakfast cereal.

Sam turned and left the room as quietly as he'd entered. The latch didn't even seem to click as it closed behind him.

Alone, Björn looked down at his phone. Shattered, in the middle of the infirmary bed, far past any possible recovery. The message was clear: he was welcome to proceed with his investigation as long as he wasn't stupid about it—without any interference from Hayden.

He left the remains of his phone where it lay for someone else to declare dead. Grabbing a tear-to-open antiseptic wipe and a Band-aid, he followed Sam out the door. When he found him, Sam took both without comment and patched his bloody knuckle.

60

He convinced Kate to join him for a walk through Siglufjörður. It was another one of those places that no foreigner could say properly, except apparently Kate Stark, who nailed it on her first try: Sig-luff-yore-door.

"So, Mr. Guide..." Kate might be teasing him, but he couldn't really tell.

"Well, once upon a time this was the key herring port for the entire North Atlantic. UK fishing fleets fought battles here with frigates against Icelandic fishing boats. Over fifty ships, on both sides, rammed one another. Plenty of shots fired. Even a couple of deaths. The Third Cod War mostly ended because, between them, they so overfished that the herring shoals stopped coming in the 1960s. After that, everyone had to leave, including the Icelanders. This was once Iceland's largest town."

Kate looked around. "I don't see the remains."

In his experience, most folks didn't think to ask the next level question. "A couple of reasons. The fall from ten thousand to thirteen hundred people did leave a lot behind. But a massive avalanche from one side," he waved a hand at the near vertical mountain that rose along one side of the narrow fjord, "blasted into the harbor missing most of the town, but throwing up a tsunami that wiped out all of the mansions ranged along the other side." The low land, wiped clean, was now the runway for the town's airport. "By the 1990s, most of the town was a wreck. The townspeople took on the project of tearing it down or fixing it up. They turned it from a ghost town to a tourist destination one. Though a few boats do still fish out of here."

"Good job of it," Kate nodded her approval.

Björn figured that he'd bought them at least twenty-four hours, but probably not forty-eight before Hayden sent in someone else to finish the job. Before leaving the ship, he'd spoken to Clara and she'd agreed to tell him of any orders Hayden issued to her before acting on them. But he needed the information to flow *to* him from Kate, not the other way around. Time for a subject change.

"Siglufjörður is attached to the national grid. Which means that it's three-quarters hydropower and a quarter geothermal. We've connected everyone except for three islands. Like Grimsey is too far offshore, so they use a diesel generator."

"I saw the building at the north edge of the village." Kate kept her head on a swivel, looking everywhere except at him. She wasn't taking in the scenery either.

Finally, it clicked in, he recognized the training. "Who are you looking for?" She'd focused on every single person they passed along the waterfront, especially those not from the ship.

"So much for remaining stealth." Kate sighed. Then she turned those crystal-blue eyes on him and studied him until he wanted to squirm.

"What?"

"I'm trying to decide how much I can trust you."

He led her away from the street over to a sculpture on one of the old fishing piers. Rusted steel sheets had been assembled to represent three herring girls and the big wooden barrels they used to fill with salted fish. Young women working brutal hours in horrid conditions had been the mainstay of processing the catch back in the day. "Why don't you trust me?"

Kate didn't look aside or avoid his gaze. "Because you said you would stay aboard only until Bret Calder's death had been solved. It's been solved, but you're still aboard and still leaping to phone calls from your boss."

Björn could only laugh. "Sam has taken care of the latter." He made a gesture as if snapping a cracker. "Okay, honesty for honesty?"

That elicited a careful nod.

"Bret's original assignment was to get close to Savannah Sachs and, if necessary, kill her before she could buy any of our geothermal plants. That assignment has now been passed on to me."

"The getting close? And now Paul's in your way?"

He shook his head.

"The execution." Kate rubbed at her eyes. "Have I ever told you how little I miss the political garbage we saw in the Secret Service? *Vikingasveitin.* Iceland's counter-terrorism squad. Even when the *terrorist* is a corporate raider."

Björn took a page from Sam's playbook and merely shrugged his acknowledgement. Except that wasn't full honesty. "I told Hayden that she *and Paul* were talking about our geothermal plants."

Kate's eyes narrowed dangerously. "Weren't you listening at breakfast?"

"I was distracted by the phone call."

"Before that."

Honesty? He was as cowardly as a goat. Well, nothing more to lose at this point. "You're a very distracting woman, Kate. I was thinking about you, not listening to the conversation."

That earned him a smile and a brush of lips against his. There and gone before he could respond or place his hands on her waist, but still a kiss. She made a thoughtful humming sound before she spoke.

"Savannah and my brother were discussing how to start a company that uses the thermal aspects of borehole technology to generate electricity. Top and bottom of a deep-drilled hole can be hundreds of degrees apart—and that's Celsius. That temperature differential can be leveraged to generate power or heating. Only the US, Iceland, and China have really studied this. The US fossil fuel companies killed that effort at the first opportunity. Relations with China being what they are, she came to Iceland. The cruise was her overview, then she *was* planning to buy up the companies to get that research. Paul, well, my brother tends to have a broader, strategic view of things. He gave her the idea of saving money upfront by *licensing* the Iceland-developed technology—and applying it in the US."

Björn couldn't believe it. Bret's death. And the chefs'. All the maneuverings. Hayden's orders because Bret had screwed up his assignment and hadn't dug deep enough. Why? Because that wasn't Bret's style any more than it was Hayden's.

All for...nothing?

Maybe he understood Sam a little better now. A quiet rage filled him, not to exploding but to a lethal spearpoint. He was going to take down Hayden if it was the last thing he did.

She rested a calm hand on his chest. "Her original *tentative* plan was outright purchase of Icelandic companies, but Paul helped her revise that. That's why they were both so excited this morning."

Okay, so Hayden had been right originally, if Björn ignored the *tentative* part. The man still needed to be ousted, with prejudice. Maybe he could enlist Clara Bragason. Or perhaps even better, Sam and Kate. That would be an attack from an unexpected angle. He glanced at Kate trying to guess at her reaction.

"I have other problems."

Right. He'd forgotten where this whole conversation had started. He nodded that it was her turn. Only then did he realize how thoroughly she'd read him without him saying a word. Intelligent might be the new sexy, but brilliance was a whole level past that.

"I have reason to believe that a member or members of the Boston Irish mob wish to harm Rikka and perhaps myself. And that they're planning to act here in Iceland."

"What? Why?"

"A long story, and trust only goes so far. Let's just say that it isn't idle speculation."

Björn turned to scan the area. Waterfront. Few people other than tourists strolling this end of town. Out here stood the old piers, five buildings of an old fish processing plant converted into the Herring Era Museum, and not much else. Nothing amiss that he could see.

He turned back to Kate, "How can I help?"

"Keep an eye peeled," she hooked a hand around his elbow, "and try not to be too obvious about it."

He bit back a sharp retort and considered. "How about if half the time I keep my attention on you instead?"

Her smile said it wasn't a brilliant line but that she'd liked it well enough.

61

Sam had to give Rikka some credit. Though she knew she'd been found, she'd refused to cower on the ship.

"I'm not leaving Kate out there on her own to risk facing what I caused," she'd told him once again as they gathered with the others outside the museum. She was smart enough to keep her head on a swivel, even if she was shorter than most people's shoulders.

Sam still couldn't speak to her, but he did like her attitude. If only she'd backed it up with action to begin with, they wouldn't be in this mess. He'd actually never been comfortable with Rikka's past. But he'd come to terms with it because it was just that, her past. Except suddenly it was her present, and that didn't sit well at all.

She'd babbled a whole explanation to him. He'd barely been able to listen.

What had she called it? Gray-hat hacking. Black hats were people who did bad *stuff*—woman couldn't even swear decently, which he normally found to be seriously cute. Not today.

White-hats were the good guys, developing and testing security systems. The Marines, like every other branch of the service, employed all of those they could find or train. But some of the agencies, the CIA certainly came to mind, he wouldn't trust with a pocket calculator, never mind a powerful computer.

Rikka insisted that her second incarnation had been strictly gray-hat hacking, following the intent of the law if not the letter of it. And that her current incarnation was strictly white-hat. *Hey, a woman has to grow up at some point.* He'd wanted to place his hand atop her head to show that she hadn't done much of that. To feel the slick weight of thick hair as she twisted enough to grin up at him for the joke. *Hey, I turned thirty this year. I'm all grown up in the ways that count.* Then she'd jump him. When she was right, she was so very right.

The problem was that right now she was so very wrong that he still couldn't stand to touch her. Trust was not to be violated. He'd never pushed her about her past, that was on him. But she'd sure as hell never offered. Doing illegal shit was one thing; the law was often stupid in many, many ways. There wasn't a deployed warrior facing the half-assed Rule of Engagement, that didn't let you shoot a known bad guy, who hadn't figured that out. But doing massively dangerous shit that endangered your friends, your comrades-in-arms...you just didn't do that—ever! Riding back to the boat side-by-side on the Zodiac from Grimsey Island, each brush of her arm against his had been an agony.

Soon, the full contingent of ship passengers had come ashore along with all the tour's escorts and guides. They crowded around an elaborate table for a herring-gutting demonstration outside the Herring Era Museum. Eight women in rough clothes and heavy rubber aprons ranging from ten to seventy years old arrived at their stations.

A load of fish was dumped in a trough that ran the full

length of the table. The women then wielded their knives. Quick slashes removed the fins. Scrub each side tail-to-head three times with the back of the blade to remove the scales. Roll the blade again. A slash at the gills, cut the head half-off, flip the fish, cut the other half, then drag the head aside to remove. All the innards slid out with it. A fast splash through a channel of running water and toss them into a trough that ran alongside each station. From there a young boy picked them up and laid them in a barrel with salt scattered over each layer.

He admired the efficiency, mere seconds to clean and process each foot-long fish.

Having seen it, he ignored the rest of the show, the narration, the manager strutting around like a boss man, and so on. Instead, he watched the crowd. All eyes focused on the show—except Kate's. And Björn's. Kate must have decided he was sufficiently safe and reliable. He knew no better judge of people and accepted her decision to recruit the third set of trained eyes.

Farther afield he saw nothing amiss.

It was only after the demonstration was over and the announcer had set about soliciting people from the crowd to demonstrate a dance common among the herring girls of old, that he heard one of the clean-up crew remark, "Hey, one of the knives has gone missing. Anyone see where it went?"

Though they kept searching, Sam would wager they weren't going to find it.

He managed to catch Kate's eye where she whirled about in the dance. When she happened to be facing his direction, Sam tapped his thigh where he'd carried his KABAR fighting knife for twenty years in the Corps. He missed having it there under the current circumstances. Then he pretended to draw it.

Kate followed his glance to the fish-cutting table. He held up one finger and shrugged to indicate a knife was missing. Then she was gone in the dance again but now warned.

He could easily imagine Rikka dancing like that. Perhaps Kate could give them lessons. If he could ever bring himself to trust Rikka again.

62

SAVANNAH DANCED ELEGANTLY. SHE HAD SLID INTO THE SIMPLE beat of the herring girls' dance, though dumbed down enough for tourists to join in, as neatly as she'd slid into his arms last night.

She made him feel like...a king. Or perhaps a very small god.

Paul liked that she'd had plans—it was more than he'd achieved in his life. But as they'd discussed them up on the viewing deck through much of yesterday, they'd felt too narrow. Brainstorming it through had carried over dinner and into the night. Beyond her suite window, the sun had set toward the northwest and reemerged three hours later to the northeast while they debated and brainstormed. The twilight had been bright enough that they'd never had to turn on the lights.

Her initial vision, to buy all of the rights to borehole drilling and exploitation in Iceland, was...limited. It also might strain even her wealth to simply acquire the right companies with little left over for development.

This isn't the age of ownership anymore, Paul had told her, impressed with his own insights. *Oh sure, it works for some people who still know how to make it work, like my sister. This is the age of licensing. What if you licensed the Icelandic technology for pennies on the dollar and developed it for the vastly larger American market? Once proven, Hawaii, Alaska, and the western continental states would create a fabulous market.*

It had taken them until that early sunrise to hash out the fuller concept. Once they had fleshed out the plans as well as could be done in a single night, they'd focused on a different kind of flesh.

He'd stopped her at that moment, not at all his normal style, but he had. He'd felt obliged to ask.

I'm not even sure why I was marrying him in the first place. He made it sound romantic and exciting, but I don't know that I did more than care for him. Finding out that he was planning to kill me explains the wills we drew up. As long as I lived, he couldn't touch my money. I have as much of everything as you do, Paul. She'd shrugged uncomfortably. *I never thought about him targeting my money.*

That had required some painful explaining on his part as she'd gone through disbelief, acceptance, rage, and whatever else a person was supposed to go through after a betrayal like that. He didn't usually stick around for those bits but, this time, they rode it out together.

My diagnosis, Savannah. Somewhere under all that flurry, there's a woman who's a little too nice.

We're not falling in love here.

Did I say a thing about love? That was a word he'd long ago sworn to never use outside of family.

You know, I was planning to use you for revenge-sex.

How about just using me for me instead?

Savannah had liked that idea. And she'd proved that, in addition to being splendidly driven, she was also gloriously agile. It may have started being all about her, but it certainly hadn't ended that way.

And after that, Paul had actually been too excited by the business idea to sleep as Savannah lay draped over his body, her skin awash in the early sunlight. That was a first for him. Paul had enjoyed plenty of sleepless nights over the years, with fine women or while cooking up a fine hoodwink on someone he didn't like.

But a fiery interest in a business venture? That was Kate's department, not his.

And it *was* hers. He'd nudged Savannah awake before breakfast. Not for sex, the only reason he'd ever woken a woman in the middle of the night—other than caught while sneaking away—but to tell her that he knew one of the top business experts anywhere. And he could prove it because she'd made them both immensely wealthy since taking over Cooks Network.

Over breakfast, Kate had been intrigued and offered suggestions neither he nor Savannah had thought of. She'd been intrigued enough to say that *they all* needed to work on this together once they were back in the States.

He and Kate had never worked together on anything important before. That alone was almost as exciting as the woman who left a kiss on his lips as she whirled into him, then whirled away during the herring girls' dance. They were the last ones dancing after the show was over and the ship's passengers had headed off to tour the museum.

Paul signaled her back into his arms, with no intent of letting her whirl away this time. As she spun toward him, she looked over his shoulder and her smile shifted to bewilderment. She plowed against him hard enough that he almost went down.

"Uncle Shane?"

63

It was a calculated risk.

Those stupid Arctic terns had forced him to be too exposed on Grimsey Island. No doubt he'd been noticed. Well, his best next move was to explain his presence in some obvious way.

He stepped forward and gathered his niece into a brief hug. "You have always danced so wonderfully, Savannah."

"Thank you. Uncle Shane, this is a friend from the ship, Paul Stark."

The man had a solid grip; Shane resisted the urge to crush his hand for where he'd seen it on Savannah's ass earlier. "You dance well yourself, Paul."

"Easy with such a skilled partner."

Well, at least he was a better choice than that Bret Calder. Stark had wealth and social standing—even if it landed closer to notoriety than fame. Now *that* was an interesting thought. Maybe he could use Paul to coerce Savannah back into Irish Pubs, Inc.'s operation? Shane had plenty of muscle, but not a honed intelligence like these two. If he pitched IPI as the glorious long con it was, Paul Stark's reputation said he'd be panting to take it on.

"What are you doing here, Uncle Shane?"

"I saw the news article on what happened at your wedding. I didn't want to, uh, interfere with your trip. So, I flew out as soon as I could and caught up with you on Grimsey Island. I only watched; I wanted to make sure you were okay. Like the old stick-in-the-mud that I am, I flew back out once I knew you were unharmed. Only after the plane took off did I realize what a fool I was being. I looked up your tour's itinerary and caught up with you here." It sounded barely credible to his ear. Hopefully it sounded better to Savannah.

Her quick hug was enough to confirm that she believed him. And that was apparently enough for the besotted Paul Stark. Most men sniffed around Savannah for her money, but Stark didn't lack in that department. It looked to be unshaded lust. That worked for him.

He'd seen the big bruiser of a guy keeping watch on the Eurasian hacker. He recognized the type; IPI hadn't fully outgrown the need for dumb muscle. He needed an excuse to get close—and, by cozying up to the male Stark, his niece had opened the perfect door.

Now he could focus on concocting a spectacularly painful demise for the hacker. This couldn't be some delicate, modern persuasion. *If you're gonna do it, do it right, Son.* He could hear Father's clear admonition as if the man wasn't thirty years dead.

He'd do it right.

He'd do it Old School.

It had been a long time since he'd dropped a body off the middle of the Harvard Bridge—dead or alive. The logistics were too complicated across national borders. But to scatter her ashes there?

He couldn't wait!

64

THE FISH-TO-OIL RENDERING MACHINERY HADN'T INTERESTED Kate or Björn. The Spartan lodgings for the herring girls' dorms emphasized what their lives had been. Björn had thought it interesting, but Kate came away angry on behalf of those women trapped in such a hard life.

But she liked the boathouse.

From a Norwegian rowboat to the thirty-eight-ton *Týr* herring netter, they'd parked nine boats inside the big building. For walkways between the exhibits, they'd fashioned wide piers of weathered wood held aloft by fat pilings and moored the boats alongside them. The boats floated on a sea made of blue acrylic, making it feel like a harbor at night with the tastefully unlit ceiling above.

Aboard the *Týr*, the wheelhouse perched above the afterdeck, offering a fine view of all the operations forward. A divider separated off the captain's cabin: a bed, a writing desk big enough for a ledger book, and little else, but it was private.

It would be a different alternate life than a Gloucester pub, roaming the sea in her own little space. She knew that reality had none of the romance, risking the brutal North Atlantic gales to bring home a meager catch as the herring shoals dwindled away. But on a steady boat, moored in a safe museum-fashioned harbor with a good roof overhead, she could imagine another way of life.

A way of life where chefs weren't murdered by wedding cakes. Where videographers weren't complicit in unleashing a disaster that made a pub brawl look like a game of checkers. Where her best friend hadn't betrayed her trust by attacking the Irish mob.

With her hands on the wheel's spokes, Kate imagined she could steer a path through it all. Past where Björn and Sam prowled the foredeck, envying the *real-man's* life that others must have lived on this craft. Past all the tourists lined up at the tables set up on the next walkway. The museum had set up samples: three different strengths of preserved herring, slices of a local cheese, and a shot of Iceland-made aquavit—a spirit strong enough to scorch out the back of your brain and leave only a thin residue of charred sawdust behind.

She'd considered swiping a bottle and throwing her own pity-party-for-one here in the captain's cabin. Maybe she'd invite Björn to join her.

Sam and Björn descended into the fo'c'sle. She'd already checked it out. A narrow door near the prow that descended a steep ladder into an impossibly small space. Six bunks stacked in tiers so tight neither Sam nor Björn would be able to roll over, blocked by the breadth of their shoulders. A tiny kitchen and a cupboard for foodstuffs. Finally, a booth-style table that couldn't seat all six at once no matter what their build.

Rikka stood on the prow of the next boat over, looking at nothing as far as Kate could tell. She wanted to forgive Rikka, knew she would, but she wasn't there yet. Two years of her life to track and catch Shirō Usagi. All the trouble of turning her state's evidence rather than throwing her to the wolves as her bosses had wanted. Getting her into WITSEC and then ripping her back out when her cover was blown.

Not merely blown. Suzi Suzuki had *personally* blown the cover that Kate had gone to so much trouble to build for her. Attacking the mob? What kind of a lunatic attacked the mob?

That almost made her smile. The money-laundering Chinese Tong that Kate had taken down with, eventually, Rikka's help was as close to being mafia as you could get without, well, being *the* Mafia. Had Rikka, consciously or not, sought vengeance upon her past? Irish Pubs, Inc. definitely fit that bill. That's probably how Rikka had blown her cover, not wanting to merely damage them but to strip them down to the bone.

Kate just wanted to be done with all of it.

A familiar movement shifted her attention to the front door of the boat house, just off her dream boat's port bow. She'd know her twin's walk anywhere, even silhouetted by the bright sunlight outside. It seemed so incongruous here inside her personal, private, executive boat.

The slender figure beside him had to be Savannah. She'd been completely rational this morning, which wasn't Paul's typical influence on women. It was as if whatever flurry of madness she'd conjured during the buildup to her brief marriage had been purged from her body. Kate would have to ask what the woman had been running away from so hard that she'd so fully invested herself in that whirlwind persona she'd presented in the lead-up to the wedding.

At breakfast, Savannah was charming and well-spoken. Her main failing was that she was young. Twenty-eight had made her both smart and curiously naïve about the world. Rikka would explain it as an alien possession. Or if Kate had guessed that, then as an exorcism requiring the Pope himself to travel to the small islands of Iceland. Or... Kate could guess what, but she was sorry to not have Rikka standing next to her in the wheelhouse and spinning stories of wedding madness cured by exploding wedding cakes.

A man she didn't recognize walked in last, clearly in company with Paul and Savannah. He looked about the boathouse, but not as if trying to get his bearings in the intriguing layout. He was scanning for...people?

For a person.

She didn't know why, but Kate had no doubt that it was the same man who had sat on the Grimsey Island hillside with the Arctic terns swirling in the air behind him.

Now he stood with Paul and Savannah? Were they targets as well?

From safe inside her wheelhouse, she looked for Rikka as the trio took the right-hand walkway toward the tables of treats. No longer on the boat next over. Kate leaned forward until her nose almost touched the glass. From her perch at the highest point in the museum looking down over the walkways and displays, she couldn't see Rikka anywhere.

Until...there. A mere shadow, glancing over her shoulder as she bolted out the front door and into the sunlight. She'd been glancing at the man who'd come in with Paul and Savannah.

At the man now staring directly at Kate's hideaway over his little plastic cup of aquavit.

65

RIKKA STUMBLED AHEAD INTO THE BLINDING SUNLIGHT, UNABLE to open her eyes for more than a blink.

Away. All she could think was—away.

At a full sprint, she ploughed into something that rattled and clanged. She squinted one eye open that was only partially adapted to the brightness. Wires! She'd run into some kind of a cage. Trapped! She tried to bat her way past a shape, but it only flopped about.

Managing to open both eyes, she saw that she'd run into a sculpture. It was made of a hundred vertical wires hung a foot apart in a grid form. From each wire hung a piece of rusted iron —in the form of a herring girl's knife. They looked like knife-shaped fish swimming through the sea. She had managed to shove her way into the very middle of the array.

She forced her way back out.

It was him. She knew it was. Shane O'Leary. The top boss of Irish Pubs, Inc. Founded by him with Tommy and Ashli Sachs.

Sachs?

Like Savannah Sachs?

How had she missed that? Didn't matter, she had.

Now she just had to get away. Far away. And once she was long gone...

Then Shane O'Leary would have no one to hunt—except Kate.

"Darn! Darn! Darn! Darn!" It would really help if she was much better at swearing. She'd practice. Real soon now.

She looked at the next sculpture over in the waterfront park. The three rusty-steel herring girls watched her. Judging her.

Why had she ever made friends with Kate? All it had done was put her in danger. Rikka had always done best on her own. Shirō Usagi had left next to no friends behind. Suzi Suzuki even fewer, if possible. As to her orphanage incarnation as Betsy Franklin, she'd had less than Shirō and Suzi combined.

Before any plan was clear in her head, she was racing back into the museum. Blasting through the entrance left her with the opposite problem than before. So dark she couldn't see crap.

She raced toward the treats table for lack of any better target.

"Hey, Rikka. What's the rush?" Paul offered her a slice of cheese on some weird Icelandic cracker.

"Where's..." And then she saw him. Shane was on the next walkway over, about to climb aboard the biggest boat. Rikka could see Kate standing in that boat's wheelhouse staring down at him.

Too little! Too late!

Screaming wasn't going to help.

Or would it?

She grabbed a plate of herring and heaved it over the gap between their two walkways.

"Hey, Shane!" she shouted at the top of her lungs. He turned just in time to watch fifty one-inch squares of pickled herring, each speared with a toothpick, scatter across the walkway five feet to his left. She was a hacker, not a sports geek, so sue her.

Rikka couldn't see his snarl—her eyes still hadn't adapted—but she could feel it and that's all that mattered.

She turned and bolted for the door, knocking Paul off the walkway in her haste. He tumbled down to land sprawled on the blue plastic sea.

A glance back showed Shane O'Leary in hot pursuit.

Great!

"Now what?" Rikka asked aloud as she raced once more into the sunlight and toward the docks.

66

THE SECRET SERVICE HAD TRAINED EVEN THE MEREST inclination to freeze out of her. When she'd identified that there was an active shooter mere feet from the Vice President-elect whose protection detail she headed, she hadn't frozen in the goal of putting herself in the way. She'd simply been four steps too far away to do so.

Watching Rikka bolt out the door as the mob's enforcer came to kill her had frozen her solid. All she could do was watch as death stalked toward her, out one walkway and then back along the one that connected to her boat. One foot on the ladder to board the boat, his eyes hadn't tracked away from hers once.

Caught, all she could do was clench her hands on the steering wheel to nowhere and watch him come. She'd seen death from inches away. Had it brush so close by that it should have wiped her away. But never in her life had she seen it stare at her with eyes like that. Not in the fury of the mistress who'd taken down the Vice President-elect. Not in any of the faces of the forty-seven gang members listening to Rikka's damning evidence spill out in the courtroom.

Berserker mad—she couldn't look away. Couldn't move. Couldn't blink away his stare.

Until she'd been as startled as he had by the loud shout of *Hey, Shane.*

Then a platter of herring had landed to one side. Together they watched as a single piece, bouncing in some form of alternate-reality slow motion, landed on the toe of his shoe.

For a moment, he'd stood as frozen as she had. Then Kate spotted a shadow racing down the far walkway and out the front door. As well as she knew Paul's walk, she knew Rikka's too.

Whoever Shane might be, he now had a new target and was running for the door.

Savannah still stood over by the tables, looking off the side of the pier. Paul was nowhere to be seen. Sam and Björn...were still down in the fo'c'sle and knew nothing.

Kate spotted a speaking tube and wondered if it still worked. She grabbed it, pulled out the plug in the end, put her mouth to the tube, and blew hard. That should make the plug on the other end, actually a whistle, sound shrilly, signaling the fo'c'sle gang to remove the plug and listen with the pipe to their ear.

But what if...she blew out an SOS: three short, three long, three short.

Sam was on deck before she'd finished. He looked straight at her. She only had to point at the front door before he vaulted over the side.

Björn, emerging as soon as Sam cleared the way, came rushing back to her. She dropped the tube and rushed out of the wheelhouse.

"I'm fine. A mob enforcer is after Rikka. She led him outside."

Björn spun on his heel and bolted after Sam.

Rikka had been clear. Clear and safely gone. But she'd

come back. Come back to draw the mob enforcer away from Kate.

No, she'd known his name. Not some mob enforcer. If she knew his name it meant he was the mob's *leader*, the man she'd tried to blackmail and who had tried to kill her once already. If he was here, that meant it was personal.

"You sure can pick 'em, Rikka." Kate raced after Björn. As she passed opposite the tables on the next walkway over, she saw Savannah on her hands and knees. She was looking down at Paul sitting on the fake ocean. "What are you doing down there?"

She didn't wait for an answer.

67

"GREAT MOVE, ALBERT. NOW WHAT?"

She really, really hoped that Shane didn't have a gun. It wasn't his style and they were illegal as snot in Iceland but, if he did, she was a dead woman. No, he was more the businessman than the thug. He'd just ruin your business, your life, and your family. Well, for anyone but her. She knew she was toast.

Still, better her than Kate. Even better yet? Not her either.

But she was fast running out of land. She'd bolted straight out the doors and all that lay before her were the piers and water.

Where was an Icelandic cop when you needed one? Probably out ticketing some rogue sheep for moving too slowly across the road.

Wait! Björn. *Vikingasveitin* was kind of a cop.

A glance back only revealed Shane stumbling into the sunlight, desperately shielding his eyes. No sign of Björn when she needed him. She'd definitely have to talk to Kate about choosing more useful love interests.

And Sam. She hated that Sam was so angry with her.

No sign of him either. ""On your own, Albert." Which only

proved her worst fear. "Only way to be." Her words of encouragement didn't do their job at all.

At the end of the pier, she raced down one of the slanted ramps to a floating dock. A Zodiac, its engine still ticking over as one of the ship ninjas stepped ashore with a line to tie it off. She took a running jump, landed in the boat, and managed to grab the throttle to steady herself.

"Bond. Jane Bond," she said in *that* voice as she cranked the throttle hard.

She raced straight ahead three feet and plowed into the back of a boat already tied off. The Zodiac bounced backward, tossing her to the floor. Okay, not so much Jane Bond.

But the rebound had shoved the nose of the boat out toward the open water and yanked the rope from the ninja's hand. She cranked the throttle again and raced away from the dock.

Wasn't this how James did it, making it up as he went? Well, she'd have to do that because she'd never driven a boat before. She quickly discovered that it was easier than all of the car-racing video games she'd conquered in her past. Throttle, wide open. Shove right to turn left and vice versa. To think she'd always been so impressed at how easy Paul made this look.

Then she jumped her first wave at an angle and was almost catapulted off the boat. Right, straight over the waves, go a little slower.

She risked a backward glance.

Nope! Not going one bit slower. She twisted the throttle to the limit.

The second Zodiac that had been tied to the pier was hot on her tail with Shane O'Leary at the controls.

And he was gaining on her.

Sticking her tongue out at him didn't strike her as an effective strategy—Jane Bond or not.

68

SAM COULDN'T BELIEVE WHAT HE WAS SEEING. RIKKA ALBERT racing across the light chop of the wide harbor. He could see by the way the boat was jouncing side-to-side that she wasn't following the best line at all. Why had he never taught her boat handling? Because she was so competent at everything that he'd never thought she lacked in anything.

She'd risked her life getting the mob enforcer away from Kate. And he was gaining on her.

What had he been doing? Fuming down below in the fo'c'sle, about to ask Björn how the hell to handle women, while Rikka was taking on the Irish mob singlehanded.

The next nearest Zodiac was out by the *Ice Adventure*. The ship's position would block the ship ninja's view from the chase off in deeper water. No help there. This was a working harbor. A few sailboats and sportfishers were tied up in the marina— three hundred meters in the wrong direction. The only option was a twenty-meter herring boat just pulling off the dock.

He shifted from run to sprint, leapt off the end of the pier, and managed to catch the gunwale with one hand and haul himself aboard.

He saw Björn skid to a halt.

The temptation to shout, *No guts. No glory.* ran strong. But the guy looked seriously pissed and Sam didn't want to rub it in. Besides, it was too far now; even an Olympic jumper would have gone in the water.

In the wheelhouse, he pushed the captain aside onto the small seat and shoved the throttle home. The old engines coughed once, then dug in. When the guy started to protest, Sam lifted him back to standing and sliced a hand at the two speeding Zodiacs. After eyeing him carefully, the man nodded and turned to face his target.

Sam quickly ransacked the boat for a weapon. A blunt gaff hook to pick up a floating line or snag a net, and a flare gun. Not even a harpoon or shotgun in case the net snagged a shark by accident.

The Zodiacs could make thirty-five to forty knots with such a light load. The deep-keeled herring boat could make six, seven if the bottom wasn't too fouled with seaweed or barnacles.

Rikka zigged when she should have zagged. No longer headed straight away from him, but the enforcer knew how to handle his boat. Leaning hard into the turn and carving an arc put him that much closer to Rikka.

He saw one of the Zodiacs nose around the back of the *Ice Adventure,* popping its nose up as he laid in the power. Someone was on the ball; Kate on the phone to the captain would be his first guess. The Zodiac didn't give chase, instead it headed straight for him. Definitely Kate.

Old Willem sat at the helm, the chief of the ninja team. His boat handling attested to a serious military past he'd mentioned no more than Sam had.

Sam turned to the herring boat caption, held up the flare gun sideways. Once he had the man's attention, Sam pulled a couple twenty dollar bills out of his pocket and pinned them to the deck under the gaff hook. When the Zodiac pulled alongside, he vaulted the gunwale to land in the bottom, taking the flare gun with him. Willem had barely slowed.

Rikka and the enforcer's boats were still a long way off.

69

RIKKA HAD TRIED EVERYTHING SHE COULD THINK OF FROM EVERY hour she'd wasted on car-race games when she should have been playing boat-race games. None of them worked. Shane kept closing on her—fast.

Watching astern, she saw Sam make the leap onto a speeding Zodiac. He made it look easy. She really wished she'd have a chance to tell him that, but something had snapped in Shane O'Leary's brain.

She'd originally found him while amusing herself by browsing through her old gang's Dark Web social media accounts. She'd had a life in Boston before Kate caught her, and Rikka had been curious about how her former pals in the Chinese Tong had gone down. There'd been a photo in Lì Huá's files of two bound-and-gagged folks being tossed in a car trunk —not by any of her people. She'd posted it with a caption: *We're not the only kings of Boston. LOL!* More than Rikka really wanted to know about her former colleague.

Curious, she'd looked up the license plate. That had led her to Shane O'Leary and the disappearance of his sister and brother-in-law that same night (which the police database she hacked said remained unsolved). While she was in there, she'd discovered what a horror show O'Leary was.

She never should have tried to blackmail him with that image. And that they were Savannah's parents? Sheesh, this just got crazier every time she connected another piece.

There was no way he'd get away with killing her in the middle of an Iceland herring town with so many witnesses.

She didn't doubt that he'd do it, only that he'd get away with it. At least, if she was dead, he'd have no reason to go after Kate. There was no way to tell either Kate or Sam how sorry she was. No way to apologize for all the things she'd done wrong.

And no time either.

Shane's boat raced twenty meters behind hers.

Ten.

At five she pulled out the knife she'd stolen from the herring girl's demo.

That's when she had an idea. She was an *itamae*. She was one trained to stand in front of the cutting board. She wished for Marnie's long *maguro* but would have to settle for the shorter blade.

The moment the nose of his Zodiac was close enough, she gave up on the steering and flipped the knife to stick point-down from her fist. With all the power she could muster, she stabbed the front pontoon of Shane's boat.

70

S<small>AM</small> <small>WATCHED THE MOVE FROM A HUNDRED METERS BACK.</small>
Willem was a good enough driver to have been Marine Force
Recon; he'd made up half the distance, but it wasn't enough.

By some crazy sleight of hand, Rikka went from doomed to
holding a flash of steel aloft that glinted in the sunlight. He had
no doubt that it was the missing knife from the fish-gutting
demo. One thing that, as a butcher, he'd always appreciated
about Rikka Albert was her knife skills.

Like a vengeful God, or at least a vengeful pixie, she
rammed the blade down into the pontoon of Shane's boat. That
she swung it hard enough to puncture the military-spec
material was impressive. That she managed to hold onto the
blade well enough to carve a long slice was a miracle—most
likely born of adrenaline-charged terror.

The right-front pontoon deflated in a single gasp and
caught against the wake of Rikka's boat. Going too fast to
recover, the bow dug in. It flipped the stern up and over.

Already sprinting up the length of his boat to attack her, the
enforcer managed to dive across and land in the bow of Rikka's
Zodiac. He was slow to get up, but not slow enough.

The flipped Zodiac lay upside down with its prop sticking up in the air, whining in a scream of protest. Then it died as the engine ingested water where it needed air. It had stopped spinning by the time Sam's boat flashed by.

The man crouched in the bow of Rikka's Zodiac.

Rikka crouched five paces away in the stern by the engine, with the knife held out before her. But he could see that she was no knife fighter. She could shave a beef tenderloin for carpaccio thinner and more evenly than anyone he'd ever met, including himself. But the angle of her blade was wrong; she was a chef, not a fighter.

Willem's grunt from manning the engine only confirmed his assessment.

He leaned forward in the skidding Zodiac, willing it to go faster.

Not fast enough.

The enforcer could see him coming up from behind. There was a madness there that Sam had seen plenty of times in the field. The wildest battle-crazed jihadi gone berserker had nothing on this man.

That's when he remembered the flare gun.

He aimed it at the man's face and fired.

71

W‍HEN HIS EYES TRACKED AWAY, R‍IKKA LUNGED FORWARD, BUT ALL she managed to do was nick his arm when she'd been aiming for his throat. Her sudden weight shift had veered the boat.

A bright flash whizzed by so close that she could feel the heat of it.

Shane also ducked as it passed close by his head, but his feral grin never changed. It was creeping her out.

The flare, fired from somewhere behind her, had overshot the boat and disappeared into the water. It created a bright orange spot that the Zodiac overran a mere second later.

She didn't dare glance back, but she knew that was the end. Her sudden move had ruined Sam's shot. He must be so close behind her, but it wouldn't be enough.

Shane reached the same conclusion as he prepared to leap at her, even though she was the one holding the knife.

Then she looked behind him.

Maybe. Just maybe.

72

Sᴀᴍ's ʜᴇᴀʀᴛ sᴛᴏᴘᴘᴇᴅ. Lɪᴛᴇʀᴀʟʟʏ, ɪᴛ ᴊᴜsᴛ sᴛᴏᴘᴘᴇᴅ ɪɴ ʜɪs ᴄʜᴇsᴛ and hung there doing nothing to send blood to his brain.

Rikka heaved the knife at her attacker.

The throw was all wrong. It spun lazily and the butt of the knife hit the berserker in the shoulder before tumbling into the boat.

Then, ever so slowly as if already dead, Rikka tipped sideways and fell overboard.

73

Shane dove to the floorboards, grabbed the knife, and rolled to his feet at the engine where the bitch had been standing a second ago. Or he tried to. It was more of an awkward fall, then struggling back to his feet and staggering toward the screaming engine. He'd sprained his knee badly when leaping over from his Zodiac.

His days as an enforcer for his father were too far behind him. Too many pints and too much good food at pubs like The Plough and Stars. Too much time wielding a phone in this new age of business than the old days of literally browbeating owners into paying protection money.

She lay there, fast falling astern. Unmoving in the water. He had to make sure she was dead. Make sure his past deeds stayed buried, and that Savannah never found out what he'd done in a drunken fit of rage that long ago night.

Her parents had wanted out. Done with the life. Done with him. Ashli, his own sister, had unleashed that vile Irish temper of hers right in his face. Calling him a weakling had been one curse too many—he'd plunged his steak knife into her heart. When Tommy drew on him, he'd had no choice, had he?

Somehow, Suzi Suzuki had found the photo of him disposing of their bodies. Probably knew they were weighted down off the middle of the Harvard Bridge.

Now she lay astern in the water and he had to make sure she was dead. He didn't even know her current name.

It didn't matter.

Keeping his eyes fixed on her, he reached for the throttle to turn the Zodiac, just as the bow impacted the rocky shore behind him.

74

SHANE O'LEARY FLEW BACKWARD, ARCING HIGH ENOUGH IN THE air to look down on the chase boat slowing beside Suzi's body and dragging it from the water. High enough to see across the harbor and spot other boats racing to come witness the spectacle.

High enough to—

Shane's back slammed into the cliff. His ears rang with loud protests of angry terns—again.

Too steep to remain where he was. His back too broken to attempt to cling to the jagged rock. He tumbled in a slow somersault onto the lower slope of the cliff, landing more or less upright, at about a BarcaLounger angle. His head, no longer in his control, tipped brokenly to the side just like that videographer Dana Winston's had. Tipped until his cheek rested on his shoulder.

Adding insult to injury, the Zodiac, continuing its flip, slammed the top of its engine into his legs, pinning him in place. At least with a broken neck he didn't feel it—though he could certainly hear it. Upside down, the prop spun at full throttle driving air into his face from an arm's length away, if he could have raised one of his arms.

Finally, it fuel-starved and died. In the sudden silence, he became aware of the sharp, pungent smell of gasoline leaking from the inverted engine. Oh God, he was going to burn. No longer halfway to hell with an arrow pointing the way. He was there.

That's when he felt the first sharp sting.

Something beat against the side of his head. He couldn't shift to see it, but he knew the sharp cry—and it wasn't his.

Another Arctic tern, angry at his proximity to their nest, pecked him hard on the temple, now his highest point. This one he saw as it circled in front of him to attack again. Soon a whole flock was peppering him with blows.

The gasoline had stopped leaking, and all he could smell was the ocean and bird poop.

Just when he'd actually welcome a nice, clean immolation.

One that would fry all these goddamn birds.

75

"WHAT... WHAT HAPPENED?" RIKKA MANAGED TO OPEN ONE EYE.
The news was so good that she opened the other. "Sam?"

He nodded his head as he stroked her hair out of her face.
She lay on the bottom of a Zodiac with her head in his lap.

"Are you still mad at me?"

He shook his head. A drop of water landed on her face, but
it hadn't come from her. She reached up to brush at his cheek
and her wet fingers came away wetter.

"Was it that close?"

Still obviously upset past speech, he nodded. That gave her
the shivers. Death had never brushed so nearby before.

"Did you get him?"

He tapped a finger in the center of her chest.

"Me?"

And he caressed her cheek with a stroke of his fingers.

She wiggled everything to make sure her body still worked.
That's when she noticed that the shivers hadn't stopped yet.

"God but I hate cold water. I'm freezing to death."

He scooped her against his nice warm chest and she

burrowed close, swearing she'd never screw up again
—hopefully.

76

"You still haven't left the ship," Kate spotted Björn sitting at the bar on the *Erebus* Deck. She'd stopped by to snag a cookie from the glass jars that Miguel always kept stocked for the passengers. "Please tell me there isn't yet another unsolved calamity."

"There isn't yet another unsolved calamity." He looked very sharp in a dark blue turtleneck and a corduroy blazer. He'd also looked amazing marooned at the tip of the pier outside the Herring Era Museum trying to call in an airstrike on a Zodiac. And felt good when he'd wrapped an arm around her shoulders as they were helpless to do more than watch the chase unfold across the water.

"Well, that's one blessing." She moved to get herself a cup of tea.

"You know that the replacement chef is already aboard. It's okay if you have a drink with me."

She glanced at Mr. Charles behind the bar. "A glass of red would be lovely."

"My pleasure, Ms. Stark. And may I thank you again for the fine job you did while we were, ah, between chefs."

"Well, if you would deign to not charge me for the repairs to the two Zodiacs we damaged, I, in turn, shall consider myself well compensated."

"Madame under-evaluates her skills. A slashed pontoon and both engines repairable is a drastically insufficient recompense."

"I won't quibble." And they shook on it.

She and Björn took their drinks to a low table in the lounge, far enough from the piano to enjoy the music yet still be able to speak easily.

Before she could repeat the question of why he remained aboard, Rikka and Sam joined them.

"Are we really okay?" Rikka asked for the fiftieth time since the doctor had cleared her. His prescription had been a hot shower to cure the chills, and ibuprofen for the battering she'd taken from hitting the water at over thirty miles an hour and knocking herself unconscious in the process.

Kate gave her a hard hug, knowing it would take many more before Rikka believed, but it was a good start for both of them. "There are nine more days to the cruise, which will hopefully be much quieter."

"From your mouth to George Carlin's ears."

"George Carlin's?" she asked as Sam delivered two beers and sat beside Rikka.

"Hey, if he didn't make it into Heaven, I don't stand a chance."

Kate knew she never should have asked. It was another Rikka non sequitur. "Anway, I look forward to learning much more about my best friend during the rest of this trip."

When Rikka had no snappy comeback, Kate knew she'd been touched.

"We've got some more ideas," Paul came over with a glass of Crown Royal whisky in one hand and Savannah in the other. She'd also opted for a glass of red.

"Stateside. I'm now officially on holiday. Nothing about business until we're Stateside." She knew it wouldn't last; Paul and Savannah were too excited about this new business, and it did have real potential. She knew she'd give in soon, if only because she wanted to see how this new facet of her twin turned out. But not today.

Savannah studied her wine in silence for the better part of a minute. "My lawyer called me this morning to let me know that I have inherited something rather...nasty." It was a very nice wine, so Kate knew that wasn't the problem.

"I actually have an answer to that," Kate told her. "Thanks to my short friend over here," she nodded at Rikka.

Rikka blinked at her in surprise.

"What matters is what you do with it, far more than where it came from."

"No, I didn't say that," Rikka protested.

"Close enough, so hush."

Shockingly, Rikka hushed. Kate would have to be patient to see how that change, too, would unfold over time.

"I can make some specific suggestions on how to take Irish Pubs, Inc. wholly legitimate as well as making it profitable for all parties involved. I'll also introduce you to a couple of friends," which she supposed they were rapidly becoming, "named Marcus and Leona, who will be thrilled to help you clean up any residual nastiness."

Savannah raised her glass in a toast of thanks.

When everyone else had toasted, sipped, and fallen into conversation about the adventures of the last three days, Kate turned to Björn.

"You haven't answered my question."

His smile looked quite smug. "I'm still aboard despite the resolution of all matters because Clara Bragason has suggested that I stay out of the way for a few days. It turns out that she is much more than she seems."

Kate doubted that, as Clara had seemed to be quite a bit, but she nodded for Björn to continue.

"She has left the cruise to work with the Prime Minister on removing Hayden from command of the *Vikingasveitin*."

"Please tell me you aren't the one replacing him."

He shook his head. "By the gods, no. Clara is. Oh, and she asked me to give you a present." He reached into an inside pocket and pulled out something only a few inches across and wrapped in a layer of tissue paper.

Kate unraveled it to reveal—

The group broke out in a mixture of laughter and groans. It was a miniature knit Arctic tern, complete with its black head and sharp orange beak.

"Next time you see her, tell her I will treasure it forever."

That earned more laughter.

Once again, she let the conversation drift aside before glancing at Björn. She didn't bother to repeat the question. Her look was enough to elicit his answer.

"I am a simple passenger until the end of the cruise. So, since neither of us does coy very well, your suite or mine?"

His was definitely nicer, but with Paul directly across the hall with Savannah... She'd rather be opposite where Rikka had moved in with Sam.

Kate rose to her feet, taking her wine glass with her. She didn't need to tell him when; her walk should take care of conveying that message.

It did.

AFTERWORD

If you enjoyed Knife's Edge
please consider leaving a review.
They really help.

Keep reading for an exciting excerpt from:
Miranda Chase #1, Drone

A list of characters and locations may be found at:
https://mlbuchman.com/people-places-planes#KS
And return afterward for a free bonus story
and a recipe from the book.

MIRANDA CHASE #1
(EXCERPT)

IF YOU ENJOYED THAT, YOU'LL LOVE…

DRONE (EXCERPT)

Flight 630 at 37,000 feet
12 nautical miles north of
Santa Fe, New Mexico, USA

THE FLIGHT ATTENDANT STEPPED UP TO HER SEAT—4E—WHICH had never been her favorite on a 767-300. At least the cabin setup was in the familiar 261-seat, 2-class configuration, currently running at a seventy-three percent load capacity with a standard crew of ten and one ride-along FAA inspector in the cockpit jump seat.

"Excuse me, are you Miranda Chase?"

She nodded.

The attendant made a face that she couldn't interpret.

A frown? Did that indicate anger?

He turned away before she could consider the possibilities and, without another word, returned to his station at the front of the cabin.

Miranda once again straightened the emergency exit plan that the flight's vibrations kept shifting askew in its pocket.

This flight from yesterday's meeting at LAX to today's DC

lunch meeting at the National Transportation Safety Board's headquarters departed so early that she'd decided to spend the night in the airline's executive lounge working on various aviation accident reports. She never slept on a flight and would have to catch up on her sleep tonight.

Miranda felt the shift as the plane turned into a modest five-degree bank to the left. The bright rays of dawn over the New Mexico desert shifted from the left-hand windows to the right side.

At due north, she heard the Rolls-Royce RB211 engines (quite a pleasant high tone compared to the Pratt & Whitney PW4000 that she always found unnerving) ease off ever so slightly, signaling a slow descent. The pilot was transitioning from an eastbound course that would be flown at an odd number of thousands of feet to a westbound one that must be flown at an even number.

The flight attendant then picked up the intercom phone and a loud squawk sounded through the cabin. Most people would be asleep and there were soft complaints and rustling down the length of the aircraft.

"We regret to inform you that there is an emergency on the ground. I repeat, there is nothing wrong with the plane. We are being routed back to Las Vegas, where we will disembark one passenger, refuel, and then continue our flight to DC. Our apologies for the inconvenience."

There were now shouts of complaint all up and down the aisle.

The flight attendant was staring straight at her as he slammed the intercom back into its cradle with significantly greater force than was required to seat it properly.

Oh. It was her they would be disembarking. That meant there was a crash in need of an NTSB investigator—a major one if they were flying back an hour in the wrong direction.

Thankfully, she always had her site kit with her.

For some reason, her seatmate was muttering something foul. Miranda ignored it and began to prepare herself.

Only the crash mattered.

She straightened the exit plan once more. It had shifted the other way with the changing harmonic from the RB2II engines.

Chengdu, Central China

AIR FORCE MAJOR WANG FAN EASED BACK ON THE JOYSTICK OF the final prototype Shenyang J-31 jet—designed exclusively for the People's Liberation Army Air Force. In response, China's newest fighter jet leapt upward like a catapult's missile from the PLAAF base in the flatlands surrounding the towering city of Chengdu.

It felt as he'd just been grasped by Chen Mei-Li.

Never had a woman made him feel like such a man. Fan hadn't known that he could be taken past the ultimate peak so many times in a single night. More than once he'd half feared that his given name would come true and he would die collapsed upon her—his fellow test pilots often teased him about his first name, Fan, meaning "mortal."

Of course, never before had he been with a woman who cost a week's salary. It would take at least a month to hide enough money from his insipid wife—now revealed to be so much less skilled than he'd thought—to buy another night with Mei-Li, the beautiful red gem.

Perhaps if this flight went well, he would get a promotion from *Shao Xiao* to *Zhong Xiao*—major to lieutenant colonel—and the money that came with it could simply never be revealed to his wife.

It was possible. After all, Lieutenant General Zhang Ru was his wife's uncle. Hadn't he lifted Fan from the officer corps to be a test pilot, and introduced Fan to his own niece and encouraged her to become his wife?

Uncle Ru personally had chosen him to be first in the Chinese Air Force to fly the new J-31—a great honor indeed.

Each successive flight in the long week of testing had built neatly on the one before. Today he had finally been given permission to truly test the J-31's limits.

And now Uncle Ru had arranged his night in heaven with Chen Mei-Li.

Fan had felt truly *immortal* this morning when he stepped up, flipped aside her robe, and entered her from behind as she'd been bent over to set their breakfast table—white rice scattering wide at her surprise. Steamed buns had fallen upon the blue-and-white floor tiles depicting ancient gardens and elegant courtesans, each pork *baozi* exploding in slow motion like a tiny bomb.

Forevermore, the fiery blend of ginger, sesame, and five-spice would season his memories of that purest sexual perfection.

In the moment of that crashing release like no other, he had indeed entered *Tian* and become Yùdi the Jade Emperor taking Mazu the Jade Empress right up her heaven-perfect ass. He hadn't been Wang the prince (as his surname meant) or even king—he'd been a god.

For the gift of last night alone, he would do anything his uncle asked.

As the first Air Force pilot to fly the J-31 *Sŭn,* Gyrfalcon in the English that Uncle kept pushing him to learn, he would also have a pilot's bragging rights for a long time to come. That too he owed to Honorable Uncle Ru.

The twin Chinese-made WS-13E engines delivered 200 kN, over 46,000 pounds of thrust, all driven straight into his aching member as a single roar of glory. The sixteen-meter-long fifth-generation fighter jet leapt for the heavens. It was only the fourth fifth-gen jet fighter in the world—and personally he felt Russia's Sukhoi Su-57 was overrated. Besides, the Russian jet was still no more than a prototype, so the J-31 was the third of the new breed (he didn't count the J-20, even though it had flown first, because with the arrival of J-31, the two-year-old jet was already obsolete).

The two American fifth-gen aircraft were, sadly, very impressive. Now it was time to put them in their place.

———

Keep reading at fine retailers everywhere.
Find at:
MIRANDA CHASE

ABOUT THE AUTHOR

USA Today and Amazon #1 Bestseller M. L. "Matt" Buchman started writing on a flight south from Japan to ride his bicycle across the Australian Outback. Just part of a solo around-the-world trip that ultimately launched his writing career.

From the very beginning, his powerful female heroines insisted on putting character first, *then* a great adventure. He's since written over 75 action-adventure thrillers and military romantic suspense novels. And more than 200 short stories, and a fast-growing pile of read-by-author audiobooks.

PW declares of his Miranda Chase action-adventure thrillers: "Tom Clancy fans open to a strong female lead will clamor for more." About his military romantic thrillers: "Like Robert Ludlum and Nora Roberts had a book baby."

His fans say: "I want more now...of everything!" That his characters are even more insistent than his fans is a hoot.

As a 30-year project manager with a geophysics degree who has designed and built houses, flown and jumped out of planes, and solo-sailed a 50' ketch, he is awed by what is possible. He and his wife presently live on the North Shore of Massachusetts. More at: www.mlbuchman.com.

Other works by M. L. Buchman: *(* - also in audio)*

Action-Adventure Thrillers

Kate Stark
Final Taste
Ice Burn
Knife's Edge

Miranda Chase
Drone*
Thunderbolt*
Condor*
Ghostrider*
Raider*
Chinook*
Havoc*
White Top*
Start the Chase*
Lightning*
Skibird*
Nightwatch*
Osprey*
Gryphon*
Wedgetail*

Science Fiction / Fantasy

Deities Anonymous
Cookbook from Hell: Reheated
Saviors 101

Contemporary Romance

Eagle Cove
Return to Eagle Cove
Recipe for Eagle Cove
Longing for Eagle Cove
Keepsake for Eagle Cove

Love Abroad
Heart of the Cotswolds: England
Path of Love: Cinque Terre, Italy

Where Dreams
Where Dreams are Born
Where Dreams Reside
Where Dreams Are of Christmas*
Where Dreams Unfold
Where Dreams Are Written
Where Dreams Continue

Non-Fiction

Strategies for Success
Managing Your Inner Artist/Writer
Estate Planning for Authors*
Character Voice
Narrate and Record Your Own Audiobook*
Beyond Prince Charming: One Guy's Guide to Writing Men in Romance

---

Short Story Series by M. L. Buchman:

Action-Adventure Thrillers

Kate Stark
Miranda Chase Stories

Romantic Suspense

Antarctic Ice Fliers
US Coast Guard

Contemporary Romance

Eagle Cove

Other

Deities Anonymous (fantasy)
Single Titles

The Emily Beale Universe
(military romantic suspense)

The Night Stalkers
MAIN FLIGHT
The Night Is Mine
I Own the Dawn
Wait Until Dark
Take Over at Midnight
Light Up the Night
Bring On the Dusk
By Break of Day
Target of the Heart
Target Lock on Love
Target of Mine
Target of One's Own
NIGHT STALKERS HOLIDAYS
*Daniel's Christmas**
*Frank's Independence Day**
*Peter's Christmas**
Christmas at Steel Beach
*Zachary's Christmas**
*Roy's Independence Day**
*Damien's Christmas**
Christmas at Peleliu Cove

Henderson's Ranch
*Nathan's Big Sky**
*Big Sky, Loyal Heart**
*Big Sky Dog Whisperer**
*Tales of Henderson's Ranch**

Shadow Force: Psi
*At the Slightest Sound**
*At the Quietest Word**
*At the Merest Glance**
*At the Clearest Sensation**

White House Protection Force
*Off the Leash**
*On Your Mark**
*In the Weeds**

Firehawks
Pure Heat
Full Blaze
*Hot Point**
*Flash of Fire**
Wild Fire
SMOKEJUMPERS
*Wildfire at Dawn**
*Wildfire at Larch Creek**
*Wildfire on the Skagit**

Delta Force
*Target Engaged**
*Heart Strike**
*Wild Justice**
*Midnight Trust**

Night Stalkers Reload
*Guard the East Flank**

Emily Beale Universe Short Story Series
The Night Stalkers
The Night Stalkers Stories
The Night Stalkers CSAR
The Night Stalkers Wedding Stories
The Future Night Stalkers

Delta Force
Th Delta Force Shooters
The Delta Force Warriors

Firehawks
The Firehawks Lookouts
The Firehawks Hotshots
The Firebirds

White House Protection Force
Stories

Future Night Stalkers
Stories (Science Fiction)

SIGN UP FOR M. L. BUCHMAN'S NEWSLETTER TODAY

and receive:
Release News
Free Short Stories
a Free Book

Get your free book today. Do it now.
free-book.mlbuchman.com